To Naomi (Lu),
Hope you enjoy this book.
Perhaps you'll see some familiar memories.

Love,
[signature]
AKA Sammy
2010

MURDER ON THE HILL

Blanche Renard Putzel

iUniverse, Inc.
New York Bloomington

Copyright © 2010 by Blanche Renard Putzel

All rights reserved. No part of this book may be used or reproduced by any means, graphic, electronic, or mechanical, including photocopying, recording, taping or by any information storage retrieval system without the written permission of the publisher except in the case of brief quotations embodied in critical articles and reviews.

This is a work of fiction. All of the characters, names, incidents, organizations, and dialogue in this novel are either the products of the author's imagination or are used fictitiously.

iUniverse books may be ordered through booksellers or by contacting:

iUniverse
1663 Liberty Drive
Bloomington, IN 47403
www.iuniverse.com
1-800-Authors (1-800-288-4677)

Because of the dynamic nature of the Internet, any Web addresses or links contained in this book may have changed since publication and may no longer be valid. The views expressed in this work are solely those of the author and do not necessarily reflect the views of the publisher, and the publisher hereby disclaims any responsibility for them.

ISBN: 978-1-4502-0663-1 (sc)
ISBN: 978-1-4502-0664-8 (ebook)

Printed in the United States of America

iUniverse rev. date: 02/15/2010

To Phil, my love, my inspiration

Schmidt's House

Chapter One

PETE PICKEN turned his truck onto Jane Street from Main and headed for the dead end. He knew Helmut Schmidt's house. In fact, he knew most of the houses and streets on the Hill. He'd been combing the town for antiques for years. Early Canadiana was his specialty.

The village of Emerald Hill sat perched on the highest lookout in the middle of a vast and ancient river valley stretching from the Ottawa River in the north to the St. Lawrence in the south. Early Canadian settlers gravitated to the hill with a view for the safety it provided; the French drifted westward from Quebec; the English, from the newly formed United States, ventured north. Eventually a mill was built to produce brick made from the mud flats in the valley, and the town grew into a picturesque Victorian village.

By the arbitrary stroke of a politician's pen, Emerald Hill landed on the west side of the Ontario-Quebec border. However, the pen did not dictate the language of the people. Residents spoke either English or French, depending on their heritage and their mood on any given day, or they spoke a mixture of the two, known colloquially as Franglaise. Newcomers were not welcomed so much as absorbed into the village life. A sign of acceptance was when a person became the subject of daily conversation.

Pete had lived on the Hill long enough to be very familiar with the contents of the houses and the secrets of their inhabitants. He earned his living trading in possessions, and his entertainment trading in gossip.

Rain pelted the windshield. Although the wipers splashed and swiped vigorously, he could hardly see the curb as rivulets filled the gutters and overflowed onto the sidewalk. This fall had been particularly wet. The Canadian maples, renowned for transforming the countryside into glorious autumn colours, were disappointingly dull. There were few colourful trees to attract tourists this year. The leaves turned dingy yellow and fell onto sodden lawns.

As he got out of the truck, Pete was glad he had worn his wide-brimmed hat, which served as a portable roof to shed the rain. His red-checked wool jacket was tattered but warm and well suited to ward off the damp fall chill. He gave little thought to the impression that torn jeans and cowboy boots would give to a prospective client. Looking poor could be very advantageous in the antiques business.

The house he was looking for was almost hidden behind wild shrubs and broken branches. Decorative Victorian gingerbread trim drooped from the porch eaves, and several boards on the steps were dangerously rotten. The house looked like a relic of better days past and forgotten.

Pete made his way carefully to the front entrance. The screen was torn, and the hinges protested as he opened the outer door to knock.

But before his knuckles rapped on the window, the door flew open without warning.

"Well, there you are. I'm not surprised it's you, and I must admit, I'm glad to see someone—anyone—at this point."

The voice that greeted him was much larger than the person to whom it obviously belonged. A small, energetic woman stood in the doorway. Her hair was wet and disheveled. She wore a raincoat over tidy black trousers and a pink cotton shirt with a silk scarf falling lopsided around her neck. Her bright eyes measured him up and down as if evaluating his worth in dollars and cents.

A rush of stale warmth greeted Pete at the door. His nostrils were assailed by odours of smoke and mould coming from the old books with rotting paper that filled the room. At the same time, the woman who stood before him wore far too much perfume, suggesting a breath of spring enveloped in sticky candy.

She blocked his entrance while peering around him to see if anyone else accompanied him. When she assured herself that he was alone, she stepped aside to let him into the dingy hallway. Then she began to chatter uncontrollably.

"He's dead. There's no question about it. When I arrived, there was no answer when I knocked; but the door was open, so I walked in. The house was quiet ... not a sound. I called out, but there was no answer. So I came into the living room, and there he was in his chair. I said his name real loud to try to wake him. You know, 'Mr.

Schmidt! Mr. Schmidt!' I was practically shouting. But when he didn't move, I shook his shoulder. Then he fell out of the chair. Landed just like that. Dead, I tell you. Dead as a doorbell."

"Nail," Pete corrected her.

"That's what I said," Emily repeated. "Dead as a doornail."

Then she went on, "And am I glad it's you showed up, Mr. Picken, and not some nosy neighbour or snoop. Now what are we going to do?"

Pete wondered how he had gotten enlisted to help her with what was quite clearly her dilemma, not his. After all, she had been here first.

He couldn't remember if he knew the woman who chattered at him while she wandered around the room, perusing the situation. He had the vague impression that he knew her from somewhere, but he couldn't place her.

She saw through his puzzled expression.

"Now, Mr. Picken, don't you go pretending that you don't know who I am. You never recognize me, even though I've met you several times already. Mrs. Blossom. Remember? Emily Blossom."

He tried to act as if he remembered the name by raising his eyebrows and smiling slightly.

"You know ... the art collector." She led him on, trying to jog his memory. "You bid against me on the vintage hunting scene at the auction last spring. Made me pay fifty dollars too much for the print even though it was water damaged."

"Oh yes, now I remember. I was bidding on the frame, actually. Why didn't you tell me you wanted the print? We could have made a deal."

"And I suppose Mr. Schmidt called you as well?" she asked, changing the subject back to their immediate predicament.

"Well yes, as a matter of fact," Pete answered. "He called me this morning at six a.m. Said he had some antiques he wanted to dispose of. Said he was in a rush to sell and asked me to come by this morning. Did he call you too?"

"Yes," she answered. "European paintings, he said. Called last night. Sounded a bit worried, if you ask me."

The room was dingy and filled with objects of all sorts. Books lined shelves and overflowed onto the floors, tumbling like rocks from an eroding cliff. Newspapers were piled in corners and lay strewn around the room, as if set aside for the reader to return to some intriguing articles at a later date. A statue stood under a table lamp next to a worn, overstuffed couch. A bronze naked knight was engaged in slaying a dragon. Brandishing a sword and clothed only in a windswept scarf, the hero slay an evil monster who stood helpless in the face of the knight's dauntless courage. Dark paintings cluttered the walls, portraying ominous scenes of ghouls and tortured humans. Some of the images were vaguely familiar, like classic depictions of famous battle scenes with all the gory details.

Emily pointed to the crumpled body lying in a heap at the foot of the tattered armchair.

The corpse was a pile of corpulence clothed in old lounging wear: moth-eaten grey cardigan, turtleneck with worn collar, stained jogging pants. The man's hands were yellow with nicotine stains; his nails were long, like claws. He clutched at his throat, as if trying to squeeze his last breath into life. His face was contorted into a crooked grin. His eyes bulged in a look of excruciating surprise, which could not let go of the final sight they beheld while in the throes of death.

Pete could hardly draw his eyes away from the specter of horror before him, until Emily's voice shattered his trance.

"Looks like he had good reason to be worried. It's murder, you know. He didn't just fall ill and die just like that."

Her words brought Pete's attention quickly back to his own predicament. He felt a shiver of panic overcome him. Not only did he have a very strong aversion to violent crime, in fact, he could do perfectly well without trouble of any kind. He preferred a life of predictable haggling. Bargains were one thing—'Buyer beware' and all that—but 'Better to be on the right side of the law,' he always said. The origins of antiques were too often questionable. In his business, a person could do without trouble with the law.

Mind you, his dread of the legal system was also well founded in personal experience, although he chose not to dwell on his past minor transgressions. The line was fine between ownership and borrowing for the purposes of making a profit. Nobody need know how familiar he was with the long arms of the police.

"Murder?" he repeated slowly, looking around him cautiously. Pete spent little time making up his mind to vacate the premises. "Well, I guess I'd better be going. There's nothing here for me to make money on."

He surreptitiously wiped his hands on his pants, as if to erase any fingerprints he might have deposited unknowingly just by standing in the middle of the room.

"Nice to have met you again, Mrs. Blossom," he whispered, as he backed toward the door.

"Oh no you don't, Pete Picken," she declared. "You're not going to sneak out of here and leave me with this mess. Like it or not, we're in this together. Now, help me figure out what's happened here and what we're going to do about it."

"I just remembered that I'm supposed to be somewhere soon," Pete excused himself as he turned to make a run for it.

However, as old and feeble as she looked, Mrs. Blossom was no antique herself. She quickly slipped between Pete and his exit, slammed the door, turned the key, and deposited it into her bodice. Then she smiled, sweet and sour at the same time.

"Now, you listen here, young man, and I'll explain the facts of life to you, you young whippersnipper."

"Snapper," Pete corrected her. "Whippersnapper."

"That's what I said," Emily answered, "whippersnapper."

Then she continued unabashedly where she had left off, "If you think that you can waltz around town with your nose stuck in the air without even bothering to remember someone's name, if you think that you're too high and mighty to give somebody the time of day when you're out scrounging around looking for a good deal, well then, you've got another thing coming.

"I've spent a good many years waiting for something exciting to happen in my life, married a decent man and paid my dues. Now, finally I get my chance to be in on the beginning of a good honest-to-goodness murder, and you want to walk out without even helping me solve the crime and be a hero on the front pages of *The Hill News*? No sirree. We're in this together, my friend. And we're going to take advantage of it."

She pushed her forefinger into his chest and practically sent him tripping over an umbrella that had been lying unnoticed on the floor behind the victim's armchair. They both looked down at the same time.

Mrs. Blossom gasped, "It's the murder weapon!"

Pete gasped as well, but for a different reason. He couldn't believe what he was hearing.

"It's the murder weapon," Emily repeated, as if he needed to be reminded. "Don't touch it."

He certainly wasn't about to.

"Don't you remember that story in the headlines about two years ago? A Russian spy was killed with the poisoned tip of an umbrella."

She paused for effect and then continued, "Notice, the umbrella's still wet from the rain."

The tone of her voice was full of suspense and intrigue.

"This man was murdered less than two hours ago. That's when the rain began, and the umbrella's still wet."

Mrs. Blossom was quite obviously enjoying herself immensely. Pete, on the other hand, was not.

The Murder Weapon

Chapter Two

EMILY QUICKLY warmed to the tasks of an astute detective. At first tentatively, and then with more assurance, she began to examine the room in more detail, commenting as she proceeded with her investigation.

"Mr. Schmidt certainly had a taste for odd and distorted pleasures," she said as she examined the titles of books on the shelves. Many of them were in German, however, others in English were plainly on similar topics.

"*Systems of Torture during the Medieval Ages* ... *Exhorting Confessions from The Criminal Element* ... *Lie Detection and Other Evasive Tactics of the Guilty Prisoner*," she read out loud.

"Nice guy," said Pete, starting to become curious in spite of himself.

He began to snoop around the room as well.

"What's this?" he asked as he picked an odd paperweight off the desk.

The cast-iron tool looked like a corkscrew combined with a small vice. Emily snatched the device from him and turned it over several times to examine it from all angles. She asserted proudly, "A thumbscrew," and then added simply, "Used."

"How do you know it's used?" Pete asked incredulously. Emily proved to be less naïve than she looked.

"Blood stains in the pitted metal." She pointed to splotches of red. "Unless it's fake, added for effect. But I don't think so. I've seen items like this as examples of ancient methods of torture."

"Imagine someone who would use that as a paperweight," she humphed.

"Probably worth a lot of money to the right buyer," Pete added, tending to the more practical side of things.

As she continued snooping and poking around the room, Emily gasped again, loudly.

"Oh no. What's really going on here?"

"I wish you wouldn't do that," Pete said with exasperation. "You make me nervous."

Ignoring his comment, she answered her own question. "It's the painting ... the one that's not there ... the painting is missing," she whispered.

"What painting? There is no painting," Pete said, following her gaze to a blank wall above the fireplace.

"Precisely," she concluded firmly. "The painting is gone. The Hieronymus Bosch. It's gone."

"How do you know there was a painting there in the first place?" he asked, feeling foolish without knowing exactly why he was listening to her at all.

"There was an original Hieronymus Bosch hanging there the last time I was here," Emily remembered. "Mr. Schmidt wanted my opinion about its value. I told him I had no idea. It was priceless, no doubt. After all, an original Bosch doesn't exist outside of museums. I don't know how he got his hands on it, but I do know it was quite valuable ... and there it is ... gone."

Her voice petered into the silence as they both stood looking at the blank wall, slightly faded where the painting once hung.

"It was a scene of terrible torture and gore. Hell on Earth," she explained. "Bosch was renowned for painting ghoulish figures in the most hideous situations and horrible agony. His imagination was like a living nightmare, and this painting was a perfect example of terror, misery, and despair."

She pronounced each of the last three words in a whisper that added to the suspense of the situation. Pete felt a chill up his back and shivered, glancing around to make sure that no one else had somehow entered the room when they hadn't been watching.

"Don't whisper like that," he said loudly. "You make me nervous." Then he added in a still louder voice as if to convince himself of the truth in his next statement, "There's nobody else here. Speak up."

She complied, almost shouting, "I wonder if the murderer was also a thief."

"We had better call the police," Pete whispered.

Just then, there was a loud banging on the door. Inadvertently Pete let out a shriek and jumped behind Emily, who tried, at the same time, to put him between her and the door.

"Open up! Police!" shouted the voice, while the banging threatened to break the lock.

They could see uniformed officers peering through the window. Emily struggled to retrieve the key which had lodged itself neatly deep into her cleavage and seemed reluctant to leave its hiding place.

"Open this door immediately!" the voice shouted, growing more angry and threatening.

Emily began to jump up and down frantically. Pete eyed her antics askance.

"Are you alright?" he whispered, as if to avoid detection by the police outside the door.

"I'm looking for the key," she said matter-of-factly as she jumped more and more vigorously.

Presently they heard a jingle on the floor as the key extracted itself from her underclothing and slid out of her pant's leg. She scrambled to retrieve it and rushed to unlock the door, while Pete considered how he might manage to disguise himself as a piece of furniture.

"Allo, Allard," said Emily, pretending squeaky innocence as she peered around the door to see Sergeant Allard just about to fracture the window with the butt of his gun.

"We were just about to ring you," said Emily cheerily.

"We were just about to call for the police," said Pete, unnecessarily repeating Emily's statement, but wanting to be sure to put in his own two cents as well.

"It's too late for that, Mr. Picken," said the loud voice belonging to Albert Allard, the local OPP officer. "We've caught you red-handed."

"But, but," Pete stammered, "I only just got here myself."

"That's right, officer," Emily piped up. "We both arrived only minutes ago."

Then quickly deflecting the officer's attention, she added dramatically, "This man has been murdered."

All three pairs of eyes followed her outstretched finger, which pointed dramatically to the corpse on the floor.

Allard looked at the body and then at Emily and then at Pete. His mouth opened, as if to speak, and then he thought better of it.

He approached the body and tested for a pulse. Presently he stood up.

"Dead alright," he affirmed. "Cold and dead."

Then he looked at the shoddy pair, who stared at him wordlessly.

"And I suppose neither of you two knows anything about this? You're just here as casual observers?" Allard's eyebrows rose suspiciously.

Both Emily and Pete answered at once.

Pete said, "She was here first."

Emily said, "He got here just after I did."

Then together they repeated, "He was already dead."

And Emily added, "Dead as a doorbell."

"Nail," Pete corrected her.

"That's what I said, 'Dead as a doornail,'" Emily answered and continued undaunted, "and that is the murder weapon!"

She reached for the umbrella to hand it to Allard, but he caught her wrist and held tight.

"Don't touch anything!" he shouted.

Emily twisted her wrist free from his grasp.

"No need to shout, officer," she said plaintively, stroking her arm with a bruised expression. "I was just trying to help."

"I told her to mind her own business, officer," said Pete quickly.

Emily looked at him with raised eyebrows.

"No you did not," she argued. "You never said a word."

Pete looked at Allard to see if he was listening to his side of the story.

"I got here, officer, and she was already snooping around. I had nothing to do with anything, so if you'll be so kind, I'll just mosey on outta here and let you get down to your police work."

Pete smiled as well as he could and stepped toward the door.

"Oh no you don't." Allard stepped in his way. "Both of you, in the cruiser. We're going down to headquarters for a little discussion."

By that time, the house was swarming with the other police officers who had accompanied Allard to the scene of the crime. Allard signaled to one officer nearby for an extra pair of handcuffs. To make his point, he cuffed both Emily and Pete and led them to the police car through the rain.

Emily glanced at Pete as they were sitting next to each other in the back seat of the cruiser. She grinned apologetically.

"I'm sorry, Pete, to get you mixed up in this mess."

Pete grunted. He couldn't stay angry at her for long. She looked like a child in an elderly lady's clothing.

"It's okay," he murmured. "After all, like it or not, we're in this predicament together."

The Country Kitchen on the Hill

Chapter Three

THE NEXT day the Hill was buzzing with the news of a murder in town. The Country Kitchen on the Hill was even busier than usual. All seven tables were full.

The tiny restaurant specialized in homemade meals and fresh baking. Clients were greeted with smells of hot bread from the oven, hearty Hungarian goulash, and delectable desserts. Ilsa Jacob and Maria Josa were partners in cooking and hospitality. Maria's specialty was Hungarian food. Ilsa kept track of the accounting. Their plaid aprons matched the plaid tablecloths, and both served the customers with casual friendliness. They knew most of their diners by name.

Conversation tended to fly between tables. Those looking for private intimacy did not tend to frequent the Country Kitchen. Those looking for company and the latest news were rarely disappointed. The latest town gossip provided extra spice to the savory dishes. Customers usually spoke English at the Country Kitchen; however, French phrases peppered the discussions when English was inadequate.

Pete was holding court at the table in the corner next to the brownies and lemon meringue pie.

"When I got to the house yesterday morning," he announced for all to hear, "Schmidt was already dead. The place was a mess."

Ears were tuned to his version of the story, even those belonging to people who tried not to eavesdrop.

Only one woman, sitting at a corner table, seemed uninterested in the conversation. She was reading a book entitled *Forgiveness Is a Way of Life*. She wore a blue hat that matched her blue coat, and she sipped tea with a blue-gloved hand. She was like a shadow hiding from the sun.

Pete's voice penetrated as far as the kitchen where Ilsa and Maria were busily preparing lunches.

"I knew it was murder right from the start," he bragged. "I sensed there was something wrong as soon as I opened the door."

Heads nodded perceptibly, impressed with his uncanny acumen.

"I thought Mrs. Blossom was on the scene first," said Mrs. Seguin suspiciously.

Mrs. Seguin considered herself an expert on all the goings-on about town. Pete referred to her as the Would-be Mayor. She made it her business to know everything about everyone in town. She definitely did not want to appear as if she did not know the whole truth, even before it happened.

"Oh, Mrs. Blossom … Well, yes," admitted Pete reluctantly, "she was there too." Then he added quickly, "But she didn't really understand the whole significance of what was going on. I had to explain it to her."

"What exactly were you doing there in the first place?" piped in Burton Barton, who was entertaining Miss Cecilia Allen expectantly.

"Well, you know I'm an expert on antiques of all kinds," answered Pete in a voice loud enough so everyone in the room could hear easily. "It just so happens Mr. Schmidt called me to ask my advice on a very important matter. I believe he wanted to know the value of his estate. He was counting on me to give him an accurate appraisal."

"I don't know this Mr. Schmidt," admitted Rose Steel. "With a name like that, surely he's not from around these parts."

"Mr. Schmidt kept to himself mostly," said Mrs. Seguin.

Someone who kept to himself would be a definite personal affront to Mrs. Seguin, who prided herself on gathering information about the citizens of the Hill. However, not easily daunted, Mrs. Seguin usually managed to gather vital statistics even if they were not actually provided firsthand by the subject in question.

"He was German," announced Mrs. Seguin, "Came here from Montreal about twenty years ago to retire. He was some kind of scientist, worked on the West Island for a research company."

"That means he must have been about eighty-five years old," calculated Burton.

"Seems to me that's old for being murdered," piped up Cecilia using the logic of her twenty-five year old brain.

"How old does one have to be to be murdered?" questioned Suzanne Duval, who often came to the Country Kitchen with her mother for tea. Sometimes Suzanne felt her life had ended at age fifty. Her mother, on the other hand, seemed to be living forever. The concept of being murdered at eighty-five had context for Suzanne.

"Well, by eighty-five, your life's almost over," said Cecilia with great authority. "Why would anyone bother?"

"How do we know he was murdered in the first place?" asked Burton.

All eyes turned to Pete, who tucked into his lunch with gusto. He didn't dare mention the umbrella. The concept of a poisoned-tip umbrella was too absurd on the one hand, and on the other hand, it had been Emily's idea in the first place. He couldn't bring himself to admit the importance of her role in the discovery of the dead body.

"Well, Mr. Schmidt was in here two days ago," said Ilsa, as she served Suzanne and her mother, seated at the far table by the door. "He liked our lemon pie. Bought one every week."

"Never once said good day to me even though I always said hello to him," Mrs. Seguin asserted, acknowledging an insult worthy of capital punishment. "He never smiled."

"He was quite polite when he came in for his pies," Ilsa contradicted her. "Always said we made the best pies in the world."

"Looked like he ate a few too many of your pies," said Pete. "I don't envy the undertaker. He must have weighed close to three hundred pounds by the look of the corpse."

"Pete Picken!" chided Ilsa. "Shame on you! Talking about the dead in such a fashion!"

"I was just complimenting Maria's cooking," retaliated Pete.

"How about some of that dessert that's gooey-in-the-middle?" Pete added, changing the subject without apologizing. "Gooey-in-the-middle is the best."

Just as Pete was about to tuck into his lemon pie, the door opened to the jingle of bells that announced a new customer. Eyes turned curiously to see the newly arrived audience. Conversation paused, hesitated like a butterfly on a petal in the sun.

Emily Blossom entered self-consciously, looking spry and hopeful. She had been rejuvenated by the excitement of her murderous discovery the previous day and her subsequent visit to the police station. She had the look of a budding genius in the disguise of a little old lady.

The generic term *little old lady* suited her well upon first impression: *little*, because she was, at most, four foot eight; *old* because her hair was gleaming white without a wisp of grey. However her eyes had the enthusiasm of a young child discovering the powers of imagination. Her smile greeted the day like a baby responding to her mother's love. Her cheeks were as rosy as a two-year-old cherub's. Therefore, upon second glance, an astute observer could not guess her age or her attitude. One had to wait, like watching a flower in bloom, in order to aptly assess her many-layered character.

The only available seat was at Pete's table. Without hesitation, Emily chose to sit opposite her accomplice.

"Good day, Mr. Picken," she said formally. "I hope you don't mind my joining you."

"Good day, Mrs. Blossom," Pete mumbled, his mouth full of gooey-in-the-middle. A dollop of meringue quivered like a droplet from the edge of his moustache.

Emily took off her coat and hung it on the back of the chair along with the silk scarf she had worn yesterday. Then she settled herself into her place like a chicken getting ready to lay an egg.

"So what time did you get back from the station?" she asked. "Did Allard keep you long?"

"Long enough ... about three hours," said Pete gruffly, revealing as few details as possible.

"Oh really?" quipped Emily. "They let me go almost immediately. They knew I had nothing to hide."

Pete cringed at her implication that he did.

Emily warmed to her topic. "When Allard found out that I was on the scene first, they relaxed about you being there as well."

Pete looked around the room to see if others had heard her statement.

Mrs. Seguin, the Would-be Mayor, looked at him accusingly, realizing that his version of yesterday's events had been rather exaggerated in his favour. Pete scowled at Emily to silence her. She ignored his expression.

"Of course, they would never suspect a little old lady of being a murderer," she said cheerily. "So since I was already at the house and had discovered the dead body before you got there, I let Allard believe that you were in on the visit with me. That way you'd be free of suspicion as well."

The droplet of meringue let go of its hold on Pete's moustache and landed squarely on the back of his hand. He licked it up quickly and affected the best of manners while eating the remainder of his pie.

"You had a perfect alibi, with a witness." She hesitated for dramatic effect. Then she punctuated her point by adding simply, "Me."

"Thanks," Pete answered sarcastically. He wiped the corners of his mouth daintily with a paper napkin, and then continued to speak, slowly and purposefully for better effect. "But I'd appreciate it if you would not get me involved in all this. I don't need you to defend me. I have nothing to hide."

He paused to let his words sink into her muddled brain.

"Please, let it be known," he raised his voice for all to hear, staring straight at Emily's innocent expression, "I am not 'in' on anything with you."

"Now, now, Mr. Picken, don't go getting huffy," she replied, tapping his broad knuckled hand gently with her dainty fingers. "You've got your standards, I know that."

Ilsa appeared beside the table.

"What would you like, Mrs. Blossom? We have some nice pear and parsnip soup."

"Oh, that would be lovely," beamed Emily. For her, everything was lovely that day.

"So, Mr. Picken," she whispered, "do you have any suspects in mind yet?"

He looked up from his empty pie plate with a startled, calculatingly dumb expression.

Pete had cold blue eyes that he used quite effectively to intimidate. He had no compunction against staring. In fact, he could direct a gaze that seemed to knife through its target, sailing beyond without hesitation. People who were susceptible cowed quickly and turned away in confusion, without really understanding why they had been so directly challenged.

Emily was amused by his attempts to wordlessly threaten her. She wondered if his icy gaze had been honed to compensate for his lack of height. Usually the stare was most effective when he was eye to eye with his opponent. When standing, he was often looking upward at other faces.

"It hadn't even occurred to me to have suspects," he said plainly, "and I have no intentions of looking for any."

At that point, Mrs. Seguin could no longer contain herself. She jumped into the conversation enthusiastically.

"What about his wife?" she gushed, obviously having given careful thought to the subject already. "Schmidt's ex-wife lives at the Seniory Lodge. She'd be a good place to start."

Emily jumped to the bait.

"Mr. Schmidt was married?" she asked.

"Oh yes," answered Mrs. Seguin. "But it wasn't a happy marriage. Quite complicated, I believe. She's a bit dotty, but very friendly."

Friendly to Mrs. Seguin meant chatty and full of information.

"I never really understood what their relationship was. She said they were married, but they weren't when she followed him to town ... something about another woman. If you're looking for suspects, you'd do well to start with Ruth Schmidt."

"Well, I'd better be going," Pete announced, as he finished off his coffee and rose to leave. "Lots to do."

At the same moment, the blue lady in the corner also decided to leave. She placed her book into a blue bag and fished out change for her tea. Without a word to Ilsa when paying the bill, she slipped out quietly. The restaurant's diners were still intent on overhearing the scraps of conversation between Emily and Pete. No one noticed that a stranger had been in their midst or that she had left wordlessly.

Emily quickly slurped the last drop of her soup.

"I'll pay for your lunch," she said through a mouthful of bread, "if you drive me over to the lodge."

He was quick to decline. "No thanks. I'll manage my own bill. Got to run."

Emily scrambled out of her chair and turned her back to the rest of the restaurant's occupants so she could corner Pete and whisper to him at the same time.

"We have something important to discuss," she mouthed quietly, "in private."

Pete was taken aback once again. She had a way of reeling him in, which he not yet learned to resist.

Emily quickly paid the bill and followed Pete to his truck. She didn't want to let him get away. He was rummaging in the cab rearranging old boxes, lamps, dolls, and smaller objects, which he had been accumulating for sale and had not yet unloaded. He did not often have passengers. He piled everything behind the seat in the crew cab of his Ford. Then he stepped back and helped her onto the running board and into the passenger seat. She sat high above the traffic, looking regal and quite smug.

Chapter Four

PETE CLIMBED into the driver's seat, but he didn't turn the key. He took his pipe from the dashboard and slowly stuffed tobacco into the pipe bowl.

Emily took the opportunity to stare and observe. His fingers were broad with dark cracks and dirty nails. *Working hands*, she thought.

She concluded she had never seen a hairstyle quite like Pete's. The moustache covered his top lip and grew around the corners of his smile as if there were not enough room for all those whiskers to settle neatly beneath his large nose. Altogether, Pete's hair was totally unruly and refused to comply with any specific shape. Beneath the broad-brimmed hat that he always wore, curls sprang in all directions into long sideburns and a puffy ponytail. She guessed that he had once been a red head, but now there was no defined colour to all those wiry kinks. White, grey, red, brown, black, and yellow all conspired to trick any attempt at generalization.

"You still have some meringue on your moustache," she remarked politely, trying to spare him embarrassment.

"I'm saving it for later," he said unabashedly, licking the side of his lips with a long, flat tongue.

Emily looked away, trying to be discreet. Pete had a few teeth missing in front. The gap made a perfect entry for the pipe stem.

Pete slowly lit his pipe and methodically puffed up a cloud of smoke large enough to fill the cab. Emily opened her window and tried to lean her head outside for some fresh air. She reminded herself that she had no right to object to a man's bad habits in his own truck, however unpleasant they might be to her. After all, it was his truck, and she was his guest.

Eventually he turned his attention to her, as if he had tried, unsuccessfully, to forget that she was there, but then had succumbed to her unavoidable presence.

"So what's so private and important that you needed to hitch a lift with me when you could very well have walked over to the lodge by yourself?" he asked gruffly.

Emily gathered herself to her biggest size so as not to be put off by his lack of civility.

"Did it occur to you to wonder why exactly the police did show up at such an opportune moment?" she asked with a tinge of defensive snootiness. "After all, we did not get around to calling them, if you remember. Yet, there they were, in full force."

Pete looked a bit disconcerted.

"No, actually, I had not given it much thought."

"Well, I did," said Emily smugly. "I found out yesterday at the police station. I overheard a very interesting conversation."

"Well?" Pete encouraged her to continue. She had his full attention now.

"Someone tipped them off," she said simply. "They got an anonymous phone call."

"Who could that have been?" asked Pete. "There was no one else there."

Emily was pleased that she had to fill in the clues. He obviously was not a deductive thinker.

"There *was* someone in the room when he died." Her emphasis of the word *was*, with a dramatic flare, implied attention to the obvious.

She continued, "That person knew Schmidt was alive when they entered, and knew he was dead when they left. Someone phoned the police to tell them about the body."

"That's what you heard?" asked Pete incredulously.

Emily nodded with a Cheshire cat grin.

"Do the police know who was phoning?" he queried.

"The police indicated that the voice was muffled. They couldn't tell whether it was a male or a female," Emily replied.

Pete let out a sigh of exclamation, which filled his cheeks and rattled his lips. Emily continued happily.

"I think it must have been the murderer," she asserted convincingly. "Who else could have known that he was dead? He or she must have slipped out the back door as I was knocking at the front. That's when they forgot the umbrella."

"I wish you'd stop jabbering about this 'murder' thing," said Pete impatiently. "You don't have any real evidence that the man was murdered. Maybe he just had a heart attack. There was no blood."

"The police are conducting an autopsy, of course," she answered with authority. "We'll know the results shortly."

"Now, how will *we* know the results shortly, may I ask?" asked Pete sarcastically.

"Well, it'll be in the *Hill News* of course," she answered confidently. "Mr. Malarkey never misses reporting a good headliner when he gets one."

"Maloney," Pete interjected. "The reporter's name is Maloney."

"That's what I said," Emily repeated. "Maloney would never miss a good headline, especially concerning a murder in town. There's never been a real murder here before that I can remember. Allard will have to make his findings public. After all, it's in the public interest. Who knows? Maybe the murderer is a serial killer just getting started."

"Give me a break," Pete parried. "Now you're going too far."

"Well, maybe that *is* a bit much," she agreed without apology, "but one never knows."

Pete started the motor of the truck and pulled onto Main Street. The thought that he might have encountered an actual murderer—let alone a serial killer—face to face the day before sent shivers through his well-fed stomach. He puffed hurriedly on his pipe, sending smoke signals out the window.

Emily settled into her passenger bucket seat with satisfaction. Not only had she managed to surprise Pete with her new information, but she had also managed to intrigue him enough to raise his eyebrows. A good sign, she deduced. Surely, at this point, he was hooked into helping her solve the crime.

Victorian House with Lookout

Chapter Five

WHEN THEY arrived at the Seniory Lodge, Emily waited for Pete to get out and to open the door for her. He didn't move from behind the steering wheel.

"Aren't you going to help me out?" she asked with a polite smile. "After all, I'm a bit old and feeble."

Pete didn't budge. "I don't think so, Tim," he said bluntly, quoting from a line in a Tim Horton's donut commercial. "You're hardly feeble, and you're not as old as you look."

"Besides," he paused for full effect, "I'm not going in there. Those places make me nervous. All those people had to be almost dying to get in there. Not me. It's not for me."

"Don't be silly," Emily chided him. "They're not contagious."

She considered threatening to withdraw her alibi if he refused to cooperate, but instead waited in silence until he let himself acquiesce. With a sigh of resignation, he opened his driver's side door and came around the back of the truck to help her out. Then he accompanied her to the door.

Strolling arm in arm, Emily and Pete presented an odd image of respectability, which was just slightly off. She, with her proper clothes, tidy hairdo and prim manner, escorted by a ragged, tough-looking character submerged under a broad-rimmed, handmade leather hat.

To encourage him, Emily complimented him graciously, saying, "I always suspected there was a true gentleman behind your rough exterior."

"A gentleman and a scholar," he added without apology.

"Well, I'm not sure I'd go that far," she quipped, not wanting to inflate his ego beyond recognition.

When he realized that they had to punch in a code to enter the building, Pete became quite uncomfortable.

"What happens if, once inside, we can't get out again?" he demanded nervously.

"That's only for the Alzheimer's patients," Emily explained. "You don't have to worry yet. You can still read the instructions which tell you how to punch out."

She strode ahead as he paused to note the sign just inside the door. "Press 1234* to exit." He figured he could manage that much and sighed with relief.

"It's not all that bad," he reassured himself under his breath, feeling more confident until he turned around and realized that the entrance hall was filled with the faces of ancient people staring at him. He hurried to catch up with Emily like a frightened child running to hide under his mother's skirts.

"Is that you, Pete Picken?"

Pete shuddered and hardly dared to look for the source of the voice that greeted him.

A very short and very round woman accosted Pete, proffering her limp hand as a greeting; it felt like an overripe plum in his palm. He tried to avoid her by looking over her head and continuing his march in Emily's footsteps, but her large volume blocked his escape. Her hips swayed provocatively as she smoothed the front of a denim skirt that gave her the shape of a rain barrel. She actually danced in his path, giggling. Her eyes disappeared behind plump, dimpled cheeks as her smile creased her face into a sea of ripples and eddies, all moving in confused expressions of mixed emotions.

"I can't tell you how happy I am to see you after all this time."

"Ah, Marie Cartier. It has been a long time," he said, wishing it had been even longer since he'd seen her.

"I'm here visiting my mother," she said, gesturing over her shoulder toward a woman hunched into her wheelchair, eyeing Pete with suspicion, but no sign of recognition. The older Mrs. Cartier's pale, crooked face scanned him from across the lobby, while a slow drool escaped the corner of her lips and made its way down her wrinkled chin.

"Ah," he mumbled, "I didn't recognize her."

"She had a series of small strokes a couple of months ago," said Marie. "We're so glad to have the Seniory staff looking after her. After all these years of mental suffering, at least she has some friendly people to make her feel welcome here. I'm so tired of caring for her at home by myself, since Father died."

"Ah. I hadn't heard."

"Yes," Marie crooned. "I'm all alone now."

Pete knew she was leering at him. *Like a spider eyeing her prey,* he thought.

"Yes, well, I hope you enjoy the change."

"Oh, I will. Especially if you drop by for a visit."

"Yes ..."

There was a stunned silence between them. Pete could hear the clock ticking, the TV droning, the murmur of elder occupants whispering among themselves.

"Well."

Pete glanced desperately after Emily's figure, fading down the hallway.

"Drop by any time," said Marie. "I'm always home in the evening after visiting hours."

Pete grimaced, excused himself, and hurried after Emily, who was asking the head nurse for directions to Ruth Schmidt's room. He didn't dare glance back over his shoulder.

"Room 17. It's down the hall on the left just past the Coke machine. Can't miss it," said the nurse abruptly. Then she added more sympathetically, "She's having a bit of a bad day. Heard her ex-husband was found dead yesterday morning. You may have difficulty following her rambling. Everything gets a bit mixed up in her head on a bad day. She'll be glad to have visitors, though. No one ever comes to see her really. I guess she doesn't have many friends in town."

Emily walked quickly down the hall. Pete, afraid of being recognized again, practically had to trot beside her to keep up. Her little feet in tennis shoes moved in short, quick steps when she was determined to get wherever she intended to be. The door to Room 17 was slightly ajar.

Emily turned to Pete and whispered at him, "When questioning a suspect, one must be direct and straightforward. We want to get her first reaction before she has time to cover up her real emotions. Remember, she may be the one who killed him. Ex-wives, you know, are the obvious suspects."

Before Pete could answer, Emily knocked loudly, and without waiting for a greeting, she entered with a smile on her face. Pete was her shadow, caught between the fear of being left behind and the fear of meeting a Looney Tunes character in person. Sticking close to Emily was his best defense. Even though she could undoubtedly get *him* into trouble, she'd also have to get *herself* out of it. He planned to be close on her heels when she made her escape.

The room was barely large enough for a single bed and simple dresser. A plastic lawn chair sat in the corner, the only seat for visitors to the tiny room.

As soon as they saw the room's occupant, they both realized she was not the murderer they were looking for. Mrs. Ruth Schmidt's frail body was no longer capable of walking. Like a bathrobe flung carelessly onto a chair, she was folded into a wheelchair squeezed between the bed and the wall. Her hair was the colour of salt. Her hands were gnarled and clutched the chair arms for support. Her legs were mere bones with slippers attached. "Hello, Mrs. Schmidt. How are you today?" Emily cheerfully launched into her best bedside manner.

Mrs. Schmidt appeared unpleasantly surprised, unaccustomed as she was to having visitors of any sort. She had obviously been crying. Tears traced tracks in wrinkles that cascaded around the edge of her downcast lips.

"Go away," she said pouting, "I'm having a bad day."

"I'm so sorry, my dear," Emily commiserated. "Everyone has a bad day now and then."

Emily led the way into the room and made herself at home, as if she were quite used to visiting invalids regularly. Without being asked, she settled into the plastic chair, apparently for a long, leisurely visit. Pete pretended not to be there at all.

"Well, your ex-husband doesn't die every day," countered Mrs. Schmidt.

"I'm so sorry for your loss. It must be terrible for you."

"Who did you say you were?" said Mrs. Schmidt, rallying slightly in the presence of sympathetic visitors.

"My name is Emily Blossom. I represent the Summit Life Insurance Company, and this is my partner, Pete Picken. We've come to see you about your husband's—rather, your ex-husband's—life insurance policy."

Pete glared at Emily, stunned by her announcement.

"Emily, what are you saying?" he whispered, so that Ruth could not hear. "Are you out of your mind?"

Emily shooed him away and continued her explanation.

"Whenever one of our clients passes on," Emily continued, as if she had been practicing her sales pitch for years, "We pay a visit to the family of the deceased to offer our most heartfelt condolences.

The company, you see, has a vested interest in the welfare of its customers."

Ruth Schmidt looked at Emily briefly, and then scanned Pete from head to toe with a critical expression.

"He looks a bit rough around the edges for an insurance salesman," she said bluntly.

Apparently, Mrs. Schmidt was not as clueless as she appeared. Emily looked Pete up and down and nodded.

"Yes, perhaps he does look a tiny bit shoddy," answered Emily, glancing up at Pete with a wink. "He's just starting out in the business. He's my assistant-in-training. We will have to have a talk to him about our dress codes."

Then she added matter-of-factly, "On the other hand, we do suggest to our representatives that they dress casually to make our clients feel more comfortable. Our salesmen used to be too well dressed. They tended to make our customers feel ill at ease."

Ruth Schmidt looked from one to the other quizzically.

"Did Helmut have a life insurance policy?" Ruth asked. "He never mentioned anything about it."

"Well, actually, it wasn't a policy as such," Emily wheedled her way through her fabrication. "It was ... well ... a remembrance. Yes, that's it, a remembrance ... He left a list of those whom he wanted us to notify in case of his death. As a caring and conscientious company, we provide that service for our clients," she started to gather steam. "We ask our customers to provide us with a list of those close family members whom they wish to be personally notified. We pay a little visit to the grieving relatives as a personal touch."

Then Emily added sweetly, "It's the least we can do at this stage." She went on. as if she were making perfectly good sense, "Has it been long since you last saw him?"

Mrs. Schmidt began to cry. Emily and Pete glanced at each other furtively to gauge each other's reaction. They raised their eyebrows simultaneously.

Maybe she's faking, thought Emily. *She can't be all that grief-stricken. He was her ex, after all.*

If this keeps up, thought Pete, who panicked whenever he saw tears, *I'm outta here.*

"I loved him so much," said Mrs. Schmidt between sobs. "And to think that he considered me a close relative upon his death. I'm so touched."

"Yes, he loved you very much," said Emily, weaving her web.

Pete rolled his eyes in exasperation.

Ruth went on, "He wouldn't even talk to me after he left me. I even followed him here to the Hill when he moved to this area, but he never acknowledged my existence. Now he's gone forever," she wailed in a loud, quavering sob.

Emily hadn't bargained on causing a crisis. She kneeled in front of the wheelchair, wrapped her arms around the grieving woman.

"Now, now," tut-tutted Emily. "It's alright. Shhh. Don't go getting yourself too worked up. It's okay."

"It's *not* okay!" cried Ruth. "You don't understand. He never lived long enough for me to tell him what I really thought of the bastard. It'll never be okay!"

Behind Ruth's back, Emily glanced at Pete, who shrugged his shoulders, lifting his palms toward the ceiling as if to say, *Don't ask me. I haven't got a clue what she's talking about.*

Eventually Ruth's sobbing quieted, as Emily rocked her in her arms.

Averting his eyes, Pete scanned the tiny, sparsely decorated bedroom. A photo in a plain silver frame sat on a hand-laced doily on the dresser. An apparently blissful couple posed for a snapshot on a stone wall overlooking a picturesque European city. A youthful Ruth in nurse's uniform clung to a rigidly handsome, thinner version of the Schmidt Pete had known. This one faded, black-and-white photograph presented a ghostly image of distant memories. The sad little memento was the only personal item in the room. No paintings adorned the walls; no knickknacks or plants cluttered the window ledge.

The room was stark and devoid of identity.

"How dreadful for you," soothed Emily. "Tell us all about it. When did you first meet Helmut Schmidt? How long ago was it?"

Without much prodding, Ruth Schmidt launched into reminiscence.

"It was just after the war in Germany. I went over to practice nursing. I had studied nursing during the forties, got my RN certification, and shipped overseas to help with the reconstruction. There were so many people in need of medical care."

"You met in Germany?" prodded Emily.

"I was young, twenty years old, and just out of college. What did I know about love? He was so handsome and confident, as if he didn't have a doubt in the world."

"How did you meet?" asked Emily. "You were Canadian, and he was German."

"Oh yes, things were very different in those days. It was after the war, and everyone was sort of numb. I was stationed in Heidelberg. There was a big American base there, and we were assigned to help with the soldiers who had been wounded but weren't well enough to be transported home. After hours, we used to go to one particular bar where there was good beer, good food, and lots of singing and laughing. Germans and foreigners, it didn't matter, we were all lost and on the lookout for a good time."

"You met at the bar?" asked Emily. "Weren't you afraid of strangers?"

"I was very naïve. I believed in basic human good, in spite of all that had happened during the war. I believed that most people tell the truth and that most people have the same basic needs: health, food, and love. I also assumed that I was essentially unimportant in the larger scheme of things. Who would want to take advantage of me? I had done nothing to anyone. I was only interested in helping others who needed my services. I loved nursing, and I was needed. I felt worthwhile in a small way."

"What was Schmidt doing when you met him? Hadn't he been in the German military?" asked Pete, who couldn't resist getting drawn into the story.

"He told me that he was a scientist doing research," said Ruth. "That's all he said at the time. Only later did I find out what kind of research and why he didn't have to fight along side other men his age."

She smiled when she mentioned how naïve she had been; but the corners of her lips curled maliciously when she spoke of Schmidt's research.

"He was only twenty-five. By rights, he should have enlisted, but he never served in the military. That's why he wasn't a prisoner of war. He never went to the front lines."

Then Ruth snickered, belying sarcasm quite incongruous with her apparent grief. "Little did I know at the time that he was much more dangerous to the enemy than any of the weapons carried by the soldiers at the Front."

"Why?" asked Emily. "What do you mean 'more dangerous'?"

"Oh, that only came out much later, after I had fallen hopelessly in love with him."

The distraught woman began to cry again. "I still believe that he didn't really mean to harm anyone," she sobbed. "Even now, I still want to believe that he was a good man at heart."

Then quickly her voice changed into bitterness. "The war did that to people—took away their goodness and made them into monsters. I always thought that he'd change after we came to Canada, that he'd forget the horrors of what he had done. I wanted him to become the kind man I always believed was underneath all that anger. I thought if I just loved him enough, he'd learn to be gentle and caring."

Pete noticed that Ruth's face changed dramatically as she spoke. One moment her eyes were streaming with tears; the next, they were flashing with anger. Her face softened when she spoke of love, but on the subject of war, a frown etched scars of pain on her forehead.

Ruth Schmidt's elevator doesn't go to the top floor, Pete thought to himself.

Emily, on the other hand, was oblivious to the conflicts that seemed to wage emotional war in Ruth's memory. She was more intent on getting to the bottom of the mystery that increasingly intrigued her.

Poor girl, she thought. *Not too clever, really.*

"I assume you were actually married?" Emily said out loud as she led Ruth back to the story. "Your name is legally Schmidt, isn't it?"

"Oh yes," Ruth nodded with a mixture of pain and pleasure playing across her face. "I had known him for only two weeks when he proposed. I desperately wanted to make love to him. My body ached whenever I was near him. We laughed so hard together, especially when we had lots to drink. When he looked directly into my eyes, it was as if he could see into my soul. And then," her voice softened to a whisper, "he was so tender and gentle with me when he walked me back to the barracks."

She paused, lost in reveries. "His lips were as soft as a breeze on my face," she confided.

Emily could see that once Ruth had been quite pretty, with soft features and delicate bone structure. Her sea blue eyes still flashed with a sparkle of beauty quite adequate to attract a young man's fancy.

"But when he kissed me ..." she hesitated briefly, took a deep breath, and remembered the feelings as if she were still in his arms.

Then her eyes searched Emily's, pleading with a pitiful gaze for female empathy. "When he kissed me, his tongue was like fire. I melted in his arms."

Silence fell between them like a spell. For a brief instant, all three occupants of the tiny, stark room were transported into the magical realm of passion. Each one of them revisited that private corner of memory where love dwells, eternal and hopeful.

Ruth could actually feel the touch of her German lover's fingers on her cheeks. She could smell the sweetness of his cologne.

Emily remembered her and her husband's first kiss on the veranda on a warm summer night. They had been swinging in a swaying chair for two. The scent of rose blossoms wafted on the evening breeze. His eyelashes tickled her skin, and his nose got in the way when their lips met.

Pete remembered a romp in the hayloft with his pal, Olivia. She had transformed from a tomboy into a young woman right before his eyes that lazy afternoon on his fourteenth birthday. Her laughter taunted him. He was nearly crazy with a desire that he did not understand.

Pots clanged in the kitchen down the hall of the seniors' residence, breaking the spell, bringing each of them away from their secrets. They all breathed a collective sigh, and let the memories slip back into the past.

"Yes, well," said Emily, getting back down to business. "Marriage does funny things to a relationship, and you were only eighteen at the time?"

"What a fool I was," Ruth resumed her narrative bitterly. "What an utter fool!"

"We all make mistakes," said Emily, trying to make excuses for the suffering woman. Ruth sniffed in response.

"Yes, well, I made a lot of them," she parried. "More than most people's share. He never really loved me. He wanted a Canadian bride, so he could get out of the country. I was a perfect mark. My friends warned me. My boss, the doctors I worked with, everyone tried to tell me that it wasn't a good idea and that I hadn't known him long enough. But I wanted him so badly. I couldn't tell the difference between wanting and needing and loving. They were all the same maddening, overwhelming desire.

"We were married by the chaplain at the barracks. We had two soldiers on the base as our witnesses because I was too embarrassed to ask my friends. I knew it was insane, but I went ahead and did it anyway. Eighteen years stupid. That's what I was, and I never really found out what a mistake I'd made until we actually came to Canada as husband and wife. Then his real colours began to show, but by then, it was too late for me. I was insanely and hopelessly in love, but worse than that, I was married to the man. For me, marriage is forever."

"Let's get on with it," Pete said to Emily, whispering in her ear so that Ruth could not hear. "Find out what she knows."

Emily realized that she had been caught up in the story, but she reminded herself, *He's right. Detectives must stay focused.*

Out loud she asked, "When you came back to Canada, that's when he changed his tune?"

"No, not right away," replied Ruth. "He was still quite civil when we first got back to Montreal. We rented an apartment. I got a good position nursing at the Montreal General, and he began to look for a job in his field."

"What did he do?" asked Pete. "You said he was a scientist."

"Yes, I found out later his specialty was pain," Ruth's voice implied much more than the simple words she uttered. "It all came out gradually. During the war, he experimented on humans. As he put it, he studied pain thresholds."

Ruth looked at Emily's face and then Pete's to measure their reaction to her revelation.

"Torture?" asked Pete harshly. "You mean that kind of pain?"

Ruth nodded without speaking. Emily shivered.

"Now we're getting somewhere," she thought, "closer to a motive."

"When he came to Canada, he was well qualified to continue his research on animals at a pharmaceutical company in the West Island of Montreal. They were all too happy to avail themselves of his extensive knowledge in the field," explained Ruth. "He got a very good offer."

"You must have been pleased in one way," commented Emily. "You had a place to live. You both had good jobs. Weren't you happy?"

Ruth shook her head. The tears welled into her eyes again.

"He was happy. He got what he wanted. But then, after about six months, his anger started to show. It was always my fault. I could never get it right. Either dinner was burned, or his laundry wasn't clean, or I was late getting home. At first he just yelled and cursed, but then, one night he hit me, knocked me against the wall. I can still feel the pain of when my head hit the baseboard. I couldn't believe he'd actually done it. That first time, I thought it was a mistake. I convinced myself that he didn't really mean it.

"Usually it was some little thing that normally wouldn't have mattered. I began to be afraid to come home because I could never predict how he was going to be. All of a sudden, he'd just start shouting, louder and louder, and then he'd work himself into a rage and start beating me. In a way, I'm lucky I was too weak to fight back. He'd just keep on hitting me until I couldn't get up any more. Then he'd leave, slamming the door, and he wouldn't come back until early morning. He'd smell of beer and smoke. Night after night it was the same."

"You never told anyone?" asked Emily softly.

Ruth's eyes showed the answer. She looked away in anguish.

"Even now I have a hard time admitting how awful it was," she said. "Even though it was so long ago.

"Sometimes, for a while, he'd seem to be better," Ruth continued. "He'd be nice to me for a while. He'd come home with a dozen roses, kiss me like he did in the beginning, and pretend that nothing bad had ever happened between us. I'd pretend too. I so wanted everything to be alright. I promised myself every day that this time I wouldn't make any mistakes. I'd look after him better, and he'd love me again. But soon, for no apparent reason that I could anticipate, he'd explode again and beat me to a pulp. At work, my colleagues were suspicious. You can only walk into so many doors before people begin to ask questions, but I'd always pretend that everything was just fine."

"Why didn't you leave him?" asked Pete, impatiently. He had little patience for illogical behaviour.

"Actually, I guess I was lucky," smiled Ruth sadly. "He left me before he killed me. I came home from work about a year after we had come to Montreal, and all his things were gone. There wasn't even a note. Nothing. He left ... just like that."

"You must have been relieved," commented Emily.

"Relieved? No. I was too devastated," Ruth went on. "I guess I really never did recover. Those first few months after he left, I was completely destroyed. I couldn't work. I couldn't eat. I just stayed in the apartment and cried, day after day, week after week. Whenever I'd call his office, his secretary said he wasn't available. I couldn't find out where he had moved or why."

Then she emitted a bitter chuckle that Pete and Emily had learned to recognize. It was like an open wound.

"Eventually I found out that he'd left me for his secretary. That's why she always covered for him. Jenny Henderson—that was her name. She was sticky sweet on the telephone. When he first hired her, she pretended to be all friendly and understanding, as if she were our best friend and would do anything to satisfy her boss's every need. Eventually I realized she was lying. They had a nice little thing going for a while. He didn't need me anymore. I'd served his purpose nicely. Little did she know that she was just a pawn as well. She thought she was better than me, but he never really loved her either. He had no capacity to love anyone, as it turned out. His heart was too twisted into hate. He actually enjoyed torturing women."

"You were better off without him then," pronounced Pete.

Ruth Schmidt dissolved once again into tears. By now she had completely exhausted herself and became like a wailing, desolate child. "I loved him. I really loved him. I'm so, so sorry he's dead."

Pete yanked at Emily's coat sleeve.

"Let's get outta here now," he said, "before she loses it altogether. This broad's two bricks short of a load."

They moved softly toward the door, but just as Pete put his hand on the doorknob, Ruth Schmidt called them back.

"What did you say your name was?" she asked.

"Blossom," replied Emily. "Emily Blossom and Pete Picken."

Ruth Schmidt seemed to revive her energy. She had not finished with them yet.

"I have a couple more things to tell you," she said, her voice suddenly strong and direct. "Important things," she added.

Emily's face flushed with excitement, and Pete caught himself getting drawn in again.

Emily approached the wheelchair and pulled her own chair closer to listen. She sensed that the secret Mrs. Schmidt was about to reveal was the reason they had come to visit in the first place.

"My ex-husband," said Ruth dramatically, "had a lot of enemies."

"He did?" prodded Emily.

Pete leaned closer so he could hear better. Mrs. Schmidt nodded authoritatively.

"Do you know who they were?" asked Pete impatiently.

"He had lots of enemies for sure," asserted Mrs. Schmidt, "but they're all dead. He made sure of that."

Emily looked at Pete, whose face drained of colour.

"He murdered them?" asked Emily breathlessly. Here was a better revelation than even she had imagined.

"You might say so," said Ruth. "If they didn't die directly as a result of his experiments, they died in the concentration camps afterward. He made sure that there were no survivors to act as witnesses after it was all over."

Emily gasped. Pete thought he was going to vomit.

"I guess I was really one of the lucky ones," Mrs. Schmidt added, beginning to cry again. "There's a fine difference between psychological and physical torture. He had his techniques down to a fine art by the time he met me."

Emily had heard enough, and Pete was all too ready to disappear. They moved in unison toward the door to make their exit, but once again Ruth Schmidt called them back.

"Just one more thing," she sobbed. "I need to tell someone … anyone … just to get it off my chest."

Emily did not move closer this time. She needed some time to figure out the significance of all she had heard. Pete's hand was already turning the doorknob.

"I'm ready to die now," confessed the sobbing woman. "Now that he's dead, I need to be with him in hell. He'll need me there. I know he will. We'll suffer together forever. It's too much torture to be living on when I know that he's no longer here. I cannot help myself. I want to die too."

Emily and Pete left the old woman sobbing into her pillow. Wordlessly they made their way down the hall and past the lobby, where ancient eyes followed their flight. Emily meticulously punched the code 1234* into the exit lock and slipped outside. Before Pete could follow, he heard Marie's sticky sweet voice just behind him.

"Pete! Pete!"

Her voice was like an electric shock, and he paused just long enough for her to block his way out of the building. He watched helplessly as the door closed behind Emily.

"I didn't want you to leave without seeing me again. Why don't you come on over and visit me soon? We could share stories about the old times. I'd like that."

Pete's face paled, and he gulped inadvertently.

"Yeah, yeah, Marie. Sometime we'll get together. Yep, that'd be swell."

He moved to leave when her hand closed tightly around his arm. He could smell stale breath when she raised herself onto her tiptoes to whisper in his ear.

"You remember when we kissed behind Old Man Henderson's shed?" She winked at him. "You were my very first boy friend."

"Don't remind me."

"We were going to be married one day," she insisted.

"We were only teenagers! What did we know?" Pete croaked and tore his arm from her grip. "Bye, Marie."

He ran for the door. Hastily he tried to punch out the numbers on the keypad: 1234. He tried three times, but still the door remained locked.

Marie eagerly approached him again. Putting her arm around his shoulders and smiling, she very gently and slowly punched in the numbers, using the star key to enter the correct code, as per the instructions beside the door.

Pete could not escape quickly enough. He squeezed himself out of the opening door as soon as there was a gap wide enough to let him through.

In the meantime, Emily had hiked herself into the truck before Pete could get into the driver's seat. She didn't want to be left behind.

Pete, on the other hand, was more than eager to leave her to her own devices. He'd had enough of snooping into other people's lives. Besides, he was totally shaken by his encounter with Marie Cartier, although he did not want to let on to Emily. He covered himself by taking the offensive.

"What's it with you?" he asked gruffly once he was behind the steering wheel. "Can't you walk?"

"We need to talk," said Emily simply. "We have to figure things out."

"Look," said Pete, being as patient as his impatience would allow, "I don't think you understand. Let me make myself perfectly clear. I've had enough of you and your figuring. That Schmidt lady back there is off her rocker, and we just waltzed on in there and sent her over the edge. I don't like crazy people. I'm certifiable enough on my own without anyone else's help."

"Don't be silly," Emily contradicted him.

She was about to go on when Pete exploded. "Silly? Silly? Where do you get off calling somebody else silly? With all your harebrained schemes! You don't know what silly is! If I say I'm certifiable, I know what I'm talking about. You ... you, on the other hand, haven't a clue what's going on. You just think you can wander in there, poking into somebody's life, pretending to be someone you're not. Then, smooth as silk, you wander on out, looking for some more little adventure, just for fun? That's silly. In fact, that's downright stupid.

"And look at that poor woman." Pete's voice rose louder as he became more animated. "Looney as a dollar. Wants to die so she can join that bastard in hell, after all he did to her. What's wrong with that woman? I don't get it, and I don't want to know nothin' from nothin'. Now, if you would please get out of my truck right now, I'm leaving and hoping, with any luck, I'll never ever see you again."

"Now, Mr. Picken," Emily began, hoping that, if she talked softly, he would quiet down. "I do agree that we did rather step into a bit of a mess. Let me explain about Ruth."

She paused just long enough to create a bit of suspense, but not long enough for him to interrupt. "Mrs. Schmidt follows the pattern of many battered women. Sometimes they actually believe that they deserve to be treated badly. It's the way they see themselves. Being beaten is the way they feel worthy."

"Exactly," said Pete, clearly exasperated with her explanation. "Now what kind of a way is that to live?"

"They say that love is blind," Emily continued, without answering Pete's comment. "I don't think that's it, really," she added pensively, as if trying to explain something that she didn't really understand herself.

"When a person is in love, she sees quite clearly who it is that she adores." She paused and then continued once she had figured out what she wanted to say. "It's just that sometimes the person she loves is not the person she wishes he were."

Pete scratched his head underneath his hat, which bobbed up and down. He scowled but had no comment in time to stop her train of chatter.

"What I can't understand is Mr. Schmidt," said Emily seriously. "How can a man be so evil?"

"Oh, brother," sneered Pete. "I can't believe you're as naïve as you pretend to be."

"I'm not naïve," she said defensively, tilting her nose with an air of conceit. "On the contrary, I cultivate open-mindedness. I choose not to judge a person based on hearsay."

"Hearsay?" repeated Pete. "You're the one who wanted to get Mrs. Schmidt's version in the first place."

"Well, you have to admit, we did get further on in our investigation," countered Emily. "After all, we do have a suspect now."

"Suspect?" he shouted. "We have ten million suspects! So what? You and the whole Nazi war crimes tribunal. The man's dead. He obviously had it coming. Whoever offed him did the world a favour. So let it go at that."

"But that's not solving the mystery," Emily rejoined.

"Look, lady," Pete began to explain. He spoke in a controlled tone that sounded as if he would detonate at any second. "Get a life … and while you're at it … I'm asking you nicely … get out of my truck … get out of my way … and leave me alone. Do you understand? Can I make it any clearer?"

Emily had a way of lifting her eyebrows and looking skyward while still facing her reluctant partner. The expression was designed to look cute and irresistible at the same time. Even though her face was rather complicated with wrinkles, she pretended to look innocently childlike and therefore quite compelling.

Unfortunately for her, Pete stared straight ahead. Since he was not looking at her, he was thus able to avoid her charms. Emily's hopeful expression changed reluctantly to one of resignation.

Her hand moved to the door latch. She heaved open the door just as a police cruiser was pulling up beside Pete's truck. They heard a sickening crunch as metal dented metal. Albert Allard grimaced.

"Oh, Allo Allard," said Emily sweetly. "Fancy meeting you here."

Officer Allard descended from the patrol car and examined the extent of damage.

"And I suppose this is just a coincidence meeting you two here?" he said suspiciously, after he had assured himself that the scratch on his own vehicle was minimal.

Pete got out of the truck and approached the passenger side. He turned green when he realized that, although the cruiser was not damaged, his truck door had been severely dented. Emily smiled serenely at the police officer, who scowled in response.

"We were just visiting with poor Mrs. Schmidt," admitted Emily innocently. "Poor woman. We knew her from the auctions, you understand," she lied, straight-faced. "We knew she'd be distraught when she heard of her ex-husband's unfortunate demise."

Allard was not to be put off. He pulled himself to his finer height of six foot two, which was quite effective in dwarfing Pete, who glanced up twelve inches to look the officer in the eye. The sergeant's badge shone brightly in the sun, along with the full component of brass buttons on his shirt.

"Now look, you two," he threatened. "I don't want to find out that you're interfering with a police investigation."

"Oh no, officer," said Emily inoffensively. "We would never think of such a thing." She paused for effect and then added pointedly, "That's your job."

Allard bristled. Pete cowed. Emily puffed herself up like a contented hen.

"And besides," she added, with what she hoped was a sweet smile, "who could ever conduct an investigation better than you do yourself?"

Allard sniffed arrogantly, and tipped his hat gallantly, but then he countered, "Just don't let me find you two messing around in something that's none of your business."

"No, sir," said Pete meekly. "Whatever you say, sir."

Pete walked quickly around the front of his truck, slipped up behind the steering wheel and started the motor. He deliberately did not look at Emily, who sat smugly in her passenger's seat. Pete drove up Mill Street and let her off outside her house.

Emily slipped down out of the truck, but she paused just before she closed the door so he could not drive away before she had her say.

"I know you didn't mean it," she stopped to give him a chance to respond. His eyebrows raised in a question.

"I mean about never seeing me again," she said coyly. "You were just upset about Mrs. Schmidt. It's okay. I'm sure we'll see each other again soon. Thanks for the ride home."

Underneath his moustache, she could see his lip twitch just a smidgen, and she knew that she was right. She smiled brightly and heaved the door shut as delicately as the truck would allow.

Emily's House with Stained Glass Window over the Entrance

Chapter Six

EMILY'S HOUSE was situated on a short lane two blocks from Main Street. After Pete had driven away, Emily paused to admire the stained glass window above the front entrance as she often did. Visitors approaching from the street could see the dark, rich colours of a simple flower pattern in the window above the door. The window was not apparent from inside but was one of the special features that Emily had admired when she bought the house, and she had resolved to appreciate the window every time she approached the house from the street.

"It's like a prayer to the house goddess," Emily explained to herself. She liked little rituals that made every day richer.

Many of the older houses on the Hill were similar to Emily's. Rust-coloured, orange-brick homes lined the narrow streets clustered on top of a broad hill surrounded by a vast river valley. The tall houses had white porches decorated in ornate gingerbread trim. The architecture represented a Victorian taste for practical conservatism with hints of forbidden pleasures. Three mansions in town had lookout towers with panoramic views of the plains stretching toward the Ottawa River in the north and the mountains in the east. Some had glass greenhouses for early planting of spring gardens.

Emily's house had been through many changes over the years.

"This house is very much like me," she realized when the real estate agent first showed it to her. "We've both been through considerable restructuring, but we have our good points just the same."

The building was no longer the elegant Victorian mansion it had once been. The decorative porch had long since been pulled down. Now the front entrance to the house was within a few feet of the block-long alley called Pearl Street. Once, the house had been an expansive six-bedroom home for a wealthy and prolific family. The floor layout originally featured two staircases with a parlour on one side and family sitting room on the other.

Shortly after the Second World War, the home had been divided into two identical halves, for two brothers who never spoke to one another. Each had renovated their halves differently. One brother had married and had children. He covered the weathered brick with vinyl siding, replaced the old windows with brown aluminum, and covered the floors with wall-to-wall carpeting. The other brother made few changes. He merely added new linoleum on top of the old, painted the walls with bright colours, and lived in virtual poverty. There was no evidence that either brother ever had very much money. All repairs had been done with the bare minimum of expense. Emily surmised that they had lost their fortunes during the depression and that they both lived on meager incomes.

Now the house was essentially two separate dwellings under a common roof. From the outside, one half-house was white with brown windows, and one half-house was brick with paint-peeling, multi-paned windows. One side appeared modernized and plain; the other side looked old and sedate with a bit of wear and tear around the edges. Inside, each apartment featured a kitchen and living/dining room area with the bedrooms and bathrooms upstairs.

This arrangement suited Emily perfectly. She had one apartment to rent and the other to live in. Having a tenant enabled her to pay her mortgage. Her pension sufficed for her living expenses, and whatever was left over contributed to her art collection.

When out and about, Emily encouraged herself to be an explorer.

"Don't let the limits of your surroundings dictate the boundaries of your imagination," Emily told herself. "To make the most of life, one must never take any day for granted."

For Emily, part of the pleasure of having a comfortable house was being secure enough to leave it. Whenever she returned home from her adventures, she felt an immediate sense of well-being. She loved being in her nest, cozy and comfortable—safe from herself and her tendency to exaggerate the mundane.

There were two inhabitants in her apartment: she was the talkative one; the other, a cat named Charlie, was bossy and demanding. Emily was well aware that, of the two residents in her apartment, she was *not* the one in charge.

Unlocking the front door, she was greeted with angry, meowing complaints.

A large cat sat on the fourth step of the stairway. He looked more like a creature from another world, housed in a very abundant fur disguise. His eyes stared out from deep inner darkness, surrounded by a whiskered face, which looked as if it had been squashed against a windowpane. The noise emanating from him sounded rather like a wolf's complaint against the full moon.

"Charlie, my boy, I know I've been away for longer than usual, but I had some important business to attend to," Emily explained, as if to a human companion. "You'll have to forgive me."

The cat descended from his perch and sauntered down the stairs toward the kitchen.

"Yes, yes, you're right," replied Emily. "I know I'm late for tea. Perhaps you'll feel better if I give you a little treat."

Dutifully Emily went to the cupboard and offered the cat some of his favourite treats. With obvious disdain, he capitulated and accepted her peace offering. Emily then put the kettle on the stove and placed a few cookies on a dish next to the teapot.

She was not surprised when there was a knock at the door.

"Come in," she shouted cheerily. "It's open."

Cassie, her tenant from next door, had an uncanny ability to show up just in time for afternoon tea. Her penchant for knowing the correct timing was aided by the fact that the walls were rather thin. Both parties could hear the activities of the occupants in the neighbouring apartment. Usually, Emily turned the radio on quite loud to muffle sounds from next door. Cassie and her boyfriend, Robert, kept a television on in each room. Nevertheless, when convenient, the neighbours could remain quite well informed of each other's activities.

"Emily, were you out again today in that cold weather?" chided Cassie. "Yesterday you were traipsing around in the rain, and again today in the cold. I hope you're wearing proper clothing. Fall is a bad time to get sick, you know."

"Oh, my dear, you needn't worry about me," replied Emily. "I'm a hardy old soul, Cassie, and besides, I can't stay cooped up in the house all the time. Actually, I've been continuing my investigation."

"Oh, my dear," said Cassie, sounding much like Emily herself, "I hope you haven't gotten yourself mixed up with Pete Picken again. That man gives me the creeps."

"Oh, Mr. Picken's a nice man," soothed Emily. "He's just a little rough on the outside, like a diamond."

"Like a diamond?" questioned Cassie.

"Yes, you've heard the phrase before," explained Emily. "A rough diamond."

"Do you mean 'a diamond in the rough'?" questioned Cassie.

"Perhaps the term is a bit old-fashioned. My mother used to say that my husband was my rough diamond," Emily chuckled. "Little did she know the whole truth, as it turned out."

"Why? Wasn't he a nice man?" asked Cassie. "You don't talk about him very often."

Emily became uncomfortable and began to fidget at the stove, waiting for the kettle to boil.

"We were talking about Mr. Picken," she said, returning the conversation to the original subject. "Mr. Picken's not as bad as he seems when you first meet him. I really believe he tries to put people off just to see if they'll take the time to get to know who he really is under that hard shell."

"He actually scares me," said Cassie, "the way he yells all the time. He pretends to know so much."

"Cassie," tut-tutted Emily, "You can't judge a cover by the book."

Cassie furrowed her eyebrows into a question mark.

"First impressions, you know," Emily continued. "First impressions are often misleading."

"It's not actually my first impression I'm worried about," countered Cassie. "I've known that man since I was knee-high to a grasshopper, and I've always thought he was a bit odd."

"Oh, he's not as bad as all that, once you get to know him," said Emily in a conciliatory tone.

Emily placed two delicate Limoges teacups on the kitchen table and poured steaming tea, the colour of carnelian, from a delicately flowered porcelain pot. Emily signaled to Cassie to sit by the window. Charlie, the cat, perched in an antique child's high chair placed next to Emily's captain's chair at the head of the table. His eyes followed the destiny of the cookies, which were a specialty from the Country Kitchen on the Hill.

Emily seldom cooked a meal. More often she bought fruit and vegetables for salad and contented herself with pre-cooked meats from the deli counter at the village grocery store. Usually Cassie and Robert invited her for dinner once a week.

"Any man driving around town in that truck of his with the sign, 'Picken In His Truck,' makes a person think twice. That's so arrogant."

"I thought the name was kind of catchy," commented Emily, "considering that antique dealers are often referred to as pickers."

"Well, my impressions of people are usually bang on, and I have a bit of difficulty with Mr. Picken," asserted Cassie. Cassie had just turned thirty, and her mannerisms implied that she thought herself quite experienced in the world. "On the other hand, when I first met you, I knew we'd be friends right off the bat."

Emily smiled with understanding. "Cassie, you're so friendly and cheerful. How could a person not be friends with you?"

Cassie continued her train of thought, "Well, come to think of it, when I first met Robert, my first impression was not great. I wasn't sure about him, but that's because of extenuating circumstances. He was with my best friend at the time, and I guess I was jealous."

"What made you change your mind?" asked Emily, who enjoyed being Cassie's confidante.

"My girlfriend and I talked about Robert and decided that we needed to put him to the test, so one night we were all out together at the bar. He was sitting next to my girlfriend with his arm around her shoulder. I walked up and accidentally-on-purpose shoved a glass of ice water off the counter."

Cassie began to giggle like a little girl with a secret. "Emily, you won't believe it. My aim was perfect. The glass landed right in his crotch. I couldn't do it again if I tried! It didn't hurt him, but the surprise on his face was unforgettable."

"You didn't really do that on purpose, did you?" exclaimed Emily, putting her delicate hand to her mouth. "I can't believe you'd really do something like that!"

Cassie's face changed from delight to innocence. "Why not? It was only a joke."

"That's such a cruel joke, Cassie. The poor boy. He must have died of embarrassment. How did he live it down?"

"That was the test, don't you see?" said Cassie simply. "At first, he was shocked, and I thought he'd be really angry. He could have hauled off and smacked me one. But then, when he saw me giggling, he laughed too. My friend and I knew immediately that he was for real … not some fake trying to impress his chick. We offered to dry him off, but he refused. We laughed about it all the way home. That was when I realized he was really a nice guy."

"Oh, Cassie, in my day we would never have dreamed of treating a boy like that. Things are so different now. When I first met my husband, we were very proper. We would never have behaved in such an unladylike manner."

"Go on," said Cassie, taunting. "Emily, I don't believe you were all that much of a wimp. Not you."

Emily's eyes twinkled. "You're right, of course. I drove my husband crazy. I just didn't fit into his mold, like the meek, mild-mannered girl he thought he had married."

"I bet you weren't. Did he appreciate you for being so special?" asked Cassie with round, questioning eyes.

"Goodness no," responded Emily bashfully. "I was a prim and dutiful wife most of the time. But then I also had a few tricks up my sleeve to keep him on his toes."

Emily quickly turned the conversation back to safer grounds before giving up any details.

"Tell me, Cassie, what was it that attracted you to Robert? After all, he was dating your good friend. What made you two get together?"

"Oh, my friend wasn't really serious about him. As it turned out, they only dated a couple of times. Robert and I hung around in the same group, but we were never really interested in each other until I overheard a conversation that I wasn't supposed to hear. When he didn't know I was listening, I heard him tell a bunch of his friends that he'd never cheat on a woman he loved. Then I knew he was really special."

Cassie had round, childlike cheeks with dimples that deepened when she smiled. Her bright blue eyes sparkled in the sunlight streaming through the kitchen window. Her bangs teased her face, as if they were taunting her to swipe them away so they could fall again against her cheeks like a flirtatious teenager.

"You're so young and idealistic," commented Emily lovingly. "I hope you never change."

Cassie was affronted. "I hate it when people say that." Her voice changed tone as if she were pouting. "I'm not as naïve as people seem to think. Besides, I know Robert. He's a really wonderful person. That's why I love him."

Emily smiled pensively. She was thinking of Mrs. Schmidt and how her love had turned so sadly against her.

"Cassie, I realize you're in love, and that's a wonderful thing," said Emily gently. "However, real love is much more complicated than you may know at this point."

"Why does everybody have to tell you all the bad things that can happen?" Cassie complained. "You sound just like my mother. I hate it when older adults always think they know so much about how hard life is. Why can't people just enjoy being young and carefree when they're young and carefree? Why does everybody always have to warn you about being hurt?"

"You're right, my dear," answered Emily. "Of course. I'm so sorry. I was letting my own fears get in the way. Be aware of the devil you know. I think that's the way to say it. No need to make things seem worse than they are. Maybe your relationship will be one of those once-in-a-lifetime opportunities. There are some people who fall in love and stay married happily ever after. I know it happens. Once in a while you see a couple who are still in love even after sixty years together. It's amazing really."

"Well, actually," said Cassie, reevaluating now that she could come off the defensive, "not too many of my friends are really happy together, now that I think about it. They seem to make such stupid decisions sometimes."

"Have another cookie, my dear," said Emily as she offered Cassie the dish.

Charlie gently reached his paw out. (His paw was more like a paddle with fur.) Carefully he scooped a cookie toward the tray on the high chair. Emily helped him to help himself. She broke the cookie into bite-size pieces more easily accessible to a cat muzzle. Delicately, Charlie munched his cookie, while purring loudly. His whiskers swept the crumbs onto the floor as he selected the tenderest morsels to crunch.

"Some people do seem to have blinkers on. Love can't see, you know. That's what they say," Emily resumed the conversation. "The woman we met today was a sorry example of unhealthy love."

"What was with that lady?" asked Cassie, glad to shift the conversation away from herself. "You seem a bit upset by what she said."

"It's hard to imagine someone committed to marriage to such an extent," answered Emily.

"Why? What happened?"

"Well, I guess you could say that she let the marriage literally drive her crazy. In the end, it actually destroyed her life. Her life is over, and she'll never be free of the love or the hate of it all."

"Ooooh," gasped Cassie. "That's sick!"

Emily nodded, "Yes, the only thing that she didn't actually follow through on was to murder the man. Someone else took care of that for her."

"You mean she hired someone else to do it for her?" Cassie's eyes were round with disbelief.

"No, no," Emily shook her head. "But she probably would have been better off if she had."

"That's bad," concluded Cassie. "That's really bad."

Emily sipped her tea and lapsed into silence. She had lots of figuring to do. Too many riddles remained unsolved.

"Now I need to move on to Plan B," said Emily, thinking out loud. "However, at this point, I have no Plan B to fall back on."

"Emily, shouldn't you leave all this up to the police?" suggested Cassie. "They're the experts in all this. Besides, the murdered man didn't mean anything to you, did he?"

"One should never be complacent," Emily answered. "That's one reason why I moved to a small town from the city. People in the city go about their business as if they were in a shell, never paying attention to anyone else. I don't ever want to get like that again.

"When I see injustice, then I'm going to do something about it. When I see someone who's in trouble, I'm going to offer to help. That's how we create a better world for everyone."

"Emily, that sounds good, and of course I agree with you, but aren't you a bit old to be traipsing around town investigating what you think is a murder but may just be some old guy who croaked of natural causes?"

"Didn't you just tell me that you don't want people judging you because you're young?"

"Yes, well, that's different," said Cassie weakly.

"No, it isn't," Emily said flatly. "There's no difference. People should not impose their expectations on anyone else. You're only as old as you think you are. As far as I'm concerned, in my heart, I'm as young as you are, Cassie, my dear."

"And you should stay that way," Cassie agreed. "I just don't want you getting hurt."

"I appreciate your concern," answered Emily as she rose to clear the table. "But let me tell you something, just between you and me.

I'd rather take a few chances in life, even if I get in trouble because of it, than to stay at home and do nothing but watch television and vegetate."

Cassie's manner softened. "Even if it means something really serious might happen to you?"

Emily nodded immediately.

"Even if it means that you might die alone with no one there to be with you?"

Emily thought briefly and then nodded again.

"Death may be my last great adventure."

Then breaking the somber tone of the conversation, she added, "We both have things to do. Run along now."

"You're right. I do have lots to do as well," said Cassie, getting up to leave. "But just promise me that you'll be careful."

"Yes, yes." Emily's mind was already racing on to Plan B.

As Emily washed up the teacups, Charlie finished the cookies.

Chapter Seven

THE NEXT morning, Emily arose before light wakened her. She had slept lightly, working out details to her Plan B instead of sleeping soundly.

Charlie was not impressed. He usually cuddled next to her under the warm duvet until he was ready to wake her for his breakfast. Six o'clock in the morning was far too early. He complained loudly and stretched his claws toward her nightgown, as if to pull her back into bed.

"I know it's early, my friend," Emily whispered, climbing out of her four-poster bed. "You can sleep in if you like, but I have to be on my way. I've got a plan now. I have to sneak into Schmidt's house before the police come back to continue their investigation. I need some more evidence. If my hunch is correct, it's still in the house, right where it was when I first saw it.

"Who knows?" she added, working herself into enthusiasm for her self-appointed mission, "Maybe I'll find even more than I'm looking for!"

Pulling the lace curtain aside just enough, Emily checked the weather before she chose what to wear.

"At least it's not raining today," she said to Charlie. "But then again, you couldn't care less, since you never go out anyway."

Emily thought about her statement for a second and then added, "Come to think of it, you're always dressed for the weather no matter what anyway, Charlie. You've got a fur coat to die for."

Charlie eyed her with an expression that made her reconsider her comment yet again. Sitting on the side of the bed, she picked up the fluffy cat and stroked him gently.

"Sorry, I didn't mean it literally," Emily retracted her quip. "'To die for' is just an expression. They only eat cats in China. There, there."

Then she put the fluff mop on his own four feet and proceeded to prepare for her morning's project. She dressed in a heavy cardigan sweater and dark jogging pants.

"Now I know why burglars dress in black," she thought, drawing from her reading of suspenseful mystery novels. "To disguise themselves in the dark ... just like me."

She donned a toque with flaps over the ears, and red woolen mittens to match. Already, early mornings in October had a hint of the approaching winter. She could see her breath in the frosty air as she hiked up the hill toward the victim's house. The streetlights flickered dimly as the daylight began to show in the distance. The scent of wet autumn leaves mingled in the air with wood smoke.

She hoped that there would be little traffic at this time of the morning so that she would not be seen. She thought, "A little old lady walking by herself so early on the streets of the village might look rather out of place."

She crossed the highway without waiting for the light to change and jaywalked across Main Street. Luckily no one passed.

She had almost arrived at her destination. Just a few steps further and she would arrive at the entrance to the house, which was cordoned off by yellow police tape stretching from one tree at the corner of the property to a bush at the opposite property line.

Then she heard a truck pull up behind her.

"Don't look now, dearie," she said out loud to herself, "but we're not alone. Just keep on walking and pretend as if nothing is unusual."

She could hear the truck slow down. Still she refused to look sideways. The motor revved down as the vehicle kept pace with her walking speed. By now she had arrived at the correct address, but of course, she did not dare to hesitate. She continued on past and climbed the hill toward the lodge.

"Surely this someone will think I'm just out for an early morning stroll," she mumbled. "I'll pretend I'm a resident and turn in at the driveway to the seniors' home."

However, just before she veered off the street, the truck's horn tooted softly.

If I were a younger woman, I'd think he was trying to pick me up, she thought, *but no one toots at an older woman.*

Finally, curiosity got the better of her, and she glanced at the driver behind the wheel.

Pete Picken's smile showed the gap under his moustache. He tipped his familiar leather hat. She slackened her pace as he pulled over to the curb and rolled down his window.

"Just out for a morning stroll, I suppose?" he taunted.

"Well, yes," she snipped. "Looking after my girlish figure, you know. One has to keep fit."

"Yes, of course," he agreed. "But isn't it strange meeting you in this neighbourhood?" He raised his eyebrows questioningly. "Just a coincidence?"

"I don't know what you mean," Emily intoned innocently. "I often come this way on my walks."

"Sure you do," he said. "Same as me, out checking for garage sales. You never know where you're going to get a good bargain."

"Funny, I didn't notice any signs out," Emily said, beginning to suspect an ulterior motive.

Pete grinned. "I was just turning onto Main Street, when I happened to notice you beetling on down here in a hurry.

"'Self', says I, 'I think Mrs. Blossom is on a mission.'" He paused to give her the impression that he was very intuitive. "'Self', I says again, 'I believe she may need our assistance ...' So ... here we is."

Emily greeted his offer of assistance with a mixture of relief and annoyance.

"Well, sir, I must thank you kindly," she said graciously. "Actually, you're right, I do have a plan. But I'm not sure that you really want to be considered an accomplice, not to mention that your truck is a bit obvious. It rather sticks out like a sore thumb."

"Ah yes, you're right," he agreed. "However, the police are well aware that I am out around town early on Saturday mornings looking for antiques. They all recognize this truck, and they don't think anything of it. You, on the other hand, look rather out of place, hiking the streets at this time of the day. Anyone might think you planned to sneak into that scene of the crime again, for some peculiar reason.

"Might I ask," he went on, as if it had just occurred to him to wonder, "what exactly are you looking for?"

"May I get in?" Emily asked politely.

Pete nodded and indicated that she was welcome. She hoisted herself into her seat and proceeded to explain with great enthusiasm.

"When we were here at the scene of the murder," she recounted, "I noticed a photograph on the desk. It's a photo of Schmidt and a younger woman. I thought this might be a clue. I wanted another look at that face. There's something vaguely familiar about the person, but I can't quite place it. Plus, I thought I might be able to find some more information about people he might have known in the past, like the address of his wife."

"Don't you think the police would have thought of all this before?" Pete asked. "What makes you think you'll find anything they haven't already picked up?"

"Well, you never know unless you look," she parried, contritely. "Do you?"

"Okay, okay," agreed Pete. "Here's what I'll do. I'll park on the street not too far away, and you go on inside and have a look around. If anyone comes, I'll pretend to be looking for something under the dash and lean against the horn. That'll give you warning to escape without getting caught."

"Would you do that for little ol' me?" she asked, surprised by his generosity, and then, more suspiciously, "Why? Why do you want to get involved again? You said yesterday you never wanted to see me again."

He shrugged his shoulders. "Just because."

"Just because, what?" she persisted, not wanting to lose her chance at an explanation.

"Let's just leave it at that," he said shyly.

"Okay," Emily capitulated. "I won't look a gift horse in the teeth."

"Mouth," he corrected her. "Gift horse in the mouth."

"Why do they say that then?" she asked petulantly. "That doesn't make any sense. It's the length of the teeth which tell the age."

"You oughta know," Pete countered.

"What do you mean by that?" she asked, getting distracted.

"Nothing really," he said. "Just about telling a person's age."

"Well, you're hardly one to talk. How old are you anyway?"

"Let's not go there, okay?" he said defensively. "We'll just leave it at that. Neither one of us has anything to brag about on that score."

"Yes, well," Emily snuffed, "let's get down to business. Where were we? Oh yes, you honk the horn if someone's coming. That's a great idea. I'll be off. Keep your eyes open."

With that, Emily clambered down to the sidewalk and retraced her steps. Looking quickly over her shoulder, she slipped under the police tape and crept around to Schmidt's back door. Pete backed the truck to a spot within sighting distance of the house she had just entered. He put his boots up on the dashboard, pulled his hat over his eyes, and pretended to have a snooze. But he kept his eyes on the rearview mirror, watching for any approaching vehicles.

House with Gingerbread

Chapter Eight

EMILY WAS relieved to find the back door opened easily. On the Hill, few people actually locked their doors.

Once inside, Emily made her way through the kitchen into the living room where the murder had occurred. Nothing had been disturbed, except that the body was no longer lying by the chair where it had fallen when Emily had tried to awaken Schmidt. There was not even a stain on the rug. The only evidence that the police had been on the scene was clumps of mud from their boots and traces of powder where they had taken fingerprints from the furniture.

She paused to survey the room and then stepped immediately to the desk. The photograph she was looking for was lying facedown beneath a pile of papers. She studied the snapshot for a moment.

This photo was similar to the one on Ruth Schmidt's dresser; however, this snapshot had been taken a few years earlier when Schmidt was a younger man.

Two young people stared at the camera solemnly. They were dressed in somber 1940s-style clothes. The background buildings looked familiar. Emily guessed that the scene was the same stone wall overlooking the city as in Ruth's photo. Schmidt's boyish features were coarse. A thatch of hair flowed across his vast forehead away from his face, revealing a generous nose and copious lips. His black eyes glared like a challenge at the photographer. The girl's face was delicately chiseled, with high cheekbones and lips like a porcelain statue. She had a look of sadness in her shining eyes.

As Emily studied the photograph, she noticed the unusual position of the girl's arms around her stomach. The boy had his hand, fingers outspread, firmly planted on her belly. With a chill, Emily realized that the girl was obviously expecting a baby shortly. Neither of the young teenagers looked thrilled at the prospect of being parents. They stood as if in resignation to the condition they found themselves in.

Returning to the task at hand, Emily slipped the photo into her pants pocket and continued her search. In the desk drawer, she found a worn and tattered address book. Just as she was about to peruse the entries, she heard the truck horn sound. However, before she could react, footsteps on the porch announced the arrival of intruders. Emily froze as she saw the front door knob turning.

"The door's locked," said a squeaky male voice.

"Duh," answered its companion. "So kick the door in."

Before waiting for the intruders to enact their plan, Emily fled into the kitchen.

She heard the thud of someone's shoulder against the front door. Then a foot slammed against the latch, splintering the lock and sending the door crashing open. Glass shattered and sprayed across the hall onto the kitchen floor.

Emily's heartbeat pounded in her ears. She realized she was too late to make an escape without being seen. Scanning the room for a hiding place, she slipped into a broom closet just as two men entered the living room.

"Way to go, Rambo," said the throaty one, clearly in charge.

The squeaky voice whispered apprehensively, "Okay, smart ass, we're in. Now what are we supposed to do? Dead people's digs give me the creeps."

"Speak up," demanded the director of the break in, "You know I can't hear on that side ever since you blasted that gun next to my ear."

"You shouldn't 've been standing right next to me," defended Rambo. "You told me to shoot the bastard."

"Let's not go through that again, Baby. Just speak up, will ya."

"Don't call me that," said Rambo. "You know I don't like that name."

"Okay, Squeaks. Let's get on with it."

"Don't call me that either. I'll call you Skinny Legs, then ... see how you like that."

"Baby, Baby, I love you," taunted the director of the break-in.

"Skinny, Minny, Miney, Moe," answered Baby. "See how it feels!"

"Cut that out," Slim demanded. "Call it quits. You're Rambo, and I'm Slim, how's that? Now, let's get on with the job."

"What're we lookin' for then, smart ass?" whined Baby. "You're the one who's supposed to know everything."

"The bishop says to look for letters. There's supposed to be a packet of letters addressed to E. Zündel. He said to look in the drawers of the desk first."

The two men proceeded to explore the living room. Emily could hear drawers opening and papers shuffling. After a few moments of silence, the searchers compared notes.

"Ain't no letters in this desk," said Baby.

"None in the bookcase either," said Slim. "Might as well look around the house just to make sure they're not here."

Emily realized with a shudder that the voices were approaching the kitchen. The men began to pull out drawers in the counter and open cupboard doors. She stood stock-still and tried to disguise herself as a mop.

"No letters in the kitchen," said Slim as he opened the broom closet where Emily was hiding.

She could barely discern his face looking the other way. She saw a tall, slim man, dressed in black: black turtleneck, black jacket, black jeans, black boots. To match his attire, the man had long black hair pulled into a ponytail and a black moustache. A gold earring flashed in the sunlight beaming through the kitchen window over the sink.

Emily held her breath. Then darkness hid her again as he shut the door.

"Nothing here the bishop would be interested in," said Slim.

"Do we have to go upstairs," complained Baby. "This place gives me the creeps, not to mention that it reeks of dead people's stuff."

"The letters are old," answered Slim. "They might be in some box upstairs in a closet somewhere. We better check, just to be sure. The bishop won't be happy if we don't find something. Although he did say that this wasn't the only place we might locate them."

The voices faded, accompanied by thumping footsteps, which carried the culprits up the stairs to the second floor.

In her relief at not being discovered, Emily allowed herself to relax and breathe more deeply. Unfortunately, she realized too late that the mop behind which she had hidden was full of dust. She felt a sneeze coming on quickly. Even though she tried to muffle the outburst, the *'achoo!'* exploded in her ears.

"Did you hear something?" asked Baby.

"Speak up, I told you!" shouted Slim.

"I thought I heard somebody sneeze."

The footsteps paused on the stairs. Emily held her breath. Silence pervaded the house.

After what seemed like an eternity to Emily, Baby said, "Probably a stray cat in the back shed."

The men proceeded upstairs.

Emily dared not breathe deeply again. Stealthily she slipped out of the closet, scooted out the back door, around the house, and across the lawn toward the street.

Pete was waiting for her with the truck running. As soon as she climbed inside, he drove off without saying a word. They headed to the Country Kitchen on the Hill for a much needed coffee.

Emily in the Broom Closet

Chapter Nine

THEY WERE both relieved to see that the restaurant was empty of diners. Although it was too early for regular customers, the room smelled deliciously inviting. Fresh bread, croissants, and muffins already lined the shelves. Ilsa and Maria were busy in the back preparing soups and goulash for lunch.

Pete and Emily chose a table in the back corner and settled in.

"Boy, could I use a good hot coffee," said Pete enthusiastically. "What took you so long? You seemed to be in there forever."

Emily glared at him, clearly annoyed. "You didn't give me much warning to get out before those two crooks came in. I had to hide in a broom closet while they wandered all over the place looking for a bunch of letters. I'm just lucky they didn't find me. I don't know what I would have said to explain what I was doing there. They could have smashed my head in as soon as look at me. Why didn't you honk sooner?"

Pete looked a bit sheepish.

"I fell asleep."

Emily gasped, "Some great accomplice you are! Thanks a lot."

"Well, you seemed to be taking your bloody time in there," Pete countered defensively. "I had to pretend to be doing something besides waiting for you to come out."

"Remind me not to count on you the next time this happens," she huffed. "I could have gotten in a lot of trouble in there."

"The next time?" said Pete. "The next time you decide to rob somebody's house, don't call on me for help. That'll be just fine with me."

Ilsa appeared at the table before either of them noticed her approach.

"Now, now, you two," she said soothingly, "Don't go having an argument so early in the morning. How about coffee to smooth things over?"

"Yes, sirree," said Pete rubbing his hands together. "Coffee's just what the doctor ordered."

Emily nodded enthusiastically as well and added, "I'd love one of your lovely muffin tops also. The blueberry ones are the best. How about you, Pete?"

"Gooey-in-the-middle, please," said Pete. "Whatever's sweet and gooey-in-the-middle."

Emily frowned at him. "You're not supposed to eat dessert for breakfast, Pete."

"And why not?" he said bluntly. "Might as well start the day out right."

Ilsa summarized, "One blueberry muffin top and one gooey-in-the-middle lemon meringue pie coming up."

Then Pete and Emily resumed where they had left off before the interruption.

"So what did you find out?" whispered Pete. "Was it worth the risk?"

Emily smiled, displaying a variety of enamel tints on her crooked teeth.

"Eurethra!" she exclaimed proudly.

Pete furrowed his ample brow.

"Eureka? Isn't that what you mean? Eureka?"

"Yes, yes," she answered impatiently. "You know what I meant. Suffice it to say that I found exactly what I was looking for ... plus some."

She reached into her pocket and pulled out the photo and the address book.

"Just look at this photograph," she said, handing the faded snapshot to Pete.

He squinted his eyes to try to make out the image more clearly.

"Here, take my glasses," said Emily, reaching into her sweater pocket for a pair of spectacles. "I always carry a pair just in case I can't read the fine print."

Pete accepted her offer and perched the glasses on his nose, while holding the photo at a distance so he could get a better focus.

"Is that Schmidt?" he asked after studying the picture intently.

"It's a younger version of the Schmidt we saw in Ruth's snapshot," Emily said. "If you look closely, you can see a scar on his cheek, probably from some dueling battle in university. They still did that in Heidelberg in those days, kind of like rights of passage. Many young German gentlemen had scars on their faces or bodies. I remember that scar made him look frightening when I first met him at an auction. It wasn't a face you'd forget easily. And look at his large forehead and the hair. He even had all that hair in his later years, only it was white instead of dark. I'm sure this is a photo of him just before or during the war."

"Well, who's the girl?" inquired Pete, by now accepting that Emily had obviously come to some conclusions that he lacked. "Does it look anything like the Mrs. Schmidt at the lodge?"

"Gimme that!" snapped Emily, yanking the photo out of his hands.

She stared at the photo, holding it close to her nose to see more clearly. Realizing that she needed a better view, she snatched the glasses off Pete's nose and placed them on her own.

"There's no resemblance that I can make out," she said after carefully studying the facial features of the young girl. "This girl has a large Semitic nose and high cheek bones, and she has two distinct dimples. The Mrs. Schmidt we met had an upturned, dainty nose and more Celtic features, fair skin and soft angles."

"How could you tell through all those wrinkles?" Pete asked, verbalizing what he thought was a logical question.

"Women know these things," said Emily with authority. "We use our intuition."

Pete raised his eyebrows skeptically.

"You wouldn't know," said Emily, glancing at him sideways while pretending to look the other way. "Men are clueless when it comes to observing details."

"Is that so?" said Pete defensively. "Then how come we notice pretty girls, but women never do unless it's themselves?"

Emily decided not to fall into his trap. "There's no arguing on that one," she said simply. "You've made a ridiculous generalization which is totally unsupervised."

"You mean *unsubstantiated*."

"Yes, that's what I said. Unsubstantiated."

Pete raised his hands in surrender and changed the subject.

"Well, if you're so smart, tell me who's the girl in the photograph then, huh?" he goaded.

"That's what I don't know," she admitted, but then added, "but I'm sure it's a clue to Schmidt's murder. You can obviously see she's expecting."

"Expecting?" Pete didn't get it. "Expecting what?"

"Expecting a baby, silly!" Emily answered with an exasperated tone.

He snatched the photo back from Emily and took her glasses to peer more closely at the girl's belly. While he studied the pose of the couple in the photograph, he grumbled under his breath.

"There's that word again—*silly*. I hate that word."

Emily realized that Pete was easily affronted.

"Oh, yes, so sorry," she capitulated. "I didn't mean it like that. It's more a term of endearment. I only use it for people I really like—like *cute*."

"That's another one I can't stand," said Pete, still staring at the photo.

"Well, I don't mean any harm by it," said Emily. "In case you didn't notice, I did not call you cute, did I? I said 'silly,' that's all. You shouldn't be so sensitive."

He raised his eyes and glared at her.

"Don't tell me what I should be," he said huffing. "I hate people telling me what I should and shouldn't be."

"Settle down," she said, dismissing his apparent hurt feelings.

She snatched the snapshot back again and pretended to direct her attention to the pursuit of missing clues.

"Is that all you two do is argue?" asked Ilsa when she arrived with their order. "One shouldn't argue with friends."

"Who said we were friends?" grumbled Pete.

Ilsa smiled. "You're an old blowhard, Pete Picken. Everybody knows you're not as mean as you make out to be."

"There's another one," Pete said, directing his comments to Emily. "*Blowhard*. I suppose that's a term of endearment too."

Emily addressed her response to Ilsa. "He's really a softy at heart, isn't he?"

"There's another one," said Pete, his voice getting louder and more agitated. "Cut that out, you two! You're really getting on my nerves."

Emily and Ilsa exchanged knowing glances, and Ilsa returned to the kitchen. Emily took a dainty nibble of her muffin top and opened the address book.

"Finally, I have a chance to look at this other treasure which I found in Schmidt's desk," she said.

"Let me have a look at that," Pete grabbed for the book, which Emily kept safely just beyond his reach.

His sleeve grazed the lemon pie that Ilsa had put in front of him. Noticing the gob on his cuff, he held his arm to his mouth and licked off the extra dessert with a long and practiced tongue. Emily pretended not to notice his bad manners.

"Hold on, I'll read it to you," she said, cocking her head in a cajoling manner.

She studied the book, slowly turning the pages, while Pete tucked into his gooey-in-the-middle pie. Presently she became quite excited.

"Listen to this," she cried. "We're in here too. 'Emily Blossom, art dealer,'" she read. "'Pete Picken, junk.'"

"Gimme that book!" said Pete as he yanked it out of her hands. "It doesn't say that!"

He thumbed through until he found the page she was referring to. She sipped her coffee, holding the cup with two hands as if it were a fragile antique bowl. She observed Pete over the rim of her spectacles while he tried to decipher the handwriting without the aid of glasses.

"I didn't think so," he said triumphantly. "'Pete Picken, antiques.' He's got the phone number right as well."

"But look at the next name," Emily added, "'Heinrich Finger, Apple Wood Antiques.' I wonder what Rich has got to do with all this."

They both knew all the antique dealers in the area on a first-name basis. They had each been dealing locally for years, and the world of antiques was small and familiar.

"I think I'll pay him a visit," said Pete. "I drop in on his shop once in a while just to see what he's got. I'll see what I can find out."

"Good idea," said Emily, taking back the book. "Now let me see ... Yes, here it is ... Jenny Henderson, 110 Rue Prince Author, St. Laurent. That's a part of Montreal, right?"

"That's Rue Prince *Arthur*," said Pete, correcting her.

"Oh yes, I did read it wrong," said Emily. "I wonder if she's still at the same address. Handy that women have to keep their maiden names in Quebec, isn't it? We might not have been able to find her if she went by her married name."

"What do you want with her?" asked Pete.

"She's the next suspect. Ex-wife number two."

"You're not planning on continuing this game, are you?" asked Pete. "Didn't almost getting caught in the closet and getting beaten to a pulp cure you of sticking your nose into everybody else's business?"

"Oh no," said Emily. "You should have felt my heart beating. It was so loud I felt sure they'd hear the pounding; I haven't had so much excitement in years. It's quite an adrenaline push."

"Rush. Adrenaline *rush*."

"Yes, yes," she said.

"Have some coffee," said Pete. "Caffeine might do the trick."

Emily added milk to her coffee. When she found no spoon on the table, she took a knife, turned it upside down and stirred the coffee with the handle. Then she licked the handle clean and returned it to Pete's plate.

"Thanks."

The address book lay on the table between them. The back spine was broken, and the last page with the final letters of the alphabet had only one entry.

"Ernst Zündel?" Pete read. "*The* Ernst Zündel? I wonder …" He raised his eyebrows and let out an exclamatory whistle.

"That's the name on the letters they were looking for," Emily said, wondering at the coincidence between the crooks' subject of conversation and Pete's comment. At first, she didn't realize that Pete was reading from the address book.

Pete looked at her without understanding where she was coming from.

"E. Zündel. That's the name on the letters those men were looking for in the house this morning."

"The Holocaust denier?"

"Who's that? The what?"

"Ernst Zündel is the guy who said the Holocaust never happened. He said there was no extermination of the Jews in the Second World War," explained Pete.

"What does that have to do with Helmut Schmidt?" asked Emily.

Pete shook his head. "Got me. I know Zündel was in Edmonton when he was arrested for hate crimes and deported to Germany."

"But, I repeat, what does that have to do with Schmidt? Why would this guy's name be in Helmut's address book?"

"That's heavy stuff," said Pete, whistling through his missing teeth. "I'm not going to touch that with a ten-foot pole."

Emily fairly glistened with excitement.

This time, Pete picked up the tab, and he drove her home without protest. They parted ways, each with a project to pursue: Pete to Apple Wood Antiques, and Emily to Montreal.

Picken in His Truck

Chapter Ten

THAT AFTERNOON, Pete set out for Apple Wood. He drove his truck more easily than he walked down the street. Slouched against the driver's door, he puffed on his pipe, holding the bowl with his left hand and steering with his right. His hat was carefully tilted just slightly to the left, and he wore sunglasses even though the day was dull and grey. He never wore a seatbelt.

He proceeded as if he owned the road and all other vehicles were expected to give way to his truck. Driving was so automatic that, since there was no oncoming traffic, he didn't bother to halt at the stop sign near his house. He pulled smoothly onto the road and drove up the lane facing oncoming traffic. He was headed for a short cut a few hundred yards further along. An approaching truck flashed its lights to indicate that Pete should stay on his side of the road.

"Cool it, man," Pete said under his breath. "I know where I'm going. Just go around me."

Pete turned left and headed up the hill on his short cut, hardly glancing in the mirror when the truck blasted its horn as it thundered past on the highway.

Every two weeks, he would load the truck full of stock and make a round of the dealers he knew. Antique dealers were often their own best customers. A good antique usually changed hands several times before eventually reaching the retail market.

"It's always good to have an unusual load," Pete reminded his customers. "That way you'll remember the sign on my truck."

Pete's Pickin' Truck carried small antique pieces behind the seat in the crew cab. With them safely stowed between the seats, there was no need for Pete to unload and reload each item. By carrying them wherever he went, Pete always had 'smalls' for sale when he stopped at dealers to peruse their stock. His truck was like a mobile store of nostalgia and memorabilia. Today his stock included a tin Coca-Cola sign, a miniature cedar strip canoe, a stenciled child's chair, several small wooden boxes, two Victorian, oval-framed portrait photographs, a red and white star-patterned quilt, and a horsehair stuffed rocking horse missing one leg and its ears.

In the truck box outside, the furniture was more likely to change. Varnished or veneered pieces were susceptible to damage by the rain, so he was more likely to unload these larger items into his warehouse. However, if he bought a particularly unusual piece, like a birch bark canoe or a Santa Claus sleigh, he tended to leave the item on the rack under the pretense that it was too difficult to lift down. Today he carried a seven-foot-long pine harvest table with turned legs, upside down on the rack.

Heading south from the Hill, he pulled into a gas station at an intersection known as Stone House. The country store with gas pumps was all that remained of what had been a thriving village at the turn of the century. The owner, Mr. Stonehouse, usually left his post behind the grocery counter to serve gas, but when he recognized Pete's truck, he stayed put and left the job of filling the tank to Pete.

While the meter ticked its way toward one hundred dollars, Pete washed the windshield, standing on his tiptoes to try to clean the centre of the glass. A silver SUV, which had already passed the intersection, slowed down, pulled over, and backed up to where Pete was attempting to scrub the last dead insect from his driver's side window. The SUV driver rolled down his window and motioned to the table on the rack.

"That table for sale?" asked the man, who was dressed in a dark business suit. He pointed past Pete's nose with a finger wearing a large diamond ring.

"Yup," said Pete, trying to squeeze one more drop of gas into his tank without spilling any on the ground. The meter read $105.97.

"How much?"

"A thousand."

"A thousand dollars? For that table? My mother had one just like that in her back shed."

Pete reached in his lapel pocket and pulled out a business card. Holding it casually between two fingers, he passed the card through the window to the diamond-ringed hand. The man glanced at the small print at the bottom of the card, which read, "We charge $1.50 to hear about what your grandmother threw out."

The SUV driver glanced at Pete, and then at the table, and drove off without comment. Pete replaced the nozzle and went into the store.

"What was that all about?" asked the storekeeper.

"I deal in wholesale. Most retail customers have no imagination," Pete commented. "The card weeds out the curiosity seekers who just want to chat. My stuff is all in original condition. No repros, no alterations. You get what you pay for."

He paid his bill with a credit card, dirty and molded to the shape of his wallet, which lived in his back jean pocket.

"Got any of those cigars?" Pete asked.

Stonehouse reached under the counter and pulled out a box of Cuban cigars. Pete chose one as if he were picking a cherry direct from the tree. He reached in his pocket for his knife. Very gingerly, he cut the tip and placed the end between his lips. With a steady hand, the grey-haired storekeeper lit the end of the cigar, careful not to set his customer's moustache on fire. Pete puffed a generous cloud of acrid-smelling smoke above his head. Then he reached into his pocket and pulled out a toonie. Stonehouse smiled, nodded, and slipped the coin into his pocket.

"You made my day," Pete said over his shoulder as he headed for the truck. "See you the next time."

Pete got back into his truck, but instead of heading toward his original destination of Apple Wood Antiques, he steered north, back toward the Hill. The cab filled with a haze of smoke, and by the time he reached the Country Kitchen on the Hill, Pete still had half a stump left to smoke. Very carefully, he brushed the lit ashes from the tip of his cigar and left the remainder in the ashtray to smoke later. The smell of cigar followed him into the restaurant.

Emerging from the kitchen to serve her newly arrived customer, Ilsa greeted Pete by saying, "Have you been smoking those smelly cigars again, Pete?"

"Cut me some slack, Ilsa," Pete said. "I left it in the truck, didn't I?"

"Well, you know I wouldn't let you in here with that thing. The other customers would vacate the premises, *tout de suite*."

Pete chose his usual chair in the corner and adjusted his seat so that he could see the occupants at all the other tables. He always spoke in a loud voice so that everyone could hear him clearly. The Country Kitchen on the Hill was as good as a podium for Pete, who figured that whatever he had to say was usually of significant interest to all who would listen.

Suzanne and her mother were just finishing their tea and croissants. Suzanne looked as if she had spent her life tending to her mother's every desire while her youthful years passed into middle age. The mother's face was empty and toothless. Her silver eyes were blank, and she stared straight ahead, regardless of what was going on around her.

"Did you ever sell that grandfather clock in the hallway?" Pete asked Suzanne bluntly.

Suzanne shook her head timidly. "No, mother couldn't bear to part with it."

"You'll let me know if you ever decide to sell, eh?"

"Yes, well …" answered Suzanne evasively. "She says she's not interested for now."

Pete nodded and scanned the room for another object of conversation.

A large gentleman with shoulder-length grey hair sipped coffee at the small corner table near the door. His wife chatted in a low, inaudible monologue, while she teased a crumb of piecrust around her plate. The husband looked mildly bored, but tolerant.

"You from around these parts?" asked Pete loudly enough to interrupt the wife's banter and cause the newcomers to look in his direction. "I don't think I've seen you here before," he said, almost as an accusation.

The man looked apologetic. "As a matter of fact, we moved in last week. We bought the old white manse down the hill. We're just getting settled."

"What can I get for you this afternoon, Pete?" asked Ilsa, interrupting the conversation, which flew like a tennis ball back and forth across the room.

"The usual," said Pete.

"Which usual?" asked the waitress. "I know better than to try to guess what your usual is at the moment. It changes regularly."

Pete was belligerent. "It may change, but it's always gooey-in-the-middle. Which one do you have today? Is that apple pie?"

"Yes."

"Do you have ice cream?"

"Yes."

"Can you heat the pie?"

"Yes."

"But I don't want it nuked."

"Well, it'll take longer to heat the pie in the oven."

"I can wait."

After Ilsa disappeared into the kitchen, Pete yelled to her without moving from his seat. "Don't forget to add an extra scoop of ice cream."

Then he turned his attention back to his new audience. "Where did you come from?"

Ilsa reappeared in the doorway, and in a voice almost as soft as a whisper, she said, "Did you say something about your order, Mr. Pete Picken?"

"Yeah. Extra ice cream on the pie," he demanded abruptly.

Ilsa stood staring at him with her hand on her hip and a confrontational expression on her face. Eventually he noticed that she had not moved. When he looked at her with a questioning expression, she raised her eyebrows without saying a word.

"Please," he said, getting her unspoken message.

Ilsa disappeared again, and Pete resumed his query with the newcomers.

"You were saying that you recently moved to the Hill from where?" he repeated his question without missing a beat.

"We moved here from the city. I happened to come here while working for a client. I went home and told my wife how pretty it is here. How people seem to take such pride in their homes and properties. The people are friendly and welcoming. We wanted to live in a small town where you're not just some number, some anonymous walking wallet. We run our businesses from home."

"Do you want tea or coffee?" asked Ilsa, reappearing from the kitchen in a continuing attempt to get Pete's order.

"What kind of business is that?" he asked, as if, whatever the man's answer, it was his business to know.

Pete ignored Ilsa's question. After a moment of hesitation, she returned to the kitchen to put the pie in the oven.

"My wife's a translator for the government, and I'm a lawyer. We each have an office in the new house."

"You'll be interested in subscribing to *The Hill News*," said Pete, warming to his self-appointed role of town tourism director. "Then there's the Gallery; they have shows every two weeks, and they're open Thursdays through Sundays. Joining the Curling Club is the best way to meet people, either that or church. Are you churchgoers?"

"Well," said the man cautiously, not really knowing why he was being asked the question.

"Well, there's the Disunited United Church on Union Street, and then there's the Allen Church and the Barton Church, or you could go to the Ladies' Tea Social Church—that's the one on the hill behind the Co-op."

"If you don't speak French, don't bother with the Catholics. The priest won't let you take communion unless you *parlez-vous*."

The wife began to send daggers across her plate of crumbs toward her husband, warning him that she was ready to depart. He got the message, and while trying to be discreet, he began to gather up the shopping bags beside his chair.

"What did you say your name was?" he asked Pete, putting his hand out as an introduction. "Greenacre's my name. I don't believe we've met."

Pete seemed somewhat taken aback that anyone would not know who he was.

"Pete's the name. Pickin's the game," he said tipping his hat, and then, toward the kitchen in a loud voice, he yelled, "Ilsa, where's my tea?"

Maria appeared from behind the counter with a sour face.

"Are you yelling for something in particular?" she asked in a flat, impatient voice.

"What's the matter with you?" asked Pete. "You look like you swallowed a sour lemon."

"The older you get, the harder it is," said Maria with a pained expression. "Once you're over sixty-five, you'll see. Just wait. It goes downhill from there."

Pete raised his eyebrows in surprise, as if such an event would never befall him.

Ilsa edged through the doorway beside Maria, pie in hand with abundant ice cream melting quickly off the top of the steaming crust. With an exaggerated gesture, she practically threw the plate down in front of Pete in an attempt to communicate her displeasure at his lack of manners. With no acknowledgement of Ilsa's frustration, Pete began to inhale the pie in generous mouthfuls.

In the meantime, the new neighbours were fumbling for their coats, apparently in a rush to escape the restaurant. They gathered up their belongings and headed out the door, toward a car parked just outside the window. The long-haired gentleman opened the door for his wife, who tucked her ankle-length coat up underneath her and folded herself neatly into the passenger side.

Suzanne exclaimed, "That's my car they're getting into."

Pete swallowed the last crumb of pie and slurped the final drop of melted ice cream. He then rose to stare out the window at the couple as they proceeded to clamber into Suzanne's car.

Pete and Suzanne and her mother and Ilsa and Maria all watched curiously as the lawyer made his way around to the driver's side of Suzanne's car and opened the door. He tried to put his long legs underneath the steering wheel. Only when he didn't fit, did he realize that they were in the wrong car. Quickly, he climbed out of the seat, back around the car, and hustled his wife out of the car, glancing toward the bakery shop window. When he realized that all the occupants of the restaurant were watching and smiling, his face turned the colour of beets. He waved weakly and smiled crookedly, two unmistakable gestures of embarrassment. Then he and his wife scuttled off toward their own vehicle parked further along the street.

At that moment, Emily was meandering along Main Street and happened to see a crowd of faces in the window of The Country Kitchen watching an awkward couple with shopping bags rushing along the sidewalk. She diverted her course and stepped into the store.

"Hello, everyone. Fancy meeting you here," she said in her usual cheerful fashion.

Pete answered her first. "Emily, I knew you'd be around. I was waiting for you. C'mon. We've got to go."

Emily was surprised, but Ilsa and Maria were more so. Ilsa was just emerging from the kitchen with a pot of tea and cup in hand.

"What about your tea?" asked Ilsa.

"What tea?" asked Pete. "I didn't order any tea. We've got to go. I'll pay you later."

He grabbed Emily by the elbow and hauled her out of the store toward his truck parked across the street.

"I was headed down to Rich Finger's place this afternoon, but then thought better of it," he said, as he pulled the truck into traffic and headed south again.

Emily looked at him questioningly. "I thought we decided that you would go by yourself, as your part of the investigation. I made plans to go to Montreal tomorrow, and you were supposed to go to Rich's."

"Yes, yes," said Pete, dismissing their previous arrangement with a shrug of his shoulders. "But then Sales got talking to Purchasing, and we had a little discussion."

Pete continued his description of the conversation, which had taken place in his truck that morning between himself and himself.

"'Purchasing,' says Sales, 'What are we heading off to look for? We have to be careful since our dead stock is piling up. We have to be more selective on the stuff we're buying these days.'"

"And how did Purchasing answer?" asked Emily, quickly catching on to the game.

"Well Purchasing was in a bit of a quandary," said Pete. "'We need some advice from that Emily chick,' said Purchasing to Sales. 'We're in a bit over our head when it comes to Art. We don't really know all that much about being an Art Dealer.'"

"Oh, I see," said Emily wisely. "You want me to identify Schmidt's paintings if they're there."

"Well, you know what they look like, don't you? I haven't a clue what a Hiroshima Bok painting would look like," admitted Pete.

"Hieronymous Bosch," Emily corrected him gently. "Yes, you're right. Of course, I would recognize them for sure. Your friend, Purchasing, has a good point. I'm glad you've asked me to come along."

The road across country led through small towns interspersed with modest dairy farms and gently rolling hills. Drooping cornfields were ready to be harvested, but the tractors remained in the farmyards, rather than get bogged down in the mud from the rainy autumn weather. The trees had lost their brilliant fall hue and stood skeletal against the drab grey horizon. The heritage homes they saw as they drove further south were either quaint log structures or more elegant stone farmhouses built by the early Scots immigrating to Glencairn County in the 1800s.

"Everyone's a MacSomething around here," Pete commented. "MacDonald, MacLeod, MacTavish. Mac (with an a) or Mc (without), they're all tight-assed and conservative as they come."

"Now, now," Emily replied, "One mustn't generalize. That's like being anti-French. One should never judge a coat by its colour."

"Why not?" countered Pete. "Call a spade a spade. That's what I say."

"What I say is, 'Life is never that simple,'" Emily stated. "The Scots came to this continent to escape the British. The Quebecois came to escape the French. No matter what language they spoke, they all came for the same reason: to live with the freedom of choice."

"Tell that to the language police in *la belle province*," said Pete.

"Well, let's hope the Separatists don't come across the border and ruin everything for us here on the Hill," answered Emily. "So far, everyone seems to get along just fine, no matter what language they speak."

Neither Pete nor Emily was willing to capitulate, and neither wanted to come to an agreement in principle.

Pete reached for his pipe and tobacco and went through the motions of preparing for a good smoke. Emily opened her window and stared purposefully at the countryside speeding past the truck. They drove on in silence.

Elegant Scottish Stone House

Chapter Eleven

"THAT MUST be the place," said Emily, as they approached the outskirts of the town of Apple Wood. "It looks like it used to be a fairly large farm at one time, but it's certainly seen its better days."

Pete recognized the Apple Wood Antiques Store by the pile of miscellaneous junk, which cluttered the yard outside an old dairy barn.

"I remember those rusted tractor wheels and that horse-drawn plow from my last visit. They look as if they're strewn randomly around the yard, but they're in exactly the same place as last time I was here, months ago. The old metal butter churn is a more recent addition though. I haven't seen that before."

"All that junk looks so abandoned and useless lying all over the place like that," commented Emily. "I can't believe anyone would pay money for those things. The old cast-iron bed is cute as a trellis, but the flowers are pretty sad, not exactly in their morning glory now."

They parked the truck and walked past a sleigh with rotting runners and full of rusted children's toys. Emily picked up a headless doll missing one arm, its dress torn and stained.

"It's been a long time since someone loved and cherished this poor old thing. I used to have a doll like this one. Her name was Plain Jane. That's what my mother always used to call me, so I thought it was a good name for a doll. I didn't know what it meant, of course."

Pete said, "The only thing I ever had to play with was my mental blocks."

Inside, the ceilings were low, and the lighting, dim.

"How are you supposed to see anything?" asked Emily, hoping that her eyes would adjust to the darkness after coming in from the bright daylight.

"You're not. It's part of the mystique of this business. People have to think they're discovering treasures that nobody else has seen before."

The vast interior of the old cow barn was full of antiques of every description.

"Since no one seems to be eager to serve us, we'll just take a look around," said Pete, obviously more comfortable than Emily in surroundings familiar to him. Emily was concerned about getting her clothes dirty.

They wandered around the store, making their way through narrow aisles of old and discarded articles of every description. Counters full of costume jewelry and beaded purses were placed along the aisleway where the cows would have stood in stanchions. Cupboards and furniture were displayed upstairs in what used to be the haymow. Row after row of painted chests, pine armoires, and cumbersome oak desks lined pathways only wide enough for one person to pass through. Stained glass windows stood piled one against another in the old feed room.

"Look at all those chairs hanging from the ceiling," whispered Emily, who was wandering like a child in awe of mysterious shapes and shadows descending from above.

Arrow-back rockers hung by their arms from the rafters; pressed-back dining chairs gathered cobwebs; and single captain's chairs swung upside down along the rough-hewn log beams.

"Some of those chairs are quite valuable," answered Pete. "But there's not one without a broken rung or split seat. Too bad. I have a customer for a matching set of good pressed-backs."

A voice boomed from the darkness behind them.

"Is there something I can help you with?"

Emily jumped at the loudness of the words, which seemed to come from a half-clothed manikin standing in a shadowy corner. The glassy eyes of the plaster model stared back at her with one arm raised and the other draped with a tattered remnant of a gown. There was no sign of a human accompaniment to the voice. Inadvertently, Emily reached for Pete's arm and peered into the darkness behind the partially naked store manikin.

"All I can see are breast implants," she whispered. "Is that a transvestite or is there someone behind there?"

"Rich Finger," said Pete. "Where the hell have you been? I haven't seen you at the auctions in a coon's age."

Presently, Emily saw a shadow move toward them. As the figure approached, she moved closer to Pete's warmth.

"Are you sure it's not a ghost?" she whispered. "All this old stuff gives me the geebie heebies."

"Heebie geebies," corrected Pete.

"That's what I said," whispered Emily. "He gives me the creeps."

Pete stepped impatiently away from her toward the light, where he could see the antique dealer from a better vantage point. Emily moved quickly to his side.

Rich Finger emerged from the shadows. Emily saw his gleaming white teeth before she noticed his towering presence. A mat of dark hair grew abundantly wild, like a hummock of grass on top of his head. He was so tall that she could see the underside of his chin. At the same time, she noticed a tuft of hair escaping from underneath his T-shirt. He wore a stained, checkered shirt. His belt buckle was an eagle with a fish in its beak. His jeans were long and tall like tree trunks.

"It's been a while since I've been down here," said Pete. "Thought I'd stop by and see if you have anything new."

"New?" repeated Rich. "New? We don't deal in anything new."

Pete laughed and relaxed, while Emily tried to reassemble her courage.

"You know what I mean," said Pete. "Got anything I'd be interested in?"

Rich slouched against a post where a stuffed moose head hung suspended with a full rack of antlers. The beady eyes of the dead animal stared down directly at Emily.

"I haven't got too much on hand that would suit you really," said Rich. "Just the usual junk. It's hard to find good stuff these days. Most of it's either already been picked, or it's too expensive."

"Too bad," said Pete, casually. "I was just saying to my friend here that I've got a customer for some pressed-back chairs. You haven't got a complete set with a deep press, do you?"

Rich scratched his chin, looking at his chair stock hanging from the ceiling, while he thought about what he had for sale. Emily poked Pete in the ribs and gestured. She attempted to describe a painting with her hands forming a rectangle. She mouthed the word *paintings* with exaggerated facial contortions. Pete frowned at her and brushed off her signals. Rich looked back toward them, just as Pete shoved Emily behind him and pretended to be looking at the ceiling of chairs as well.

"Is that a complete set of six there?" he pointed to the ones that he knew were not matching.

"Naw, they don't match. The rungs are different," answered Rich.

"Too bad," said Pete, turning as if to go. "These people want a set in the worst way."

He headed for the door, even though he was aware that Emily was dragging her feet. Over his shoulder, he continued the conversation with Rich, who accompanied them toward the light.

"How's business lately? Is it picking up at all?"

"Oh, I've got the odd customer up from the States that comes in pretty regular. You gotta know what they'll buy. Snowshoes are a big thing right now. I could sell every pair of snowshoes I can get my hands on."

"Snowshoes?" quipped Emily in spite of herself.

Rich nodded from his great height. "Snowshoes and wood shovels. They hang them on the walls in restaurants."

Just as they reached the door, Pete tossed over his shoulder, "You wouldn't have any interesting art on hand, would you? My friend, Emily, here is an art collector. She's looking for old paintings."

Rich shook his head. "Nope, nothing at the moment."

Pete added as nonchalantly as possible, "Did you ever buy anything off that old man from the hill? He supposedly had some paintings he wanted to get rid of."

Rich's face showed a mixture of emotions before he could mask his expression.

"You must mean Old Man Schmidt."

"Yes, that's the guy. His name slipped my mind. That's it—Schmidt. Supposedly he had some good stuff at one time."

Emily felt her palms begin to sweat. With great difficulty, she refrained from comment.

"Oh yeah, I bought some of that bastard's paintings alright," said Rich bitterly. "I thought he was making me a good offer because we're both German. My real name's Heinrich. I thought we were buddies, that he trusted me as a fellow countryman. I met Schmidt at an auction one day, and we got to talking. He let on about these paintings and said as how he'd let me have first dibs on them because we're *deutsche freunde* and all that. He set me up good ... real good."

Pete raised his eyebrows, and Emily knew her eyes were wide like saucers as she held her breath.

"Why? What happened?"

"I'll tell you what happened. You probably heard rumours about it anyway. The word was all over the countryside that I was dealing in stolen paintings."

"Really? I never heard anything about it," lied Pete.

"Yeah, the old guy called me up and said he was ready to sell his paintings. Originals, he said, which he brought with him from Europe. I went up there, and I couldn't believe what they were. He even had an original Hieronymus Bosch. Creepy painting. Ever seen anything by him?"

Pete signaled no, while Emily nodded her head eagerly.

"A real original Bosch? I thought they only existed in museums," she said.

"Oh they were originals alright. Complete with blood and gore. The one painting was full of tortured demons, and freaky people and creatures doing weird things to each other. The artist was famous for depicting life in heaven and hell during the medieval ages. He had a really twisted imagination. If you ask me, he must have been on drugs," said Rich.

"Schmidt offered you this painting? And you bought it?" Pete urged him to continue his story.

"Yep. I bought that one and a few others that he had. I knew they were good quality. You could tell. The frames were originals, and the way the canvases were mounted and protected was very old. I couldn't find signatures on all the paintings, but you could tell they were done by artists who knew their stuff."

"I won't ask what you paid for them."

"They weren't cheap," said Rich. "The bastard knew their value, but he couldn't sell them on the market. I was too stupid to realize that he knew exactly what they were. He knew how he got them, and he knew he couldn't get away with advertising them in public or anywhere where dealers would know what they really were. Somebody was bound to recognize them."

"Were they stolen, then?" asked Pete, finally getting to the point of their visit.

"He said he brought them over from Europe after the war. He said there were a lot of paintings that had been confiscated as part of the reconstruction process. I believed him. I thought he probably bought them on the black market or something, but I never thought they were really hot."

"So, how did you find out what they were?"

Rich attempted a laugh, but it turned into a sneer.

"When the cops showed up here in four cop cars, I had a pretty good idea I was in trouble for something."

"The cops? The cops showed up here?" asked Pete.

"The cops?" echoed Emily.

"The cops," affirmed Rich. "I put the paintings on eBay myself. I took digital pictures of them and put them on the net. Now do you think I would've done that if I thought they were stolen?"

"You could have sold them privately, no?"

"Yes, well, I thought I'd get a better value if I auctioned them off. I was right, too. The prices went up into the thousands. I would've made a bundle if they'd 've been legit."

"So what did the cops do?"

"They had a search warrant and demanded to see the paintings. They had some kind of an expert with them who identified the paintings and said they had been reported as stolen after the war. The Nazis supposedly stole priceless paintings from Jews mostly before they were shipped off to the concentration camps. I guess that's when Schmidt got his hands on some of those works of art. He thought he'd foist them off on some dumb antique dealer, and I was the patsy. The cops arrested me and took me to the station for questioning. Believe me, they weren't nice about it."

"No!" gasped Emily.

"Yes!" Rich mocked her.

"But Helmut was such a nice man!" she couldn't help but say.

"Nice man, my ass!" said Rich. "That man knew exactly where he got those paintings and where they came from before he got his grubby mitts on them. He told me he needed to get rid of his things and that he wanted to raise money to leave to his daughter. That's why he said he was selling them."

"His daughter?" exclaimed Pete and Emily at the same time.

"That's what he said."

"So what happened after that?" asked Pete. "How'd you get off?"

Rich changed his tone. He became confidential. "Promise you won't tell anyone?" he asked softly, as if someone might overhear his next confession.

"I promise," said Pete.

"I promise, too," said Emily, as if she were included in on the secret, even though she knew that she didn't count.

"Cops make deals," said Rich. "They said if I gave them a list of all the dealers whom I do business with, then they'd let me off."

"Dealers around here?"

"Yeah. I did, but I didn't know why, until the next month when the tax people showed up on my doorstep. They did a complete audit of all my books. I ended up paying them fifty thousand dollars in back taxes. Lots of the other dealers on that list I gave them got dinged as well ... big time."

"Fifty thousand dollars? That's a lot of taxes," exclaimed Pete.

Rich grinned. "They figured I had a new house and a new truck every year and that I had the money from somewhere."

"That's a lot of taxes," Pete repeated.

"I'd appreciate it if you wouldn't spread it around," said Rich. "I know the word's out, but not many people know the whole story."

"It's okay," Pete reassured him. "My lips are sealed."

"So are mine," said Emily.

Having thus been sworn to secrecy, Emily and Pete bade Heinrich Finger goodbye and headed for the truck.

Just as Emily was scrambling into the truck while Pete held the door open for her, Rich approached them with a package in his hands. He handed Emily a dusty bundle of tattered sheets wrapped in an old newspaper and tied with string.

"I've had these old prints and articles hanging around ever since my arrest," he said. "They came with Schmidt's stuff."

Emily was surprised that Rich actually spoke to her and not to Pete. He had seemed so aloof in her presence.

"Thank you so much, sir," she said trying to sound truly grateful.

"Might be something interesting for you, and I sure don't have any use for it. I don't need any more grief from the cops."

Rich winked at Pete, as if they had secrets of the trade in common.

"What a nice man," said Emily, as they drove out the driveway and headed for home. "I guess I'll have to change my song."

"Tune," Pete corrected her. "Change your tune."

"Yes, well, he was much nicer than I thought at first. I'll look through these old papers later when I get home," said Emily, as she stowed the package in the back seat, on top of an old trunk beneath a duck decoy.

"You never can tell what might come in handy at some later date."

"Don't forget to take it with you when we get home," Pete said. "I've got enough junk stored back there to last me till a much later date, as it is."

"Yes, yes," agreed Emily. "I'm so glad we made the trip down here, Pete, even if we didn't find any paintings. That was such an interesting story about what happened to Rich."

"Well, I don't necessarily believe everything he says," said Pete. "But I sure am glad it didn't happen to me."

"There but for the grace of God, as they say," said Emily.

"God's got nothin' to do with it," said Pete, putting an end to that discussion in no uncertain terms.

Chapter Twelve

WHEN THEY were back in the truck and speeding toward home, Emily was bubbling.

"You were wonderful back there, Pete," she complimented him. "So calm and cool. Rich Finger was putty in your hands."

Pete's smile betrayed itself under his moustache.

"Did you ever study the art of interrogation?" she asked, buttering him up. "Hercule Poirot had nothing on you."

"Who?"

"Oh, he was just one of the very best detectives in the world. I've studied his methods thoroughly. You could probably teach him a thing or two."

Pete grinned in spite of himself. Emily was quiet for a moment, as the tires kept track of the cracks in the pavement.

"Do you really have a customer for those chairs?"

Pete feigned indignation. "Of course I do," he said. "It's just that Rich never has anything for me to buy. His stuff's all junk."

"He must have some good things," said Emily. "He didn't get a new house and a new truck every year for nothing."

"Oh, he pretends that he didn't do anything to deserve being falsely accused and that he's all innocence, but the guy's no fool. He's dealt some hot little items with some pretty shoddy characters."

"How do you know that, Pete Picken?"

"Let's just put it this way," he said coolly, "I wasn't born yesterday."

Presently they approached the Stone House intersection, and Pete pulled in to the gas station.

"You want something?" he asked Emily.

"I'll have what you're having."

"Oh, no you won't. What d'ya want?"

"Surprise me."

Pete disappeared into the store and returned a moment later. He tossed a cigar into Emily's lap and proceeded to fill the cab with clouds of smoke. Emily took the cigar from its package and lit it with the cigarette lighter. However, after two or three puffs, she gave up the effort.

"Ugh," she said, looking rather green. "I don't know how you can smoke those things. I thought I'd try it in self-defense, but be my guest to the rest of this one. I'd never make it home without being ill."

Pete puffed contentedly on his cigar, while Emily rolled her window down. She leaned her face out the window and breathed in as much fresh air as possible.

"Would you please close the window?" he asked. "It's cold outside."

Reluctantly she rolled up the window and sat for a moment before she asked, "Would you roll down your side a bit to let the smoke out? I feel ill."

Still slouching against the door, he opened a crack in his driver's side window. Gradually the cab cleared of smoke.

"What was that about Schmidt's daughter?" asked Pete.

"He never mentioned a daughter to me," said Emily. "Do you think that Jenny Henderson had a child? I'm pretty certain that Ruth Schmidt said she never had children."

"Maybe it was just a lie," said Pete, "like all the other lies he told."

"I wonder if it had anything to do with that photograph. Perhaps we can assume that baby was his."

"Yes, but, during the war, we don't know what happened to the woman in the picture."

"Or to her baby either," added Emily.

"Seems like he had a change of heart toward the end of his life," said Pete.

"Like I said, he always seemed like a nice man to me," commented Emily.

Pete glanced sideways at Emily's profile. Her pert little nose poked the air like that of a mouse sniffing for cheese. Her eyes were blue and dreamy. As usual, a lock of hair had broken lose from the bun where it was supposed to stay tucked away. Emily tried to give off an air of conservative composure, but the wisp of hair betrayed her. She could not keep it under control any better than she could keep her emotions hidden.

"You are an incurable optimist," he stated. "There's no hope for you."

Her nose sniffed higher in the air, and she shrugged her shoulders as if to shake off his comments.

"I'd rather see the good in people. It makes life much more enjoyable."

"Maybe so," agreed Pete, as he puffed on his cigar, "as long as you don't ever wake up."

"Pete, you don't know anything about me. What makes you so high and mighty that you think you know so much about other people? Maybe you should look at yourself once in a while, and maybe you'd see you're not all that perfect either."

"I know I'm not perfect, Emily. But at least I don't go around pretending to be somebody I'm not."

"What makes you think I'm somebody I'm not?" she sniffed.

"You cover up too much."

"Cover up for what? How do you know?"

As Emily spoke, the stray lock of hair tickled her nose. Impatiently, she tucked her hair behind her ear and patted her head with both hands to make sure every wayward strand was in place.

"You think nobody knows about the real Emily Blossom."

"I am the real Emily Blossom."

"Really?" She clutched her collar to make sure there was no skin showing beneath her chin. "I try really hard to be honest and genuine."

Pete sensed that his comments were hitting home, so he persisted with his interrogation.

"You've got secrets like all of us."

"What do you mean?"

"For instance, were you as happily married as you say?"

"What do you mean?"

"What did your husband ever do to make you feel good about yourself?"

"How do you know what my husband did or didn't do?"

"You never say anything bad about him."

Emily paused and considered her next line of defense. Her fingers battled with themselves in her lap, as if she were trying to figure out from which direction to begin an offense. She was acutely aware that she had always been a very poor chess player.

"So? You never say anything at all about your wife."

"I'm not married and never was."

"My point exactly," Emily snapped.

"What's your point exactly?"

"If you never were married, there's a reason. You don't go to all that trouble to keep to yourself for no reason at all. I'd guess you loved somebody once, and she hurt you badly. That's why you're the way you are."

"Shows what you know," said Pete evasively.

"Tell me I'm wrong then," taunted Emily.

"You tell me I'm wrong about your husband," Pete countered.

Emily was silent for a moment before she answered.

"Alright, I'll say it. He had a mistress on the side. We both pretended she didn't exist, but it was never the same after. We stayed married, and I looked after him when he was dying. I collect his pension, but we were not really very close at all. We tolerated each other. That's all."

"That's what I thought," he said with finality.

Emily sat quietly looking out the window. When Pete glanced at her again, he noticed a trickle of tears wet her cheeks. He cleared his throat uncomfortably but didn't know what to say. They drove the rest of the way to the Hill in silence.

Chapter Thirteen

PETE DROPPED Emily off in front of her house and skidded his tires as he drove away. Without reacting to his hasty departure, Emily reminded herself to notice the sun reflected in the stained glass above the front entrance. She convinced herself to smile and sighed with contentment.

"So far, it's been a very fine day, Charlie. Thank you for asking," she said to the fluffy cat when he greeted her at the door. "How about your morning? Did you enjoy sleeping in?"

The large ball of fur complained miserably, meowing in loud, colourful yowls.

"What, no breakfast yet? I suggest you fire the cook, Charlie. Imagine being treated so poorly. You've only had dry cat food so far today? You do look rather like a large shadow of your former self, I agree. You definitely should complain to the manager of the household."

Emily chattered as if the cat spoke English; all the while, the irate feline relayed his message in no uncertain terms. They understood each other perfectly. She made her way immediately to the cupboard in the kitchen and dished some gourmet cat food onto a Limoges saucer. He wound around her feet impatiently until she placed the dish on his feeding mat.

"There, there, Charlie, don't despair," she soothed him. "Life has not come to an end just yet. Now you have enough to ward off starvation for at least another hour or two."

Once she had looked after Charlie's needs, Emily shed her heavy sweater and put the kettle on for a cup of tea.

When she had first moved to the village from the Big City, her nickname for Ottawa, Emily promised herself the luxury of a substantial budget for the interior design of her new house. She had handpicked each piece of furniture from local houses and shops in the area.

"I want my home to live through the history of its contents," she explained to the real estate agent who showed her the house. "I want to pretend that everyone who ever lived here was happy, healthy, and comfortable. Moreover, I intend to live here exactly that way myself."

Her home was like her memory, selective, yet calculating. Every table, armoire, and chair represented an era, the styles of décor that would have been found in a house of the Victorian period. In the kitchen, she had a long pine harvest table representing rustic Canadiana from the early 1800s. The living room featured an Edwardian sideboard and side table of manufactured inlaid mahogany. Her Limoges china in the dining room was displayed in a Victorian curved-glass china cabinet. She slept in a four-poster bed that matched her chest of drawers and mirrored dressing table. Even Charlie's seat at the table was an eighteenth-century child's high chair with hand-carved rungs, forged cast-iron hinges for the tray, and a hooked rug mat for his cushion.

Once she was comfortably installed in her new home, Emily decided that she needed a new career to go with her new home. She became an art collector. Her goal was to surround herself with exceptional works of art.

Her taste for art tended toward surprise. She was not contented with ordinary expectations of traditional landscapes and pretty nostalgia. In the entrance to the front hall was a portrait of a young Tibetan child, which had caught her fancy. The child was, at once, laughing and tearful, dressed in an abundance of rags to protect her from the brutality of her winter surroundings. In the living room were modern abstracts by a local artist whom Emily admired for his ability to portray barren wastelands in perspective, with a promise of hope in the light within muted shadows. The kitchen featured photographs of flowers at strange angles and drawings of rocks underwater. Whimsical sculptures and abstract stained glass adorned the windowsills and corners, each with a unique twist of space out of context.

Once she had completed furnishing her nest, Emily still continued to buy knickknacks and small intriguing objects that caught her fancy. As a result, the house was filled to the brim with memorabilia, and every nook and cranny was full with stuff.

When Emily ran out of room on the walls of her cozy home, she began selling the overflow. She became well known among art dealers as a source of eclectic and interesting works. She also cultivated a reputation among antique dealers as a person who paid well for good pieces and had little patience for incompetence.

Once the water had boiled, Emily fixed herself a cup of steaming tea and carried it to the sitting room. She settled herself comfortably into her favourite rocking chair and picked up her current Agatha Christie novel.

"Research," she thought as she looked through books in the library. "Every good detective reads up on the experts."

She was just leafing through the chapters to find her place when a gentle knock on the door interrupted her browsing. She called over her shoulder without rising, "Come in. It's open."

Cassie entered the room, quiet and subdued. Emily sensed immediately that behind her attempt at cheer was a bowlful of tears. Cassie was usually bright and energetic; however, this afternoon, she was restless and preoccupied.

She wandered around the room, aimlessly tracing the edges of the tables and chairs with her finger, until her attention settled on a photograph sitting on a side table next to the couch. The photo looked like an artist's rendition of portraiture: the sepia figures were tinted by hand in pale pastels; the folk art frame was adorned with hand-carved roses and daisies. Both faces posed in smiles that could have belonged to anyone saying "cheese."

"Is this somebody you once knew?" asked Cassie.

"Yes," admitted Emily. "That's me and my husband when we were first engaged."

Cassie's face brightened. "Really? That's you? But you looked so young."

"Yes, too young," said Emily.

"He was handsome, too," said Cassie, teasing.

"Yes, too handsome."

Emily was relieved when Cassie let the subject drop, replaced the photograph, and continued her meandering around the room.

"It always smells so good in your apartment, Emily," commented Cassie.

"I don't know why."

"It's a mixture of soft perfume, herbs, Charlie, musty comfort of old things, and fresh flowers, all at once," said Cassie, as she sniffed the air for a description of each wafting scent.

"Must be the Cherry Rose Festival tea," answered Emily. "One should always be careful to choose the right tea for the right occasion.

"Serve yourself a cup of tea, my dear. I've just boiled the kettle. Come sit and join me. It's lovely here in the sun."

After having watched Emily make many, many cups of tea, Cassie knew her way around the kitchen by heart. She poured the tea and chose a chair by the window near the coffee table. Emily pretended to be reading. When she looked up after a moment of silence between them, she could tell that Cassie had been crying. The young girl's soft blue eyes were now red and swollen. Her cheeks were puffy, and her face flushed.

"So, my dear, what's new?" Emily asked casually.

Cassie pretended cheer, but her voice was shaky and weak. "New? New? Oh nothing, really. Everything's going along just fine."

A long pause settled between them. Charlie leaped into Emily's lap and proceeded to curl into a comfortable ball, accompanied by very loud purring. Emily regarded Cassie patiently.

"Everything doesn't look just fine to me," she commented.

Cassie looked at her blankly, and her eyes filled with tears.

"Emily, you were right," she blurted out. "When you said I was naïve and innocent. I didn't want to believe it, but of course, you were right."

She buried her face in her hands and sobbed loudly, her shoulders shaking with every breath. Emily waited.

"We had our first fight," Cassie cried. "We've never had a fight before."

The sobs began to quiet down. Charlie's purring settled into a low idling motor. Presently Cassie came to herself and reached into her pocket for a Kleenex. She blew loudly. Charlie bothered to glance at the disturbance but did not move from Emily's cozy lap. Emily sipped her tea and waited again.

"We went to bed arguing. I didn't sleep all night. Neither did Robert. In the morning, he left without kissing me goodbye. Oh Emily, I don't like fighting. It's an awful feeling."

Emily searched her memory for comforting words.

"I'm not sure what to say that would make you feel better, dear," she said. "If I were Pete Picken, I'd say, 'You think you got troubles? I just found out that I've got a cousin who's a Republican ... and to top it off, he's converted to Jews for Jesus. You think you've got troubles? You've got nothing on having a Republican cousin.'"

Cassie's sweet smile broke through her somber mood, like the sun from behind the clouds. Emily breathed a sigh of relief, and her hand strayed toward Charlie's favourite scratching spot behind his ears. The cat's purring intensified.

"There, there," said Emily softly. "That's better. At least I got a smile. Now, what was it all about? Can you tell me, or is it too personal?"

Cassie's forehead wrinkled into puzzlement. "You know, Emily, I can't even remember how it started. Somehow we ended up yelling at each other, and it all seems so stupid now, so pointless. It started when he came home late from work. I asked him where he'd been and what took him so long. He just blew up ... just like that."

Emily felt her hands tighten on Charlie's scruff. Her breath caught imperceptibly in her throat. How well she remembered those long nights alone. When her husband finally did come home, the excuses were usually lame and hollow. They both knew he was lying, and they both pretended he wasn't.

Emily reminded herself with great relief that she had left that old life behind. Now, hoping that Cassie would have a better experience than her own marriage had been, Emily commanded her voice to remain calm and even.

"Cassie, my dear, men do not like to be challenged. After a hard day's work, they need their space."

"I didn't mean anything by it," Cassie defended herself. "I'd been working too, and supper was already burned. He hates burned steak. I had a bad day, and I was already upset and tired. I go and make supper, and he's the one who's late. What gives him the right to be all huffy?"

"It's always about who's right and who's wrong," said Emily softly, "but both people have to give more than their share to make up for the bad feelings."

Cassie began to cry again. "I don't know what to say to him. I wish he hadn't left without saying goodbye. It's the awfullest feeling when he doesn't talk. I just wish he'd come back, and we could talk about it."

"There, there, Cassie. Things will be alright. If you really love each other, you'll work it out together."

"I don't think he'll be back, Emily," Cassie sobbed. "He didn't even say goodbye or tell me where he was going. I'm so frightened. All those things come to your mind, 'Will he have a car accident because he's so angry and drives too fast, and I'll never see him again?' 'What happens if he goes to see another woman for sympathy?' I can't even call him on his cell phone. He was in such a hurry, he left it on the dresser. What happens if he gets in trouble and needs to call home?"

Cassie looked up from her worries and searched Emily's face for answers. "Emily, it's so awful, not knowing."

"Cassie, it'll all work out. You'll see. He's probably just gone out for a breath of fresh air. He needs some time to think. Give him time. He'll be back."

"This is the hardest thing I've ever done in my whole life," complained the girl.

"Cassie, there's nothing simple about a relationship between a man and a woman. People have been trying to figure it out since Adam met Eve. They had their first fight over an apple. If you're right for each other, you'll be able to talk it all out. It'll be like it was before, only better."

"Emily, it will never be better after all we said to each other. He made me so mad." Cassie's voice was bitter. "He knows exactly what to say to push my buttons, and he said some pretty mean things."

"And you didn't?"

Cassie's face fell.

"I guess I wasn't too nice either." She paused, and then asked helplessly, "How can you be so nasty to someone you love so much?"

"If you didn't love him," said Emily, "it wouldn't matter what you said. It's when it really matters that you hurt the person you care about most."

"Love is so complicated," whined Cassie.

Emily nodded in agreement. Charlie snuggled deeper into her lap. The grandfather clock in the upstairs hallway chimed. The Tibetan child stared plaintively from her portrait on the wall.

"I'm going to Montreal tomorrow," said Emily to break the somber mood and lead the conversation in a different direction.

"Are you going by yourself?" asked Cassie, genuinely surprised.

"Don't you think I'm old enough to go by myself," quipped Emily with a smile. "I've been to the city before, once in a while, in my younger days. In fact, it may surprise you to know that I actually grew up in a city."

"That's not what I mean, Emily, and you know it. You never know what can happen."

"Nobody notices an old maid like me. Cassie, you wouldn't know this, but when you're over fifty you become invisible."

"Get real! You're still quite beautiful in my eyes."

"It's true," asserted Emily. "Young men only notice young women. Middle-aged men might look sideways at an attractive forty-ish woman on the lookout for an affair … second childhood, last fling, sort of thing. But no one notices women over sixty. They have nothing to offer."

"Emily, I think you're being a bit hard on yourself. Besides, I hate to say it, but older women get murdered just like young women do," said Cassie bluntly.

Emily winced.

"That only happens when there's some sort of relationship between the victim and the perpetrator. I don't know anyone who would do me any harm, especially in Montreal."

"Why are you going then?"

Emily hesitated. "Just a whim," she answered evasively. "I'm going to see a man about a horse."

"You're what?" asked Cassie.

"You don't know the expression, I guess," laughed Emily. "I just … it means …"

"I get it," Cassie interrupted. "You don't want to tell me. It's a nice way to say, 'Mind your own business.'"

"Well, not exactly that," said Emily. "It's more that I don't really know who I'm going to see exactly, or what I want to find out."

"Well, you be careful," said Cassie. "I couldn't stand to lose Robert, and you too."

"Now, now, Cassie. Robert will be home soon. You'll see. You're not going to lose him or me."

Cassie stood up and carried her teacup to the kitchen.

"I guess I'll be going home," she said. "I've taken up enough of your time."

Emily put Charlie gently on the floor. She wrapped the young girl in her arms, rocking slightly to and fro. Cassie yielded into Emily's hug like a small child needing comfort. They held each other tightly.

"Do something special for yourself," suggested Emily. "A good hot bath with lots of bubbles usually does the trick."

"Thanks, Emily," said Cassie. "Thanks for listening."

Cassie went back to her apartment next door. Emily returned to her chair to resume her reading. Her eyes fell on the photo of two young faces staring back at her as if from the distant past, so familiar, yet forgotten so long ago. Charlie jumped into her chair and kneaded a cozy nest for himself in her lap. Emily turned the pages in her book to find the place where she had left off. Soon she heard the bath running in Cassie's upstairs bathroom.

Quebecoise Habitant Stone House

Chapter Fourteen

ON SUNDAY morning, Emily prepared to travel to Montreal.
    She did not drive. Shortly after moving to the Hill, after a minor car accident, Emily had lost her nerve for driving. She sold her car and walked anywhere she needed to go in the village. For the past two years, Emily never ventured beyond the Main Street where she shopped for her daily requirements. Nevertheless, she prided herself on her independence. No one, not even Mrs. Seguin, and especially not Pete Picken, was aware that Emily no longer had the freedom of going where and when she pleased.
    Emerald Hill was equidistant from two large cities. Ottawa was one hundred kilometers to the west, and Montreal one hundred to the east. Village residents with cars could easily drive to either city in one hour. However, public transportation was limited to one bus per day.
    Emily approached her trip with trepidation. Her comfortable home on Pearl Street had become her refuge and her hiding place. Even though some days she felt confined by small spaces, when it came to traveling, Emily was reluctant to leave her cozy nest.
    She announced her intentions to Charlie over breakfast. The cat was perched in his high chair, enjoying a bit of scrambled eggs and bacon. Emily's appetite was not as enthusiastic as usual. Charlie was happy to help her finish off the leftovers.
    "Charlie, my man, I'm counting on you to hold down the fort," she said, as they dined together. "I'm taking the ten o'clock bus to the city, and I'll be back by six. I hope that you can stave off starvation until I return. Keep the bed warm, and don't open the door to strangers. No need to answer the telephone. Whoever calls can leave a message. Do you understand all that, Charlie?"

The cat responded by licking his whiskers and meticulously cleaning his face with a large furry paw. He purred contentedly as Emily sipped the last of her coffee.

"Why is it, Charlie," she asked pensively, "that whenever one has to leave, one appreciates being at home even more than usual?"

As if in hearty agreement, Charlie jumped down from the table, strolled over to his favourite armchair, and curled up for a nap.

Resigned to her decision, Emily did up the dishes.

"A person likes to have everything in order before leaving on a trip," she used to say to her husband. "Even the underwear drawer should be in order. You never know what might happen. In case you end up in the hospital, someone may need to get some things while you're away. Besides, coming back to a home that's neat and tidy is more welcoming than coming home to housework."

She decided to wear her warm cardigan sweater and loose slacks. To match, she chose her black over-the-shoulder bag. She checked her wallet to make sure she had enough cash for her trip.

"Forty dollars should be plenty," she figured.

Emily paid cash for everything she bought. She rarely used credit and had never bothered to get a debit card, since she could not imagine having need of one.

Before leaving, Emily approached Charlie's chair and squatted down to his level. She scratched him behind the ears just the way he liked being cuddled. His purring grew loud enough to fill up the room with motoring.

"You're my very best boy, Mister Charlie, my sweet. We're so very lucky to have each other. Isn't life grand?" Emily crooned.

"Now, you have a big responsibility. You have to enjoy today enough for the both of us. Take care, and I'll be back as soon as I can."

Only when she opened the door to leave did she realize how unpleasant the weather was. Sheets of rain pelted the pavement. The wind snatched reluctant leaves from their branches, sending them flying with the gusts, down the street.

"Oh, Charlie, I think you have the right idea!" she commented as she reached for a raincoat and umbrella. "I wish I didn't have to go out today, but I have a better chance of finding Jennifer at home on the weekend.

"Besides," she added, furrowing her brow, "a committed detective must persevere. We'll never get closer to the truth, if we don't strike while the trail is still hot."

Thus convincing herself to follow through on her intentions, Emily closed the door behind her, leaving Charlie comfortably snoring in his chair. She clasped her umbrella tightly against the wind and faced the rain with determination. She was glad that she had been smart enough to wear her galoshes, instead of her more comfortable walking sneakers. At least her feet would be dry, even if her toes were already cold.

She hiked quickly to the gas station where the bus stopped briefly to pick up passengers getting on in the village.

Only one other passenger waited at the same stop. Emily thought she had seen her recently but could not place exactly where or when. The tall, middle-aged woman wore a blue hat and carried a blue umbrella. Even her eyes, as blue as the sky on a summer's day, matched her colour coordination. Blue-gloved hands clutched a blue suede bag. The woman smiled shyly as Emily approached, but neither said a word as they climbed into the bus. The blue lady made her way to the back of the bus. She seemed to disappear into the shadows of the daylight.

Hoping for a friendly conversation to make the trip seem shorter, Emily chose a seat in front, just behind the driver. Emily noticed that he wore his hat tipped to one side. His hair was cut primly in straight, even lines. His hands, with clean, round fingernails, gripped the steering wheel with ease. A diamond ring sparkled on his ring finger. The driver hunched in his seat with the bus idling, until departure time. Emily filled in the silence while waiting.

"Not very nice driving weather, is it?"

"No, ma'am," he answered.

"You know, I love living in Canada," she said. "If nothing else, we can always talk about the weather. You never know what the weather's going to be from one hour to the next. Don't you agree?"

"Mm-hm."

"Canadians love to complain, especially about the weather. In other countries, where it's warm all the time, people would look at you very strangely if you open a conversation by saying 'Nice weather, isn't it?' Of course it's nice—then there's nothing else to talk about.

"Canadians, on the other hand, can go on for hours about the weather. If you're a farmer, it's too wet, or it's too dry. If you live in the city, it's too hot, or it's too cold. For skiers, there's either too much ice or not enough snow. For hikers, it's either too windy or too rainy or too dusty. Canadians always have something to complain about. Don't you agree?"

"Mm-hm."

The driver looked at his watch and prepared to leave the station. Just as the bus was pulling away from the curb, Emily saw someone's fist banging on the door window.

"Stop, stop! There's another passenger!" she shouted.

The bus lurched to a halt, and the driver pulled the handle to open the doors. A short, tent-like figure draped in a cape clambered on board; shaking a dripping umbrella and panting with great effort, she heaved herself up the steps.

"Thank you so much for stopping," she said, gasping for breath. "I can't believe I almost missed the bus. I never would have forgiven myself."

The driver grunted and held his hand out for the ticket. The woman rooted in her purse desperately.

"Oh, I hope I haven't lost it. I just purchased it a minute ago. Oh dear. Oh dear. Where could I have put it?"

"Try your pockets," Emily suggested.

The woman glanced at her, grasping at any possibility, riffled around in her coat pocket, and produced a soggy bus ticket. A smile lit her face and seemed to turn the dreary atmosphere of the bus into a ray of sunshine.

"Thank you. Thank you," she said to Emily, the bus driver, and the universe all at the same time.

Then she comfortably established herself and her belongings in the seat across the aisle. Emily noted that she was almost large enough to fill two spaces, but her toes did not touch the floor. When she leaned back against the seat, her chest provided a comfortable cushion for her ample chin. Her breath came in large gulps, and sweat dotted her forehead with the exertion of running for the bus.

As the bus navigated onto the highway, Emily looked out the window. Visibility was poor. There was not much to see through the grey fog and dreary showers. The wipers swished monotonously. The bus rode smoothly in spite of the rough pavement and accumulating puddles. Emily enjoyed being above the traffic. As they passed slow-moving cars, the bus left a trail of spray and muddy water in its wake.

"Didn't I see you at the Seniory Lodge recently?" asked the woman sitting across the aisle. "You were with Pete Picken, weren't you?"

Emily looked more closely at the passenger's face, but her face wasn't familiar.

"Oh, I'm terribly sorry," added the stranger. "Let me introduce myself. I'm Marie Cartier. I live just outside of town on the left-hand side of County Road—the little brick bungalow. I used to live with my parents; but my father died last month, and my mother is in the Seniory Lodge now. That's when I saw you with Pete. I was visiting my mother, and you were visiting Ruth Schmidt, I believe."

Emily vaguely remembered Pete talking with a woman in the lobby. Pete had seemed out of sorts, but she hadn't really paid much attention. She was intent on her meeting with Mrs. Schmidt and hadn't bothered to be sociable.

"How do you do?" Emily said, welcoming the distraction of meeting someone in town whom she did not know. "Emily Blossom."

"Are you a friend of Mrs. Schmidt's, then?" asked Marie Cartier.

Emily cleared her throat, trying to think of an appropriate answer.

"You might say that," she said. "I was offering my condolences after Mr. Schmidt's death."

"Good riddance is what I say," scoffed Marie.

Emily continued as if she had not heard the remark. "I thought someone from the town should pay Ruth Schmidt some respect. After all, just because you're in the Seniory Lodge doesn't mean you've vanished from the world now, does it?"

"No, no, of course not," Marie answered quickly. "My mother is well situated there. They look after her ... actually, better than I could, finally. I just wasn't equipped to handle her health problems all alone. I'm quite satisfied that she's well cared for."

"We are certainly fortunate to have a place like that to look after our elderly residents," said Emily, taking great care to clarify that she was not one of them.

"Did you know Mr. Schmidt then?"

Marie persisted in questioning Emily, as if she had an ulterior motive. Emily noticed an edge to her voice that was inconsistent with the friendly tone she had demonstrated earlier.

"I knew him."

"Well? Did you know him well?"

"Why do you ask?"

Emily was becoming extremely uncomfortable with Marie's tone of voice. Her questions implied accusation, not just curiosity. Emily was used to being the one to ask the questions.

"Oh," said Marie, on the defensive, "I was just wondering."

Emily had the distinct impression that Marie was either fishing for information or she wanted to share an opinion. In either case, Emily was suspicious of her motives. She hoped that eventually Marie would explain her interest in the Schmidts, without Emily having to divulge her own involvement. She allowed silence to fill the space between them.

Presently she noticed a large sign indicating that they were crossing the border between the province of Ontario and the province of Quebec. A gigantic fleur-de-lis, in white on blue, the colours of the provincial flag, signaled entry into *la belle province*.

Almost immediately, the surface of the asphalt changed; the pavement became rougher, and cracks widened in the road. The countryside changed subtly. The signs were no longer bilingual but announced their messages in French only. Unlike the straight-walled, sparse Scottish stone houses in Glencairn, the early Quebec cottages of stone had scooped roofs and gables. The Quebecois had built their homes with flare, but also for practical reasons, to shed the winter snows and deflect the wind. In the distance, a cross at the summit of Rigaud Mountain declared the predominance of the French Catholic religion. Its message of salvation was glaringly apparent in neon brightness against the black trees and gloomy horizon.

"Thank goodness we don't have to go through customs to change provinces," Emily said to Marie, expecting to introduce a more objective topic of conversation. "The two provinces have such different languages, different cultures, different ways of doing things."

"Strange things happen in this province," said Marie mysteriously. "I know. I used to live here."

"You sound as if you're glad not to live here anymore," Emily observed.

"You're so right!"

Marie's tone was bitter and full of import. Emily couldn't resist asking for more details.

"You moved out of Quebec for the usual reasons? Taxes, language, health care?"

"If only it was that simple," answered Marie.

"Were you a child growing up in Montreal?"

"Oh yes. But that wasn't the worst of it. It's what happened before I was born that was the worst."

Emily waited for her to continue. She never would have guessed where this line of questioning would lead.

"It's your friend, Dr. Schmidt, whom I have to thank," said Marie, with pure hatred in her voice.

Emily gasped inadvertently. Her face reddened self-consciously. She couldn't believe her luck. As a detective she could not have wished for a better lead into her investigation.

"It's such a coincidence that we ended up in the same town as he did, after so many years of trying to escape what he did to us."

"What on earth are you talking about?" asked Emily, flabbergasted by the turn in the conversation.

"Look," said Marie, "I don't want to offend you. If Dr. Schmidt was a friend of yours, let's just drop the subject right now. I really don't want to discuss it."

"No, no," said Emily, trying to calm her beating heart. "I'm not naïve about what kind of a man Helmut was. I know he had a checkered history."

"That's one way to put it, I suppose," said Marie bitterly.

"Did something happen to your family in Germany? Perhaps during the war?" asked Emily, trying to piece together the facts she knew with the insinuations that Marie was making.

"Oh no, this was in the late fifties," said Marie, "long after he came from Germany. He had become an illustrious doctor of psychiatry by the time we came in contact with him ... rather, by the time my parents went to him for help. Little did they know what kind of a nightmare they would be living, thanks to the great Herr Doktor."

"Are we talking about the same Dr. Helmut Schmidt?" asked Emily, just to be certain. "The medical scientist, Dr. Helmut Schmidt, with a specialty in psychopharmaceuticals?"

"Oh yes, the one and the same," affirmed Marie. "He eventually ended up at the Allan Memorial Hospital, working for the CIA in the late fifties."

"The CIA?" echoed Emily.

"Oh yes," said Marie bitterly. "Didn't you know? The Canadian government was in cahoots with the CIA, doing research into the psychological effects of drugs on the brain. They called it mind control and chemical interrogation."

"That was Schmidt's specialty during the war in Germany," Emily whispered, feeling a chill ripple its way up her spine.

"The Office of Scientific Intelligence is what they called it," explained Marie. "But nobody knew it at the time. Also known as Operation Paperclip. All of this came out much later. By then, of course, it was too late for my mother … too late for any of his victims whose lives were ruined forever. Nobody really talks about them all that much."

"His victims?"

"Oh yes. All the patients who went to the Allan for help … the poor people who were mentally ill and never really had a chance to defend themselves. Nobody believed them at the time. They were mentally deranged and depressed. Who would ever believe them? They were only paranoid.

"That's what happened to my mother … and my father never forgave himself afterward. But it was too late by then. Their marriage was destroyed, along with her brain, and my childhood. No one could ever repay us for all that we lost. No one."

Emily was beginning to understand Marie Cartier's changing facial expressions, which punctuated her sentences as she spoke of her past. Anger, resentment, tenderness, and love all flowed in succession in wrinkles and gestures across her face. Tears etched paths down her cheeks, like the raindrops on the windshield of the bus. This woman had been deeply wounded beyond anything Emily could imagine or explain.

"What happened exactly?" she asked. "Can you tell me the whole story?"

Marie began from the beginning, in a vague, distant tone, which seemed to reach back into her memory, delving into pain that she had long ago tried to bury. Finally, she had found someone to listen. Finally, in a bus hurtling through time, through the cleansing rain, in the autumn of the year, in the autumn of her life, she had found a stranger who wanted to understand her suffering.

Her story flowed into words, to the rhythm of the wipers beating away rivulets coursing down the window. Emily listened with her heart, feeling this woman's torment as if it were her own.

"My mother was born in la Ville de Montréal. Both her parents, and my father's parents, were Montréalais. Generations of small, strong, hard-working people. Spoke French to each other, and English to their bosses. Worked hard, drank hard, played hard. Good Catholics, lots of kids.

"She lived on the same street as my father. They had known each other since childhood. At sixteen, she had all her teeth pulled out, dentures put in, and then she was ready for marriage. He was her only boyfriend. Of course, they'd have a large family of kids, and he'd support them all on his salary as a garage mechanic. They were married in La Cathédrale Marie-Reine-du-Monde. When she became pregnant, no one was surprised. Her mother told her everything would be fine; both her grandmothers knitted sweaters and blankets for the baby. The baby would be born in L'Hôpital Notre-Dame. Mme Clarisse Cartier's life was unfolding as it should.

"Until things went terribly wrong. Clarisse was not a big person to begin with. Like lots of Quebec women, she was less than five feet tall, small-boned and petite. The baby came to term; she was a month past the delivery date when she felt her first contractions. The baby was breach, and labour continued for three days. When I was born, nine pounds, ten ounces, we were both exhausted. Needless to say, even though both mother and child survived, the whole birthing process was painful and draining. I really don't think my mother ever got over it; her health was never the same. She had no breast milk; I was raised on formula. My mother went into a deep depression, and my grandmothers had to take over raising me. My father worked seven days a week to pay for the groceries, rent, and drugs. Six months later, my mother attempted suicide, and she was taken to Allan Memorial Hospital for treatment of postpartum depression."

"This is where she met Helmut Schmidt for the first time?" asked Emily.

"Yes. Things were bad for her at this point, but they got a lot worse in his capable hands."

Marie paused in her story, as if to recollect more of the details. Emily waited, sensing her anguish.

"I don't know if my father ever actually met with Herr Doktor. He didn't understand depression, had no concept that it was a disease. I believe he just thought it was all in my mother's head, like so many people do. He thought she could get over it, if she just made the effort. According to the priest, suicide was a mortal sin. My mother needed to go to confession. One hundred Hail Marys would absolve her of her sins, and then she could get on with having more children. In the meantime, she couldn't eat or sleep. She had no strength to get out of bed, let alone make meals for her husband and child. I was at my grandmother's house. She used a kitchen knife to cut her wrists just before Father was scheduled to come home from work. He found her on the bathroom floor in a pool of blood. After the doctors stitched her up, she was admitted to the Allan for a psychological evaluation."

Marie snickered and wiped her eyes with the back of her sleeve before she continued her story.

"They told my father that my mother was a perfect candidate for a new method of drug treatment. Effective drugs had been developed to erase bad memories. They assured him that, since his wife was suffering from depression resulting from a specific traumatic experience, all they had to do was to administer a mind-altering drug. They would erase memory of the incident from her mind. Then she would forget everything that had happened to her and soon recover to her previous good health. How could he not believe the expert doctors? By now, he was clutching at straws. Besides, they were all English, and he was Francophone. They were right."

"It sounds like it makes sense. I can see why they convinced him that the treatment would work," said Emily.

"That's the point," Marie answered. "They didn't actually care about treatment of depression. One of the programs at the Allan was to study the permanent effects of LSD on the brain. It had nothing to do with medical treatment or recovery. Dr. Schmidt had done many experiments in torture and psychological manipulation during the war. He was one of several Nazi scientists recruited from Europe after the war. The drug experimentation in Canada was just a continuation of his research. Of course the CIA was very interested in the results of the program. They wanted to expand their arsenal to include effective methods of drug warfare and interrogation of prisoners of war. Even though the experiments could never have been sanctioned in the United States, the Canadian government of the time seemed quite amenable to supporting such research."

"I never knew about this," said Emily.

"My mother was in the wrong place at the wrong time," Marie continued. "She and hundreds of other victims like her."

"Why didn't anyone do anything to stop it?" As Emily said the words out loud, she realized how naïve they sounded.

"Not until 1974 was the program finally uncovered in an article in the *New York Times* and followed up by investigations by the U.S. Congress. By that time, I was in my late teens; my mother was still suffering from flashbacks and extended periods of depression; and my parents' relationship was in shambles. Hundreds, maybe even thousands of other victims had their lives destroyed before the practice of nonconsensual experimentation was exposed and the practice was outlawed."

"You must be angry," said Emily, not knowing what else to say. "Although that's probably an understatement."

"Angry? Yes," Marie agreed. "But it's much more complicated than that. How can I possibly describe it to you?

"For such a long time, I hated my mother with such a passion. How could she have abandoned me like that? How can a person whom you love so deeply do that to herself? Sometimes she took it out on me. See this?"

Marie pulled up her sleeve and exposed an ugly burn mark on her arm. Emily saw in Marie's eyes that she was seething.

"Your mother did that?"

"With an iron."

"She burned you?"

"When I was six, I had a temper tantrum. She pinned me down on the kitchen table and pressed a hot iron into my arm until I stopped crying."

"Why?"

Marie looked away and stared at the rain pelting the windows. Her voice wavered.

"She said it was demons who told her to straighten me out. Later on, she denied ever having done it. She was like that ... crazy. One minute laughing; the next minute, a raving maniac. I never knew anything different. For me, that was just the way she was."

"And yet, you still looked after her?" said Emily.

"For a while, I thought I was protecting my dad."

"Protecting him against what?" asked Emily, mystified by Marie's process of rationalization.

"Against the truth."

"He didn't know what she was doing to her own daughter? You never told him?"

"She told me that if I said anything, she would kill us in our beds while we were sleeping."

"He never divorced her?"

"He was a good Catholic. Divorce is not an option."

Emily was silent. She tried to comprehend how a person would cope in such a situation, how a child could survive without being consumed by resentment against all those who failed to protect her against this terrible wrongdoing. Marie seemed to read her mind.

"Long ago, I concluded that I had a choice: I could allow myself the luxury of hatred, or I could let it go and try to build a healthy life. For a while, I was consumed by anger. I embraced it. I wallowed in it. I convinced myself that I deserved to hate everyone who contributed to my unhappiness. But then, I realized the only person I was hurting was myself. It took me a while, but eventually I was able to accept the worst and make the best out of whatever was left."

Marie's blue eyes pleaded with Emily for understanding. "What choice do I have?"

Emily wavered, mumbling, "Lots of others would choose differently."

"I saw what hatred did to my mother and to our family, Mrs. Blossom," said Marie flatly. "One thing I knew for certain: I didn't want to be like her."

"You're a brave person," said Emily.

Marie sniffed. "Brave or stupid. Sometimes I'm not sure which."

The two passengers lapsed into silence, as the bus carried them toward the city.

Then the tone of Marie's voice cut the air between them.

"There is only one person I never could forgive, and I hated him with an all-consuming passion."

Emily listened carefully, as the words substantiated her lingering suspicions about Marie Cartier.

"I hated Helmut Schmidt. I spent my days plotting what I would do to him if I ever had the chance. I spent my nights dreaming of the ultimate methods of torture I would use. For years, every time my mother beat me, every time I saw her eyes burning with insanity, every time my parents argued, threw furniture, slammed the walls ... for all those years, I blamed Herr Doktor Helmut Schmidt. He was a monster in every sense of the word. I loved hating him."

Emily thought carefully before she asked the next question, but she decided that the direct approach would be the most likely to get an honest response.

"Did you murder him?" she asked in a whisper.

"I only wish I had," said Marie bitterly. "I would be proud to admit having had the courage to end his life as brutally as he did mine."

"Are you saying you did not murder him then?" asked Emily again.

Marie Cartier looked Emily directly in the eye and sneered.

"No, I did not murder him, but I am celebrating his death with great joy. Today I am going to Montreal to celebrate my freedom."

Marie leaned back against the seat. She closed her eyes as if to shut out the horrible memories, which had haunted her all her life. A serene smile trembled on the corner of her lips, and her eyelids fluttered like butterfly wings. The conversation was over.

Emily's thoughts drifted to the image she had of Helmut Schmidt, as she had known him over the past few years. She tried to reconcile the deeds she had recently learned about with her impression of him as her friend, when she sat in his living room over tea, listening to his reminiscences and memories of the old country. What she now knew of him was frightening for many reasons: That he had been capable of unfathomable evil was terrifying in itself; however, that Emily had been oblivious to his capacity for inflicting pain and suffering was perhaps more disconcerting. How could she have been so very, very naïve? Positive attitude was one thing, unconditional love, and all that; but such complete ignorance of a man's potential for evil? Emily realized she needed to question herself much more deeply than she had until now. How little did she know about her own self? How little did she know about true evil in its purest form?

I wonder how a person goes about convincing himself that murder and torture are alright. What kind of a man was he, that he seemed to enjoy seeing people in pain?

She tried to remember the conversations they had had. She recalled that Schmidt had been particularly fond of talking about Crazy Ludwig and his castles.

"If you ever go to Germany," he'd say, "you must visit those old castles in the Schwartz Wald. Amazing how one man could conceive of constructing such monstrosities just for his own amusement."

He also seemed quite fascinated with the images of the Bosch painting. Somehow the suffering of the everyman held some kind of allure for him. Emily tried to grasp Schmidt's character in her mind.

He must not have thought of his victims as real people, she rationalized. *Surely he couldn't have considered them humans, individuals with feelings and emotions, or he would never have been able to live with himself, knowing that he inflicted such pain ... Still, he didn't seem to be psychopathic to me. He seemed to be quite ordinary. He liked growing flowers in his garden. He seemed to enjoy watching the children play in the park on his way to The Country Kitchen for his pie. He was polite, and he loved telling stories about the days of the old Kaiser. He knew a lot about history. How could he have so totally blocked out any feelings of guilt or remorse?*

Emily found herself incapable of understanding the psyche of a methodical torturer and murderer. The mechanism by which a person could convince himself to inflict excruciating pain on another human being was beyond her imagination.

There must have been just cause, she concluded. *Somehow he must have thought that his research was for the betterment of mankind. I know the Germans considered the Aryan race superior, but how could they justify annihilating people of other races so completely?*

Eventually, Emily had to find an explanation that suited her. *He had no conscience. The same as his Crazy Ludwig, there was no accountability. Whatever he did was okay, just because he could do it. There cannot have been any question of right or wrong. He was told to torture subjects, so he did. He never thought of his victims as people.*

The theory, she realized, worked only in so far as strangers were concerned. But what about those he loved, his wife and his girlfriend?

Maybe he was badly hurt as a child, Emily theorized, *rejected by his mother and tortured by his father. Maybe such behaviour was all he knew. He learned it from the time he was a baby. He didn't know any better.*

Emily considered this option, but could not really accept this scenario as an excuse for the behaviour of all the Nazis who perpetrated crimes against humanity during the Second World War. She concluded that Schmidt's treatment of those he loved had to have been tainted by guilty feelings and misdirected anger.

If he hated himself, then he probably thought that he was not worthy of being loved by anyone else. He had to destroy those who loved him in the same way his innocence had been destroyed by the war.

Emily found herself almost satisfied with this explanation. Still, she realized, there would be aspects of such evil personified that she would never be able to understand. She had managed to protect herself through her whole life against hatred and violence. So completely had she succeeded, that she could not even imagine the depths a person would go to to sink into the reality of inflicting torture on another human being.

"Tell me about Pete," said Marie, interrupting Emily's thoughts.

Emily was glad for the diversion. She realized her questions were taking her in circles. Some aspects of Helmut Schmidt's personality were incomprehensible.

"Pete? Pete Picken?" Emily stuttered, sensing a trap.

"Is he a good friend of yours?" asked Marie.

"Oh, I haven't known him all that long," said Emily, stalling for time. "I met him soon after I moved to the Hill. We did some business together. I believe he sold me a painting."

"I've known him for years," offered Marie. "We go back a long way."

"Is that so?"

"I think I'd like to resume where we left off," Marie continued for some reason, which Emily could not fathom. "We used to be quite close."

"Is that so?"

"I suppose he's one of the more eligible bachelors in town, don't you agree?"

"Is that so?" repeated Emily, at a loss as to a proper answer that would not get her or Pete into further trouble.

"Do you think he's looking for a companion?" Marie persisted in spite of Emily's reluctance to hold up her end of the conversation.

Emily looked out the window and realized, with relief, that they were downtown. The tall buildings loomed over the highway, and the side streets narrowed.

"Excuse me a moment," said Emily, gladly interrupting Marie's train of thought. "I see we're approaching the terminal. I need to ask the driver directions."

She leaned forward in her seat and addressed the back of the driver's head.

"Can you tell me, driver, how one gets from the bus terminal to St. Laurent?" she asked.

"Ville St. Laurent?" he specified over his shoulder.

"Yes, I guess that's it," she answered, assuming that the entry in the book just omitted the 'Ville' part of the address.

"You can get there on the Metro," he said. "Look on the map when you get into the station. The entrance to the Metro is inside the terminal. Take the orange line to the last station at Cote Vertu."

"Is it a long ride?" she asked.

"No, ma'am," he said. "Not too far."

"It's been such a long time since I've been to Montreal," she reminisced. "I'm afraid I've gotten too used to being at home in my little village. I've forgotten all the tricks of getting around in a big city."

"It's not hard to find," said the driver. "Just look for the Metro signs. The map's easy to read."

When the bus pulled into the Terminus on Berri Street, Emily's heart was racing with anticipation.

She and Marie gathered up their coats and umbrellas and scrambled out of the bus and down the steps to the street. Emily had forgotten about the Blue Lady seated in the back of the bus, until she felt her brush past the two of them as they paused to say goodbye to each other. The blue coat quickly melted into the press of pedestrians and travelers in the terminal building.

"I'd quite forgotten how exciting it is to be in a strange city," she said.

"It's been ages since I've been back," said Marie. "Brings back all kinds of memories."

"Well, I hope you have a good visit here. Enjoy your freedom," said Emily.

"Will you give my regards to Pete when you see him next?" asked Marie.

"Yes, yes, of course."

"Thank you for the chat."

"It's been most informative," agreed Emily. "I thank you."

Chapter Fifteen

AFTER WATCHING Marie Cartier disappear into the crowd, Emily directed her steps into the terminal building, intent on finding her way downstairs to the Metro. According to the map of Montreal, the district of Ville St. Laurent was north of the Metropolitain Autoroute. The orange subway line, destination Cote Vertu, serviced that area of the city.

She had no way of knowing whether the notation in Schmidt's address book was accurate. The address she had noted for Jennifer Henderson read "Rue St. Author, St. Laurent"

"It can't be all that difficult to track down," she had remarked to Pete yesterday. "Surely when I get closer to the address, I'll be able to find someone who can direct me to the exact location."

The bus driver was right. The Metro was clearly marked. St. Laurent district was indicated on the map. The orange line was simple to follow. Emily felt quite confident that she was finding her way quite easily.

"Traveling is like riding a bicycle," she reassured herself. "One never forgets the tricks one learns from experience."

Happily, she boarded the subway when it slipped into the station. She tracked her progress by watching the stops on the map above the sliding doors. She stayed on board until the final stop, when the computer voice announced, "*Ville St. Laurent. Descendez, s'il vous plaît. Terminus.*"

However, once she reached street level, her confidence began to ebb. She was no longer quite so certain that she was on the right track. There was no street by the name of St. Author on the map of St. Laurent. She consulted the telephone book. No Jennifer Henderson listed. She stopped several passersby to ask directions. They were wet, and miserable, and impatient to be on their way. No one could tell her which direction to go. Time was getting on, and she was no closer to her goal of finding Schmidt's ex-wife. The rain showed no signs of letting up. The autumn wind was cold and blustery. By this time, Emily's raincoat was soaked through, and her toes felt like icicles. Usually undaunted, her spirits began to wane.

"The day is not unfolding as it should," she muttered.

Although it was usually against her principles to be so extravagant, eventually Emily decided to take a taxi. She flagged down the first available cab and tucked herself into the backseat.

"*Cent dix Rue St. Author,*" she said with authority.

The taxi eased into the lanes of traffic and headed down the busy thoroughfare.

"Good," thought Emily, "this is the best way to get there quickly. The cabby obviously knows where we're headed."

After weaving skillfully in and out of traffic for about ten blocks, the cab driver reached for his walkie-talkie. The dispatcher had been calling directions in a garbled Quebecois accent to various taxis throughout the district.

"*Rue St. Author,*" the cab driver mumbled. "*Où est ce que c'est?*"

Emily knew enough French that she began to feel a bit shaky.

"Perhaps my plan isn't working out as well as I thought," she mused.

Silence protruded from the speaker, then static.

"*Rue St. Author,*" repeated the taxi driver, who was now headed west in heavy traffic. "*Je suis sur Cote Vertu, pas trop loin de la Décarie.*"

Emily detected the cab driver's accent and guessed that he was from a foreign country.

"Perhaps he's just new to the area," she surmised. "I'm sure the dispatcher has a map of all the streets in the area."

"Maybe it's Rue des Auteurs," she suggested over the cabby's shoulder. "Maybe it's the French version of the street name."

"*Est ce que vous avez une Rue des Auteurs?*" asked the cabby to the microphone.

All the while, the cab was hurtling through the rain-soaked streets, turning first onto one street and then onto another. With each turn they drove further and further from the Metro station. Emily became more and more uncomfortable. She watched the meter gradually rising. Already the amount approached ten dollars. She had paid fifteen for her round trip bus ticket into the city, and she still needed enough to get back to the Main Bus Terminal. The dispatcher remained agonizingly unresponsive.

"Pull over," cried Emily. "Pull over and wait for him to give us directions."

The cabby glanced over his shoulder impatiently.

"Hey, lady, I ain't got all day. It's getting late."

"Well, ask him again. If he doesn't come up with directions, pull into that gas station, and I'll ask the attendant."

The cabby repeated his request for directions to 110 Rue des Auteurs or rue St. Author, but the dispatcher failed to respond.

"Let me out then," said Emily. "I'll go ask someone."

"Hey, lady, you ain't getting out of this cab until you pay me for what's on the meter."

"Don't be silly," she answered. "I'm only getting directions."

"Gimme the ten bucks first," he demanded.

"No need to go getting all huffy about it," said Emily. She reached in her bag and pulled out exactly nine dollars and fifty cents, the amount indicated on the meter.

"Just wait here. I'll be right back," she said as she slipped out of the cab.

Before she could get the gas attendant's attention, she realized that the taxi had pulled back into the traffic as soon as the light turned green.

"Wait! Wait!" she cried, running after him. "Don't leave me out here! I have to get back to the station!"

The taxi disappeared around the corner. Emily stood, desolately, in the pouring rain. She had left her umbrella on the seat of the cab.

The young man at the gas pumps watched her curiously while he served the cars that pulled into the station for fill-ups.

He was thin and tall. His face was pockmarked with acne scars, and a shadow of hair on his chin indicated that he was just approaching the age of having to shave in the morning. He wore his baseball cap backward, and his heavy coat was dripping from the rain. He smelled of gasoline. His green eyes sparkled with a gentle kindness. He had not yet learned to be cynical while serving impatient strangers.

Bedraggled and discouraged, Emily approached him hopefully.

"Do you have any idea where I can find Rue St. Author?" she asked. "The cabby didn't seem to know where it was."

"No, ma'am. I'm sorry. I've lived around here all my life, and I've never heard of any street by that name."

Suddenly, Emily realized why the taxi driver had abandoned her. There was no such street as Rue St Author, or anything resembling such a name.

"The taxi driver probably knew he couldn't find the street," she said to the nice young man. "Now I'm really stuck."

"Are you sure that you have the correct address, miss?" asked the teenager politely. "Perhaps you've read it wrong."

Emily was tremendously relieved to find someone who would help her. Between the bus driver and the cabby, she felt lost and alone. Finally this young lad seemed to appreciate her predicament, and he was willing to help her find a solution.

Only at this point did Emily consult Schmidt's address book. She had been so confident of her destination, she had not bothered to check the actual entry under Jenny Henderson's name. She thought she had remembered it correctly.

"Here's the entry," she said, leafing through the book to find the H's. "Yes, yes, here it is."

She showed the lad the book. He leaned over and studied the handwritten address.

"It says, 'Prince Arthur,'" he read. "Could that be what you're looking for? Prince Arthur's Downtown Montreal ... Yep, that's it. Look here. It says, 'St. Laurent.' That must mean Boulevard St Laurent. That's a main north-south street downtown. Prince Arthur runs perpendicular to St. Laurent in the garment district. I think that's your best bet."

Emily groaned when she realized what a mistake she'd made. Not only had she let herself be cheated by the taxi driver and spent money needlessly, but she had also wasted precious time. Her return bus was scheduled to leave at four o'clock. Already it was two o'clock. She had no time to lose.

The pleasant teenager directed her back to the Metro station. The crooked cabby had managed to charge her almost ten dollars for driving her around in circles. She only had to walk two blocks to get back to the Cote Vertu subway stop. Her new destination was the corner of St. Laurent Boulevard and Prince Arthur just a few blocks from the main bus station and the hub of the Metro lines. She would have just enough time to find Schmidt's second ex-wife and to ask her a few pertinent questions before her return bus ride.

Sitting on the subway and back on course, Emily began to feel more energetic. She did not have time to stop for lunch yet;

however, after she had accomplished her mission, she'd grab a snack at the terminal to take with her on the ride home. She took the opportunity to count the cash remaining from her forty dollars. Nine dollars.

"That's plenty for a good lunch after I've earned it," she calculated. "For a while there, I was getting pretty discouraged, I admit. But a detective shouldn't let little setbacks get her down. Onward and upward, that's what I always say."

She nodded her head assertively and promptly dozed off as the train shot across the city toward downtown. Luckily, the voice over the loudspeaker was penetrating enough to roust her out of her nap just as the subway pulled into the transfer station. Emily jumped off the train, just as the doors slid closed behind her, and the train whooshed away from the platform into a tunnel of darkness. Emily changed to the Angrignon green line and rode one stop to St. Laurent. Then she made her way up the stairs toward the street level and the drenching rain.

Chapter Sixteen

COMING OUT of the station, Emily felt she was entering a strange world in a foreign country. The sights and sounds of a bustling metropolis pummeled her senses. Truck brakes screeched. Car horns blasted. Vehicles splashed through overflowing gutters, drenching pedestrians on the sidewalks. The air was heavy with exhaust fumes, and fleeting aromas of french fries, garbage, and wet newspaper wafted on the blustering wind. Most of the road signs and advertisements were in French. The streets were lined with tall buildings, punctuated by spiral staircases and elaborate entranceways. The storefronts were full of products and items, which bore little resemblance to the shops of Emerald Hill. Furniture, clothing, textiles, herbs, health products (none of which Hill residents would find any use for) were featured in attractive displays designed to catch the attention of passersby.

Emily wondered how she had ever lived without some of the products she saw advertised. While she paused to consider the prospect of buying items displayed in each window, pedestrians rushed past her with their heads bowed to the rain, hardly bothering to look where they were going. When she stopped to gape at the architectural details of the buildings, the exterior spiral staircases and brightly painted corbels and door facades, crowds streamed past her like gushing torrents. Amongst all the strangers, Emily found herself searching for someone she knew.

Surely I must know at least one person on these streets, she thought. *All the faces look vaguely familiar, yet I can't place a single name to any one of the hundreds of people here. At home, I would recognize at least four out of the five people I see on the street.*

As she studied the passing crowds, she realized some vagrants had no destination. One man stood at the entrance to the SAQ liquor store. He wore several layers of clothes, and a bag of belongings sat by his feet. His eyes stared blankly ahead, and he proffered a Styrofoam coffee cup toward the customers going in and out of the store.

"*Pour un café, s'il vous plaît*," he repeated to each person passing. "*Un peu de monnaies pour un café.*"

Every so often, a figure paused and reached into a pocket. Change would clink into the extended cup. The man nodded in appreciation but never cracked a smile.

"*Merci*," he said, extracting the change from the bottom of the cup.

Emily noticed that he left a loonie and a toonie in the bottom of the cup to give passersby the impression that this was how much they should donate. Emily guessed that he made a handsome day's income this way.

Probably doesn't use it all on coffee, though.

As she approached an intersection, she noticed a gang of rough and ragged teenagers with squeegies making their way along the lines of stopped cars. It seemed a bizarre undertaking, since the rain washed the cars and the windshields hardly needed cleaning. Although some drivers waved them off, some actually rolled down the windows and passed a handful of change toward the drenched youngsters, who shouted jubilantly to each other whenever they made a score.

After the initial shock of emerging into the noisy, lively city, Emily drew herself away from the distractions. She realized she would have to hurry in order to accomplish her mission. She still had to walk four blocks to Prince Arthur Street, and then she had to find Jenny Henderson's apartment.

As she hustled along the sidewalks, she missed her umbrella terribly. With only her skimpy, wet raincoat to ward off the damp cold, she was soaked through to the skin. She could no longer ignore the various pains in her body. Her toes felt like frozen lumps at the end of sore, tired feet. Her hips complained with every step, and her lower back refused to relax into her willful stride. Her neck was stiff; her head throbbed, and her shoulders sagged under the weight of her raincoat and bag. Still she argued with her body's ailments.

Don't you tell me that you're getting older. We do not allow age to become an excuse. Even if you were younger, you'd still be complaining. It's been a long day. Tomorrow you can rest. Today we still have work to do.

She chided herself as she hurried through the rain, not even allowing herself the luxury of resting to catch her breath. At last she saw the sign for Rue Prince Arthur, which she repeated to herself with a French accent, just to give herself the full flavour of being in a truly *quartier français*.

"*Cent dix Prince Arthur,*" she said out loud as she read the numbers on the buildings. "It must be in the second block up from St. Laurent. All the streets running east and west begin at this intersection. Jenny must live in an upstairs apartment, since most of the first floors seem to be taken up by storefronts and restaurants."

Presently she found the number she was looking for. She felt a flutter of excitement when she recognized the name *J. Henderson* on the mailbox at the entrance to a walk-up. Apartment 5A.

"That must mean the fifth floor," Emily said unhappily. "This isn't exactly the kind of a place with an elevator either."

The building was dingy. Paint was peeling in the hallway. The banister railing was loose. A strong smell of urine emanated from dark corners. The treads on the steps were worn and slippery. The flights of stairs seemed to rise upward forever. Each step became more and more difficult, and Emily had to pause on the landings to catch her breath. Finally she reached the top floor and found the door marked 5A.

She knocked tentatively and listened. Nothing.

"Oh, please don't tell me they're not home," she begged no one in particular.

She knocked again.

Presently she heard someone moving inside. An eye appeared behind the peephole that allowed the occupant to view whomever stood in the hallway. Slowly the knob turned, and the door opened wide enough for a face to appear behind a chain holding it shut.

"Hello," said Emily in her most cheerful voice. "My name is Emily Blossom. I'm looking for Jenny Henderson. I have a message for her."

The face disappeared. A finger slid the chain from its latch, and slowly the door opened just enough to reveal the slim figure of a woman stooped with age and poverty. Her hair hung limp against sculpted cheekbones. Her sad grey eyes were sunken, and her skin was the colour of weak chicken soup. She wore a simple print dress, which hung loosely from her shoulders as if on a hanger in a closet.

Instinctively, Emily whispered, although she did not know exactly why she felt compelled to do so.

"Are you Jenny?" she asked softly. "I've come about Helmut Schmidt."

Jenny's eyes widened, and she gasped. She tried to close the door, but Emily had her foot firmly planted against it.

"He was murdered last Thursday. I didn't know if you had heard," Emily blurted out her message and came quickly to the point. "I wonder if I could come in?"

Suddenly a husky voice boomed from somewhere inside the apartment.

"Who the hell is it?" demanded the voice. "Get rid of them. Tell 'em we don't want any."

Jenny whispered desperately, "Go away, please, whoever you are. Leave now, before he finds out."

Emily fished into her bag and produced a business card she used as an art collector.

The woman's gnarled fingers grasped the card and slipped it into her pocket. Her eyes were full of fear, and she kept glancing back over her shoulders.

"I'd like to talk to you about him," Emily persisted.

"Go away. Please ... now, quickly," hissed Jenny, panic-stricken.

Before Jenny could close the door, a large hand grasped her shoulder and shoved her into the background. The door flew open, and Emily found herself facing the belly of a giant of a man. He wore a Hell's Angels T-shirt. Tattoos of skulls and snakes covered both arms. Beneath a handlebar moustache, his teeth were black. His hair, in a braided ponytail, reached almost to his waist.

"What d'ya want?" he growled. His black eyes flashed menacingly.

She was nose to nose with the head of a snake printed on the man's T-shirt. The image stared directly at her with beady eyes, its forked tongue aimed threateningly in her direction. She tried to raise her eyes to speak to the man who confronted her, but she was mesmerized by the vision of a rattlesnake poised to strike.

Emily trembled, and her voice shook. She couldn't think quickly enough to fabricate a good excuse.

"I've come about Helmut Schmidt," she muttered. "Thought Jenny might want to know what happened to him."

The Hell's Angel's fist grabbed Emily by the collar of her raincoat and raised her up to the level of his eyes. She stood on the very tip of her toes and could barely breathe since he held her so tightly she was choking. She could smell cigarettes on his breath, and as he spoke, his spit soaked her cheeks.

"Now you listen here, you old fart! Whatever happened to that piece of shit, he had it coming. He beat my old lady so bad, she's lucky to be alive. She's got nothin' to say.

"First those thugs show up looking for some letters, and now you, with some story about murder. If you ask me, Schmidt had it coming. We don't want nothin' to do with no trouble. Now beat it!"

He shoved Emily's tired body down, across the hall and toward the banister. She landed on her knees and remained crouching lest he chose to push her over the railing.

As he slammed the door, he yelled over his shoulder, "Don't ever show your mug around here again."

Emily could hardly breathe from fear. She waited until his steps retreated away from the door, and then she sidled toward the stairway.

Suddenly, the apartment door opened again, and a package flew across the hallway at her.

"Take this crap, if that's what you're looking for. It's no good to us and only causes us shit for trouble."

The door slammed shut again, and Emily shivered. In the dim light of the hallway, she could see a package of letters lying at her feet. She stooped to pick them up and noticed the neat handwriting on the address of the first envelope: *To: Mr. E. Zündel.*

Emily picked up the bundle, stowed the papers in her purse, and fled down the worn stairs to the street level. When she reached the entranceway, she tried to rearrange her clothes and regain her composure. She patted down her wet hair and tucked the stray strands behind her ears.

"An old fart," she muttered to herself. "Imagine that!"

She chuckled as she buttoned her coat and straightened her shoulders.

"I've been called lots of things, but never an old fart."

She shook her head and proceeded out into the pouring rain once again. Then, on second thought, she returned to the protection of the stairwell. She extracted the letters from her purse and tucked them into the inside zippered pocket of the lining of her raincoat.

"That'll keep them dry until I can look at them more closely."

Then she hurried down the street toward the bus terminal

Chapter Seventeen

SHE GLANCED at the time on a clock in a jewelry store. "Fifteen minutes to four," she calculated. "Just enough time to make it back."

Pedestrians streamed past her. Emily studied the faces in the flow of the crowd swirling around her. Individual expressions flashed one after another in unsuspecting candor: idle curiosity, boredom, preoccupation, emptiness.

"Each person lives inside his or her brain carried by a body of flesh and blood," Emily mused. "Humans in cities, like thousands of cells in a vein of blood, flow along predetermined paths toward their destinations. They coexist shoulder to shoulder, yet they are totally isolated one from another. Each individual is totally absorbed in his or her own self-importance."

Emily let her mind wander through her impressions as she made her way along the street. For variety, she decided to walk to the bus terminal on the other side of the boulevard.

She reached an intersection and waited for the lights to turn in her favour. Rush hour traffic was beginning to build. She concluded that jaywalking was not really a very good idea considering the aggressiveness of the Quebecois.

"They drive with their horns rather than their brakes," Emily said to no one in particular.

As she watched the cars inching forward, each trying to get an advantage over others in the next lanes, she mused at the impatience of the drivers.

Everybody's in such a hurry these days, she observed. *In a hurry to get nowhere fast. They all arrive at the same place within a few seconds of each other, yet they're all trying to get ahead of one another.*

She studied the traffic and counted seconds for the light to turn green, waiting intently for the pedestrian crossing sign to indicate that she could cross safely. In the back of her mind, she heard snatches of a conversation behind her, but the meaning of the words did not make sense.

A voice whispered, "There she is. She's the one."

"I'll catch her off balance. You grab the purse."

The voices sounded vaguely familiar, but by this time Emily was used to the false similarity of city impressions and discounted her instinct to turn around.

Surely they can't be talking about little ol' me, she thought.

The light changed, and she was about to step into the street, when a taxi careened around the corner nearly knocking her down. She stepped back and collided with somebody advancing close behind her. Before she realized what was happening, she felt her purse slip off her shoulder. Caught off balance, she reached too late to retrieve the strap. She stumbled into a puddle in the gutter. Clambering to regain her balance, she saw a stocky young man with a bald head and drooping trousers disappear down an alleyway clutching her favourite black purse.

Before she could call out, she heard brakes squeal. A car skidded to a stop just as a pair of strong hands grabbed her by the shoulders and yanked her onto the sidewalk. Her rescuer held her upright until she could recoup her senses. Becoming aware how close she had come to losing her life, Emily became weak-kneed and light-headed. Her whole body began to shake uncontrollably. A vague darkness overwhelmed her.

When she came to, she was sitting in a café. A concerned tall, thin man watched over her. Her raincoat had been removed and was hanging over a chair beside her. Her cardigan sweater drooped, lopsided off one shoulder, and she slouched dangerously close to falling off her chair. Still the strong arms held her steady until she could regain her strength. Gradually she recouped her composure.

"Well," she heard herself say breathlessly. "That was an adventure! I never had my purse snatched before."

The rough-looking character who had been supporting her stepped back, watching her closely for signs of relapse. She tried to smile as convincingly as possible.

"My, my, one does get into quite a pickle, doesn't one? But I'm okay now, thank you very much."

"Did you lose anything else?" asked the slim man through his moustache. "Did anything drop out of your pockets?"

He looked strangely incongruous. Emily could not place where she had seen this fellow before, with his black hair, black moustache, and gold earring, but he seemed out of place, and oddly, out of character. His concern for her seemed genuine, but she sensed ulterior motives.

"No, no, I'm all in one piece," said Emily. Starting with straightening her hair, she began to pat her body all over to reassure herself. "Yes, yes, I'm quite alright. Everything's in working order, I'm sure."

"Did you have any belongings with you other than your purse?"

Emily tried to place the young man's voice. His intonation was so familiar, yet she was sure the fellow was a complete stranger. She reassured him that everything was accounted for, and that she could look after herself.

"I can't thank you enough for pulling me out of the way of that vehicle," she said, remembering vaguely the sequence of events that had led her to this sorry state of affairs. "I can't imagine how many pedestrians are run down in this city by reckless drivers. Perhaps I can make it up to you some day, in some way."

The tall man signaled to the waitress to bring a cup of tea. He paid the bill immediately and indicated to Emily that she should drink. Then he pointed to his watch.

"If you're sure you're okay, I'll be going now. I have to meet my friend down the street," the man explained in a deep-throated, raspy voice.

Emily thanked him as profusely as possible, while reassuring him that she was fine. She sipped her tea, and watched her rescuer disappear into the crowd streaming by the window.

After the tall man left her, Emily began to take stock in her predicament. She had her raincoat. The letters from Jenny were still in the inside pocket. Her umbrella and purse were long gone. No change jingled in her pockets, only a soggy Kleenex. She was totally drenched. Her clothes were soggy and dirty; her hair was bedraggled. All in all, she felt rather like an old rag.

Crowds of pedestrians on the street streamed past the shop window. The numbers had grown considerably as people left work for the day. Rain pelted the umbrellas tipped toward the biting wind. Streetlights flickered as daylight faded, indicative of the shortened autumn days and early chilly evenings.

Everyone else is heading home to their comfortable apartments. It's getting late. Soon it will be dark, and the rubbies will be out on the streets. My clothes are soaking. I'm cold and wet. I have no money. I've missed my bus. I'm all by myself in a strange city. What a mess I've managed to get myself into.

As she evaluated her situation, gradually Emily became overwhelmed by feelings of exhaustion and despair. Uncharacteristic tears rolled down her cheeks. Rarely was she without energy to cheer up. Usually, she could convince herself of the bright side of things. But now, sitting alone in a strange café, without knowing exactly where she was, Emily's resources were depleted. She had nowhere to turn, and no one to call upon. She watched the faces of strangers as they passed by the window, and she felt completely alone in the midst of multitudes.

The waitress who had served her tea appeared at the table. A tag on her shirt pocket indicated her name was Tarnisia.

"Excuse me, madame," she said apologetically. "I'm just ending my shift. Can I get you anything before I go? I hope you're feeling a bit better. You've had quite a shock."

Emily shook off her feelings of self-pity and gathered her spirits together, like a hen gathering her chicks under her feathers.

"Thank you very much. I'm fine, really. It's time I should be going along as well."

She clucked confidently, with no actual idea of where she would go or how she might get along.

Tarnisia helped her put her raincoat on. Although she had no purse to carry, out of habit, she checked her pockets again. Her fingers came across Schmidt's address book, which she had absent-mindedly deposited into her coat after showing it to the gas station attendant.

"Actually, Tarnisia, there is something you could do for me, if I could ask you a huge favour," Emily called after the waitress, who was preparing to leave the restaurant. "Might I use the telephone? I have no money, but I need to make a call to a friend to ask for a ride. It would be hugely helpful. You see, I'm from out of town, and I don't have any way to get home. I would appreciate it tremendously."

Emily tried to sound friendly, appreciative, and helpless at the same time.

"Well, the boss isn't here right now," the waitress responded weakly.

"I'm sure if he knew my situation, he wouldn't refuse," cajoled Emily. "I won't stay on long. You can dial for me and listen to make sure I don't cheat you."

"Perhaps you should go to the police," suggested Tarnisia. "They'll help you, and maybe they'll get your purse back."

"You know as well as I do that they have more important things to do than to chase after a purse snatcher," said the practical Emily. "I just need to call for a ride. I can't use a pay phone because I have no change and no credit card. Please help me. I would appreciate it so very much."

The young girl glanced over her shoulder, as if to reassure herself that no one else was listening. Then she capitulated. "Alright, just a short call. Here's the phone. I'll wait right here. Then we'll leave together."

Emily leafed through the address book for Pete Picken's phone number. She found it under *A* for Antiques. As she dialed the number, her fingers were shaking.

"Please, please, be home, Pete! I hope I don't get an answering machine," she said loud enough for Tarnisia to overhear.

The phone rang three times, and she was about to hang up, when a gruff voice answered.

"There's no one home," said Pete with familiar gruffness.

"Oh, Pete," Emily said excitedly, "I'm so glad you answered."

"Pete died," said the voice, "and this is a recording."

"Pete, stop fooling," Emily rebuked him. "I'm in a bit of trouble."

In spite of her resolve to stay calm and pretend that everything was okay, Emily's voice quavered. "I'm in Montreal. I've missed the bus. My purse was snatched. I have no money, and I have no way to get back to the Hill."

She punctuated her news by sniffing back unwanted tears.

"What's the matter? Where are you? What's happened?" asked Pete, detecting her tone of desperation.

"I'm sorry, Pete. I know you hate women who whine."

Then Emily covered the receiver with her hand and whispered to the waitress who was trying not to eavesdrop, "What's the address here? Where am I? I don't even know that."

"St. Laurent Boulevard," said Tarnisia. "Corner of Ste. Famille."

"I'm on St. Laurent Boulevard," repeated Emily into the phone. "They stole my purse, and I don't know anyone in the city."

"Emily, now listen carefully," said Pete quickly sensing her predicament and taking charge. "Go to Schwartz's Delicatessen.

It's not far from where you are. Go there, order a smoked meat sandwich, and wait until I come to get you. I'll leave right away. It'll take me about an hour and a half."

Emily covered the receiver again and asked the waitress, "Do you know Schwartz's Delicatessen?"

Tarnisia nodded. "It's just up the street. I'll take you there."

Emily thanked Pete and hung up the phone with a shaking hand. She explained to the waitress what Pete had told her, and together they left the restaurant.

In spite of the rain, Boulevard St. Laurent was bustling, as the lights of the city began to take over for the sunshine. The storefronts blurted their message to passersby: Coiffure, Boutique Atomic, Sports, Fruits et Legumes. Narrow side streets with cobblestones were lined with cars on both sides. Graffiti decorated brick walls depicting masked, angry caricatures and exaggerated abstract pronouncements.

"It's as if the artists are desperately trying to call attention to their anonymity and to their genius at the same time," Emily commented to Tarnisia as they made their way up the boulevard against the blustery wet wind.

"They just don't have anything better to do," Tarnisia countered. "None of them have jobs, and most of them are druggies."

From a block away, Emily spotted the sign Chez Schwartz opposite the corner from Bain Shubert. She read several different pronouncements over the door advertising the specialties of the house: Schwartz's Bifteck, Coca-Cola, Charcuterie Hebraique de Montreal Inc.

When they arrived outside of Schwartz's, Emily hugged her young companion and thanked her profusely.

"I hope, if you ever get in trouble, that someone like you will help you the way you've helped me." She patted Tarnisia's cheek in a kindly manner. "Thank you so much."

She lingered and watched the tall, slim body of her new friend disappear into the crowds, which streamed along the main.

"Some people restore your faith in humanity with such simple acts of kindness," Emily commented to no one as anonymous faces streamed by her frail body. "And they don't even realize how much difference they've made in an old life."

Then she turned to enter the restaurant where she would wait for Pete to rescue her.

Emily's Purse Snatching

Chapter Eighteen

THE ENTRANCE was crowded, and people lined up on the sidewalk, huddling under the awning, out of the rain. Emily took her place behind the latest arrivals. She raised her collar to the wind and clutched her raincoat close to her chest, while she waited her turn to enter the restaurant.

Being so accustomed to her small town, Emily was not used to seeing people of different races, colours, and cultures. On the Hill everyone was pretty much white-skinned and conservative in dress. The couple waiting in line ahead of her tweaked her curiosity, and she could not help but stare. The man wore a shiny black leather motorcycle jacket and had dreadlocks reaching to his knees. His skin was the colour of milk chocolate; his lips were sumptuous, and his eyelashes seemed to flicker, highlighting the twinkle in his dark eyes. His girlfriend, blond and buxom, had a tattoo of a bird with a snake in its beak on her left buttock, just above a low-slung, silver-studded belt keeping her tattered jeans from falling off her hips.

I'm sure her pants would actually slip right down to her ankles if they weren't so tight, Emily thought. *She must have taken at least half an hour to pull those on ... and then they don't even cover her belly. Bare bellies, especially with belly button rings, must get very cold in the winter.*

Emily could not help but stare when the woman turned to face her boyfriend. She had rings everywhere on her face, through her upper lip, in the centre of her lower lip, through both eyebrows, and a diamond stud in her left nostril. When the woman opened her mouth to speak, Emily noticed her tongue was also pierced.

So intent was Emily on the couple in front of her that she hardly noticed the line advancing through the entrance of the restaurant. Suddenly she felt a blast of warm air engulf her, accompanied by an overwhelming aroma of smoked meat.

It smells like wet, hot, peppered fat cooking on charcoal... cholesterol, all dressed.

Inside the restaurant she realized that she had been standing in the line for take-out orders. As she stepped out of line, the people behind her crowded into her space. The dining hall was crammed with tables, where strangers were seated together, and customers, who were waiting to be seated, filled every vacancy as soon as it became available. Stools at the counter were occupied as well.

No shortage of customers. A far cry from The Country Kitchen.

A dark-haired, middle-aged waiter appeared to usher her to her seat. His eyebrows were bushy and greying, and his large nose was more bulbous on the left side than the right. He smiled as he greeted her. He had two large dimples and a bushy Groucho Marx moustache. With little time wasted, he hustled Emily to the next available place setting. He said he'd return for her order. Emily assumed he would bring a menu shortly.

She was seated beside a twenty-something couple, who seemed quite absorbed in each other. The woman looked very *française* with delicate facial features except for a large, hooked nose, which, on another face, would have seemed sadly grotesque.

French women are so stylish, thought Emily. *They can get away with being ugly just by virtue of pretending to be beautiful.*

Although the couple seemed totally engrossed with each other, and the woman appeared quite haughty, Emily refused to be put off by their arrogant mannerisms. She tried to strike up a conversation with them.

"Not very nice weather outside, is it?" she said, smiling broadly when she sat down at their table.

"*Non, pas très agréable*," mumbled the young woman unenthusiastically.

"*Il fait mauvais*," commented Emily in very English French.

Without further response, the woman returned to her conversation with her companion. She spoke softly in heavily accented French, intently leaning over the table toward her boyfriend, whose cheeks were shadowed with a day's growth of whiskers.

Emily dubbed her table companions Frenchie and Whiskers.

Frenchie's lips puckered around her words, and her cheeks puffed full of air, as if she were practicing diction with a mouthful of pebbles. Her lips were delicate and sculptured; her eyes, dark and impenetrable. Her wispy hair and her fingernails were black, like ebony.

Too black, said Emily to herself. *Frenchie obviously dyes her hair and paints her fingernails to match. But heavens, those fake nails look like black claws. I'm surprised she doesn't get arrested for carrying a lethal weapon. She could easily scratch Whisker's eyes out.*

Actually, they make a good pair. Frenchie looks like the bad stepmother from Cinderella, and Whisker's cheeks haven't seen a razor in days. I know it's the style these days, but men with peach fuzz beards look as if they've forgotten to look at the mirror in the mornings. They're both right in fashion.

Since she was unsuccessful in engaging her neighbours in conversation, Emily took the opportunity to assess Pete's choice of restaurants. Tables were crammed into a long hall-like room. Diners ate elbow to shoulder; couples sat opposite each other, strangers occupied the same tables, and every stool at the counter was taken. At least ten paintings and photographs hung on the wall depicting Schwartz's over the years, open *"depuis 1928,"* according to a sign hanging over the entranceway. There was Schwartz's in a thirties black-and-white photo showing a food lineup, Schwartz's painted in oils as a part of a street scene, Schwartz's in watercolour, Schwartz's in charcoal sketch, Schwartz's in a child's drawing. Newspaper articles set in period frames featured alluring headlines: "The Best Smoked Meat in Montreal," "Smoked Meat Lovers' Heaven," and "Fifty years of Specialty Smoked Meat."

Emily observed that Schwartz's was obviously a popular place. Most of the people seemed to have been there before, and the regulars knew exactly what they were hungry for.

There was no menu, no list of daily specials, and no prices that Emily could see. Whiskers listened intently to Frenchie's monologue without comment. He nodded at the appropriate pauses and grinned agreeably to show that he knew he was supposed to be listening.

Really he is just thinking of sex, observed Emily, pleased with her talent for astute observation. *Look at how he watches Frenchie's expressions and gets all soft in the face when she smiles. He doesn't hear a word she's saying. He's trying to imagine what she will look like with no clothes on. He'll pay the bill for dinner, and then she'll pay him back with a kiss. That'll be a nice start to the evening. There's something about those French people who are sexy just by the way they talk and look at each other. Not like that couple in the corner who are talking in loud English about politics.*

Emily shifted her attention to an English-looking couple seated at the next table over. They were dressed in tweed and cashmere.

He'll not get it on with her tonight. He doesn't know enough to keep his mouth shut. He keeps defending his point of view and acting arrogant. He should agree with her if he wants to impress her. Women need to think that they're being listened to, even if what they say is gibberish.

Presently Groucho, the waiter, returned, and Emily focused on the task of ordering dinner. Her tablemates selected the specialty of the house, smoked meat on rye with a pickle, french fries on the side, and Coke to drink.

Who needs a menu? she asked herself.

When it came Emily's turn to order, she indicated the couple beside her with a nod of her head and said, "I'll have what they're having, *s'il vous plaît*."

The waiter scribbled shorthand on a piece of paper and disappeared behind the counter.

At this point, Emily busied herself with a study of how the food was prepared. She concluded this restaurant had been serving the same specialty in the same manner since 1928. Periodic thudding of a bread-slicing machine, which looked to be as old as the restaurant itself, sounded like an industrial sewing machine. Each loaf of rye bread became a tower of quarter-inch slices. Rows of sliced loaves stood on end in a glass counter beside the meat table. Shelves at ceiling height above the ovens were lined with quart jars of yellow, orange, and red hot peppers, interspersed with three different kinds of mustard. However, the layer of dust on the jars indicated that the condiments were really more for show, and Emily suspected that few customers deviated from the regular fare.

The meat-carving man looked as if he had been slicing smoked meat his whole life. His entire body was involved in the act of meat slicing. His lips twisted and contorted, as his knife carved paper-thin pieces from a succulent shank of steaming beef the size of a man's torso. His jaw flexed in unison with his sawing arm, and his mouth opened and shut as the blade carved its way toward the chopping block. His once white apron was covered in blood-red palm prints, left when he wiped his hands after handling the dripping hunks of meat.

The waiters shouted their orders to the chef; grease spattered in the frying vats; plates clattered; customers conversed over the din of cooking and serving.

Within a few moments, Groucho appeared with plates overflowing with french fries and smoked meat sandwiches at least three inches high. A large dill pickle garnished each meal. Magically, the waiter carried the whole order in one trip. He opened each can of Coke with a flick of his fingertip as he placed them on the table with a flourish. Emily wondered briefly why he placed a pile of extra paper napkins in the centre of the table.

The use for the napkins became quickly apparent when she saw her fellow diners dig into their meals. Whiskers devoured his sandwich as if he were inhaling it. His moustache was soon decorated colourfully with ketchup and mustard. Even the meticulous Frenchie seemed to have no qualms about stuffing her face. Meat juice and mustard trickled down her chin, before she had a chance to wipe her face and taste the juicy pickle. She slurped her Coke from the can, all the while gazing into her lover's eyes with a twinkle of flirtatious allure. She actually stopped talking long enough to ingest her dinner before resuming her monologue of comments. Whiskers consumed every drop, every crumb, and every tidbit of gossip with equal enthusiasm.

In the meantime, Emily wondered, *How on earth am I going to get my mouth around this sandwich without spilling the contents down the front of my dress?*

She began by the safer route of picking up a fry with her fingers and taking a delicate bite to test its temperature. She squeezed a dab of ketchup onto her plate and was embarrassed when the bottle emitted a disgusting belch. She looked around to see if anyone thought it was her, who had made the noise. No one in her vicinity seemed to have noticed. Self-consciously, she dabbed a tip of her French fry into a ketchup puddle and popped it smugly into her mouth. Then she attempted a bite of the sandwich. The first taste sparked her appetite. She remembered she had not eaten since her morning breakfast with Charlie. She tucked into her smoked meat feast ravenously. She paid little attention to the trickle of tasty juice dribbling onto the napkin that she had had the foresight to tuck into her collar like a bib. She ate with gusto. To quench her thirst she sipped at the Coke, which tickled her throat and fizzed in her stomach.

A pleasant burp surprised her when it punctuated the end of her first smoked meat dinner. She looked around again to see if anyone had noticed this time. No one paid her the slightest attention. She sat back and prepared to relax and digest in leisure.

However, almost as soon as they had finished their meal, Whiskers and Frenchie asked Groucho for their bill, and made their way to the teller who was collecting payments. Emily realized that there was still a line of people waiting to be seated and served. The turnover of customers was steady. The waiters were quick to clear the plates. As soon as customers left their places, the busboys laid new table settings for the stream of hungry customers who crowded into the entryway.

In a quandary since she had no money, Emily watched to see how people paid their bills. An older woman sat behind a raised counter beside the exit, high above the dining room. She surveyed the crowd. Waiters presented the diners with handwritten bills as soon as they had finished eating. Receiving the chit was a not-so-subtle hint that diners were not encouraged to linger over dessert. In fact, there was no dessert offered. Meals were served and cleared, and a place reset as soon as each customer put down his or her fork. Seats did not remain vacant for long.

Emily received her bill at the same time as Whiskers and Frenchie. Groucho cleared the plates immediately, including Emily's.

This could be a problem, Emily thought. *I wonder how long it will be before Pete gets here. I forgot to look at the time when I called him. He said about an hour and a half. It's probably been about forty-five minutes. I cannot leave because I have no money. I cannot stay without ordering more food. The solution is clear ...*

Groucho showed the next customer to her place beside Emily. The woman held a cell phone to her ear as she approached the table. She wore rings on three fingers of her left hand. Fake stones were set in cheap costume jewelry. A cluster of bracelets weighted down her telephone arm.

As her companion continued a telephone conversation, Emily studied her new tablemate. The woman was a bleached blonde, whose roots revealed the pepper and salt of her real hair colour. Her blonde split ends were tangled around the cell phone she held to her ear. Her cheeks were sallow and drawn, while wrinkles outlined her eyelids and the corners of her incessantly moving mouth.

Emily decided that the woman looked older than she actually was. *She must be a smoker. They age prematurely*, she thought. In Emily's experience, smokers usually had pale complexions, and their skin looked half-dead and withered. She figured that somehow the smoke from the cigarettes must dry out the facial features.

She's got the voice of a smoker, too. Deep and raspy. Some people think it's sexy, but not this lady. She's too rough around the edges.

"What do you mean you haven't got any money?" the woman shouted into the phone. "You can't spend money you don't have—that's just asking for trouble."

Emily felt suddenly self-conscious, although she had no compunction against eavesdropping, especially if a person had no problem with talking about private problems in the middle of a restaurant. She realized the woman could have been scolding her. After all, she also was just asking for trouble by spending money she did not have.

Groucho appeared for the cell phone woman's order.

She covered her phone receiver and, without missing a beat, said, "Smoked meat with fries and a pickle. Coke to drink, please."

Emily smiled at the dimpled waiter, who looked at her questioningly.

"The same again, please," she said. "It really was superb."

Groucho raised his bus180hy eyebrows very slightly.

"Another Coke, too?" he asked.

"Yes, please," said Emily in her most charming manner to cover for her nervousness. She was afraid he might have heard the woman's comment into the phone and get the idea that she, also, did not have any money.

"You can add it to my bill."

Groucho returned to the kitchen to place the new orders. In the meantime, the telephone lady finished her call and closed her cell phone.

"Nice day except for all that rain," said Emily. "I guess the weather will get a lot worse before it gets better, eh?"

"A lot worse," her companion agreed. "Now, if you'll excuse me, I have one more call to make before the food arrives."

Emily smiled at the woman's bad manners. As she opened her cell again and began dialing, Emily shrugged and shifted in her chair. By moving around, she tried to digest her previous smoked meat sandwich quickly to make room for the second meal. To distract herself, she glanced around the restaurant, searching the crowd for familiar faces. She never really thought she would see anyone she actually knew.

All of a sudden, she felt an unexpected chill of recognition. She spotted two men following Groucho to their table. The image of the tall man's gold earring, dark moustache, and dark clothing tweaked her memory. She remembered his profile from the darkness of the broom closet. With a shiver, she put two and two together and realized that she had already encountered these two thugs twice: once in Schmidt's house, and once on the street corner. The tall one, Slim, was also her rescuer from the purse snatching incident. Emily knew instinctively that his companion must be Baby. She could picture his shorter and stockier build, shaved head, and baggy pants disappearing down the street with her purse.

She felt blood rush to her cheeks as she tried to slouch down into her seat, pulling up her collar to hide her face.

They couldn't have recognized me from the closet incident, she reasoned, *but if they saw me sitting here, surely they would know who I am.*

Emily was horrified to realize that Groucho was seating them just behind her table.

Then she recognized their familiar voices.

"There was nothing' in that purse," said Baby's high-pitched, nasal tone, which Emily knew well. "Only a bit of cash and a handkerchief. I pocketed the change and dumped the purse in a container down the alley. There was nothin' in it, I swear."

"Then where's the package of letters that guy was ranting about?" Slim's deep-throated drawl was unforgettable.

Emily's emotions somersaulted. She shivered with fear at the intimidation in his words but at the same time recalled the kindness he had shown her after her shaky ordeal.

One thing's for sure. I can't trust either one of them if they recognize me, she thought.

Baby continued, "She must have hidden the letters somewhere."

"Yeah, right!" Slim's sarcastic tone cut to the quick. "Just where would she find a place to hide a package that big between the apartment and where we grabbed the purse?"

"Under the stairs?"

"No, she's got to have them on her."

Emily slowly, casually lowered her hand to feel the inside pocket of her raincoat. Sure enough, the packet bulged inside the lining. Emily dared not move quickly. She didn't want to draw any attention to herself.

"The bishop is offering big bucks for those letters," said Slim. "He won't be impressed if we let her get away with them. In fact, I'd venture to bet we'll be dead meat if we don't produce."

"What's so important about a bunch of rotten old letters?" asked Baby.

"The bishop seems to think they're important to his career."

"A bishop has a career? I thought the church looked after its own."

"I dunno. The Catholic Church has plenty of problems these days. Is anybody's future guaranteed?"

"What happens if we botch the job?"

"Let's just put it this way," answered Slim, "I wouldn't bother to save money for your retirement."

Just then the woman at Emily's table cupped her hand over the cell phone receiver.

"Are you alright?" she asked Emily. "You don't look so good."

Emily managed a faint smile, feeling the blood drain from her face.

She whispered, "Actually, I'm not feeling all that well. Excuse me for a moment."

Emily desperately scanned the restaurant, hoping that the bathrooms were in an opposite direction from where Slim and Baby were seated.

"They're in the back corner," said the woman, gesturing to the sign that read *"Femmes"* in the shadows of the large dining hall.

Emily grabbed her raincoat and hurried away, making sure to keep her back turned to the men seated behind her. Not daring to glance over her shoulder, she scurried among the tables, inadvertently knocking a man's elbow as he was drinking from a Coke can. She could hear him gasp and choke, and scrape his chair from the table to avoid getting his clothes soaked, but she didn't slow her flight toward the safety of the ladies' room. Once inside a booth, she sat down on the toilet seat, panting, trying to calm her thundering heartbeat and think carefully about how to handle the situation.

Perhaps I could safely stow the letters in the sanitary napkin container. Then I could come back later to pick them up when Pete gets here, before we leave.

Still, she could feel the power of Slim's hand on her shoulder, lifting her from the path of the speeding car less than an hour ago. She thought of Baby's bulging muscles, carrying her purse down the street. She shuddered when she tried to estimate the extent of their anger when they realized that their attempts to find the letters had been foiled by a little old lady.

Do I dare to confront them in public? What if they hurt me?

Then reason got the better of her fear. She tried to picture the scenario of Slim and Baby accosting her for the letters in the middle of a crowded restaurant.

They wouldn't dare cause a disturbance, she reasoned. *I don't know what I'm so worried about. I know how to scream at the top of my lungs if I have to.*

Just then she heard the bathroom door open slowly. She saw a pair of shoes pause outside of the booth where she was hiding. There was a gentle knock on the door.

"Are you okay in there?"

Emily recognized the raspy voice of the cell phone lady.

"I don't want to disturb you, but I just wanted to be sure you're alright."

Emily stood up and slid the bolt from its keeper. She opened the door just enough to peek out and scan the row of sinks to make sure no one else was listening.

"Are we alone?" she asked.

Both women surveyed the room. When they were sure they were the only ones in the bathroom, Emily emerged guardedly.

"There are two men out there who might be dangerous," she explained. "But I don't think they'll do anything in the middle of the restaurant."

The cell phone lady watched her suspiciously, trying to determine whether Emily's fears were well founded or whether she was a nut case.

"They can't do anything as long as you're surrounded by people. Come and eat. Follow me," said the raspy voice. "The smoked meat is getting cold."

Cautiously Emily followed her new friend back to the table where the smoked meat sandwiches and french fries were waiting. She did not dare to look at Slim and Baby to see whether they recognized her. While she was in the ladies' room they had received their meal and their conversation had subsided. She could discern sounds of slurps and satisfying smacks as they devoured their dinner. Apparently discussion about their next move was delayed, pending further consultation.

The phone lady studied her reaction for a moment to try to determine whether or not Emily would recover from her fears.

"There, you see?" she said reassuringly. "There's nothing to be afraid of. *Bon appetit!*"

Apparently satisfied that there was no further need for surveillance, she tucked into her sandwich with enthusiasm. Juice and mustard dripped from her jeweled fingers onto the floor.

Emily thought that she had totally lost her appetite, but she went through the motions as if she were hungry. Soon, she managed to consume the first mouthful of her second sandwich as if she had not eaten for days. Then surprisingly her taste for good food did revive itself. The tartness of the pickle helped to mitigate the effect of fat slithering down her throat. She used three napkins this time to keep her fingers from soiling her dress. Three french fries and a large blob of ketchup remained on the plate. She had underestimated—but only slightly—the extent of her recuperative powers.

Just as she bit into her sour dill pickle with a satisfying crunch, Emily felt a heavy hand gripping her shoulder. A shot of pain stabbed at the base of her jugular, where a steely thumb neatly paralyzed her from the neck down. Her latest swallow caught in her throat, and she choked. The phone lady looked up from concentrating on her sandwich, and gasped.

"This very fine lady is coming with us, now aren't you?" said Slim in a smooth and slimy tone. "We have a little business to discuss outside."

Emily's eyebrows expressed her astonishment at the audacity of such a manoeuvre. Her eyes met the phone lady's blue and empty expression. Neither one of them moved, waiting—for what, they did not know.

"Perhaps I can help you with your coat, madame," said Baby with a sneer, as he helped himself to her coat from her lap.

"Unhand me, you brute!" Emily shouted as loud as she could.

The language was a bit outdated, but it did the trick. Slim hesitated and softened his grip. Emily stood up, scraping her chair back, knocking it to the ground with a loud crash.

"And you," Emily said to Baby as she snatched her raincoat from his hands, "Take your grimy mitts off my coat."

"Leave that woman alone!" said Telephone Lady. "She's not going anywhere with you! Waiter! Waiter! Get rid of these two thugs!"

Groucho appeared silently and took a stance between Slim, Baby, and Emily.

"The lady does not wish to accompany you, sir. Pay your bill before you leave."

Slim glared around the restaurant. A hush had descended on the room. Even the dishes ceased to clatter. All eyes were directed at him and Baby, as if willing them to burst into flames and disintegrate. He looked at Groucho and Telephone Lady, evaluating their combined strength against his. Then he let his hand drop from Emily's shoulder, sniffed loudly, twirled his moustache, and strode to the counter to pay his bill. Baby slithered after him, like a beaten servant.

Emily looked around the room and smiled at all the faces waiting expectantly to see what she would do.

"Thank you all very much for your support," she said to the whole room with a polite curtsey. "*Merci beaucoups.*"

She turned to Telephone Lady.

"How can I thank you enough?"

She reached across the table and offered her new friend a hearty two-handed handshake. Then Emily sat down, smoothed her clothes, cocked her head with a gesture of pride and arrogance, and downed her last sip of Coke with a slurp.

Telephone Lady finished her meal quickly. Groucho delivered her bill and Emily's second bill and cleared away the plates.

"What are you going to do now?" asked Phone Lady.

"Actually, I'm waiting for a friend to come here to pick me up," explained Emily. "He should be arriving shortly."

"Are you sure? Would you like me to stay until he arrives?"

"Oh no, thank you so much. That's not necessary. I'm sure that as long as I stay here, I'll be safely in a crowd."

The woman looked at her quizzically. "Safety in numbers, you mean?"

"Yes, yes, that's what I said. Safety in numbers."

Emily smiled, stood and shook her friend's hand, and said goodbye. The phone lady paid her bill, and as she left the restaurant, Emily could see that she was already dialing another number on her cell phone, no doubt to tell her friends all about what had happened to her while eating smoked meat at Schwartz's Deli.

However, Emily's predicament was still quite precarious. Feeling relatively safe among the company of strangers, she needed to find more excuses to stay seated until Pete's arrival.

Surely he won't be much longer, she consoled herself, *unless he gets caught in a traffic jam. If he doesn't get here soon, I'll be the one in a jam.*

In Telephone Lady's place sat an older man with Einstein hair, white and flying in all directions as if aroused by static electricity. His lips were stained with nicotine, and the first two fingers of his right hand were an orange-green colour down to the first knuckle. His eyes gleamed, and a smile flickered across his face. He appeared shy and curious at the same time.

Finally, here was someone Emily could talk to.

She was quite prepared to open the conversation with Mr. Einstein if need be. She was afraid Groucho would lose patience with her if she looked as if she were stalling. Luckily, this time her new companion seemed quite willing to engage in conversation.

"Terrible weather we're having," he said. "We've had a very wet fall."

Emily happily joined in with her comments. "They say that if the fall is wet, there'll be lots of snow for winter. I'd rather have snow than ice if we have to go through the cold months until spring."

"Yes, yes," agreed Einstein. "Disagreeable in the city, though. Rain or snow always turns into dirty mush."

"I'm not from here," offered Emily as an explanation. "Snow stays white longer in the country."

The older man looked at Emily closely, squinting his eyes as if to get a better focus.

"Don't I know you from somewhere?" he asked. His voice was friendly and gentle. "I'm sure I've seen you before."

Emily glanced over her shoulder to see whether he was speaking to someone behind her. She whisked away a stray lock of soggy hair that threatened to block her view. She eyed Einstein askance.

"I don't believe we've met," she answered. "Your face is vaguely familiar, but then again, every one in the city reminds me of someone I've met at some time or other. They say that no matter where one travels in the world, the chances are good that you'll meet someone you know eventually. The world is that small."

Einstein peered at her face with his twinkling eyes. He cocked his head sideways and knit his bushy eyebrows together, as if to evaluate her features more accurately.

"No, I'm sure I've met you somewhere," he asserted. "Are you by any chance an art collector?"

Emily felt a chill of apprehension.

"Yes," she said slowly. "You might say that. Do you collect art?"

"Not exactly," he answered. "I'm a painter. I have some paintings hanging in the National Gallery, actually. I'm sure you must have been at one of my openings. I never forget a face."

Groucho appeared at the table for their order. At the sight of the waiter, Emily realized that she felt very, very full.

"Smoked meat on rye," said the painter. "With a pickle on the side. French fries and a Coke."

The waiter's dimples deepened when he waited for Emily to state her wishes.

I'm sure he realizes I'm stalling, she thought. But out loud, she heard herself ordering once again.

"Smoked meat sandwich," she said, and then added, "Forget the fries and pickle. And I'll just have water to drink, please."

Groucho scribbled on his pad and disappeared behind the meat counter.

Einstein looked at Emily quizzically. "Is that all you're going to have?" he asked. "Surely you're not watching your waistline. You certainly don't need to worry about your looks."

Emily couldn't decide whether he was teasing her or offering her a compliment. In the art world, she remembered, artists often tried to butter up potential buyers.

Even though she knew she was beyond the age of eligibility, she chose to believe he was flirting with her. She laughed as provocatively as she knew how.

"It's been my experience," she said with a giggle, "that the more successful the artist, the more likely he is to be generous with his compliments."

Einstein chuckled. His teeth were stained and crooked, but his mannerisms were charming and disarming.

"It's been *my* experience, my dear young lady," he retorted gallantly, "that the more beautiful the woman, the more likely she is to be extravagant with her praise."

Emily blushed. When it came to flirtation, she felt quite out of practice; however, she realized she was beginning to enjoy herself tremendously. Slim and Baby were nowhere to be seen, and this man seemed capable of getting her out of a mess if need be.

So it was with a bit of disappointment that she spotted Pete approaching the table. His familiar swagger, the cock of his hat, and his toothless grin caught her off guard. She felt torn and confused. Her precarious predicament suddenly melted into the background, and she greeted Pete with a mixture of relief and annoyance.

"Well, Pete Picken," she declared, "It's taken you long enough to get here."

Pete's face fell. Unconsciously, he readjusted his hat, smoothing his hair back and positioning the brim low over his eyes to disguise his discomfort.

"What kind of a greeting is that?" he asked in an injured tone. "Here I thought I was rescuing a damsel in distress, and all I get for thanks is, 'It's taken you long enough to get here'?"

Suspiciously he glanced at the nicotine-stained man with scattered hair sitting opposite Emily at her table. Emily ruffled her feathers, and self-consciously, shifted her eyes from one man to the other.

"If I'm interrupting something, I'll just be on my way back to the country," Pete said in a loud, edgy voice.

Emily jumped up and put her hand on his arm to soothe him.

"No, no, Pete," she said, recovering her composure and trying to retract her mistake. "I'm sorry. I didn't mean it like that. I'm really, really glad to see you."

Then she turned toward her new acquaintance. "May I introduce you to … Mr. … Actually, I don't believe I remember who you are exactly. You said you were a painter, but you didn't mention your name."

"Bryant," said the artist, reaching his hand out to shake Pete's hand. "S. T. Bryant. Pleased to make your acquaintance. Are you an art collector as well?"

Pete seemed slightly mollified by the painter's friendly introduction and relaxed his defensive approach.

"No, actually, I'm an antique dealer. Pickin's the trade; Picken's my name. Just call me Pete."

"Well, Mr. Picken, pleased to meet you. Won't you join us?"

The three of them sat down, just as Groucho arrived with Emily and Bryant's orders. The waiter paused, looked at Emily, at Bryant, then at Pete, and shook his head in wonder. Emily was relieved that he chose not to acknowledge the length of time she'd been seated at his table.

"Bring me the works," said Pete with the confidence of a regular customer. "Smoked meat sandwich, fries, a big pickle, and red pop, please."

Then, just as the waiter finished scribbling the order, Pete added, "Oh yes, and a few slices of fresh onion. Don't forget the onion—thick like this."

The distance between his thumb and forefinger indicated at least a half an inch of onion. Groucho scribbled furiously and disappeared to fill Pete's order.

Emily looked at her sandwich and secretly groaned. However, in view of her two charming companions, she dared not comment. She pretended to wait for Pete's meal to arrive, in a desperate attempt to stall off eating and to let her food settle so that her appetite could regain its enthusiasm. She hoped her reluctance to dine was not too obvious.

Pete glanced at his hands and excused himself to go to the washroom.

Since Pete's arrival, Bryant seemed less interested in pursuing conversation with Emily. She was obviously spoken for. Emily, for her part, was relieved when the artist turned his attention to the task of eating. His previous attempts at impressing Emily by his good manners became of secondary importance compared to a gaping smoked meat sandwich. Soon his face was dripping with succulent juices, and his stained fingers were covered in ketchup and mustard. The ketchup bottle burped; and the Coke can slurped; and Emily was no longer attracted to his charisma.

When Pete's dinner arrived, Emily was relieved that he concentrated on making short work of the meal. He approached the challenge of sandwich eating differently from the other eaters she had observed. Using fork and knife, Pete meticulously cut the bread and meat into bite-sized pieces, alternating mouthfuls with tastes of pickle and onion. He remained relatively unsullied, and only needed one napkin to wipe his mouth after dinner. The red pop, on the other hand, tinged his moustache with a cherry-coloured fringe.

He did not attempt small talk, and she, for once, did not try to fill the silence between them with idle chatter. The din of the restaurant enveloped them comfortably in a pillow of noise: the clattering of dinner dishes, the chattering of the bread-slicing machine, waiters calling out their orders, and snatches of conversation caught out of context, like abandoned words on the wind.

Emily took dainty bites around the edge of her third helping. She was loath to present Pete with her three bills. She wished she did not have to offer him any explanations, and she was fresh out of excuses for her ridiculous behaviour. Fatigue washed over her like a wave of resentment, and all she wanted to do was to curl up in her own bed and disappear.

As soon as Pete's plate was empty, Groucho promptly cleared the dishes. Without a word, Pete gathered up Emily's three bills and his own. He helped Emily put her coat on and went to the checkout counter to pay. Emily felt the weight of the precious package of letters bump against her leg. She nodded goodbye to Bryant, and he returned her acknowledgement with a bow. As they left the delicatessen, Emily glanced up and down the boulevard to assure herself that her assailants had given up their pursuit, at least for the time being. To her relief, they were nowhere in sight. Pete took Emily by the elbow, and escorted her through the rain, down St. Lawrence to where the truck was parked.

"Thanks for paying the bill, Pete," said Emily quietly, as he hustled her down the street.

"Look, Emily, I don't mind helping you out, but ..." he hesitated, as if unsure how to proceed.

"How much was it?" she asked.

"Twenty-seven-dollars' worth of smoked meat sandwiches?"

"I had to do something while I waited for you to rescue me."

He was silent, not really knowing what to more to say.

"Knights in shining armour sometimes come in strange disguises," she murmured.

"What's that supposed to mean?"

"Look, I'll pay you back. I promise."

"That's not the point."

"What is the point then, exactly?" she asked, not able to let the subject drop, but sensing that she would be better advised not to pursue it.

"The point is that you put yourself in considerable danger with your crazy schemes."

He shouted loud enough that passersby glanced in their direction, and Emily became self-conscious. She tucked her hair back behind her ear and checked that her bun was in place. She resisted the impulse to reply with a snide "Little do you know."

"You're just lucky you didn't really get hurt."

Emily smiled secretly to herself, holding tightly onto Pete's arm, as he propelled her down the boulevard.

"Yes, but I didn't now, did I?"

"F'n lucky," he mumbled.

"Pete," she snuggled against his arm, enjoying the strength of his stride, "What would I do without you?"

He grunted in response.

They arrived at the truck, parked illegally in a delivery zone. He opened the passenger door and helped her onto the running board. Trying to find a handhold, she had to climb awkwardly up into the cab to reach the seat. Once she was safely installed, he strode in front of the hood and swung open the door on the driver's side. In spite of his small stature, he glided into the elevated seat behind the steering wheel as if it were second nature. The truck motor roared into action. Pete navigated his way into traffic and headed for the highway.

Not another word was spoken between the two of them until the city lights disappeared into the darkness of the countryside, as they drove west toward Emerald Hill and home. The only sounds were the tires spraying through the puddles on the pavement and the slapping of the windshield wipers, wiping away tears of rain.

Chapter Nineteen

THE TRUCK cab smelled of pipe smoke, and cigars, and musty boxes. The backseat was filled, as usual, with small antiques. Several bigger pieces of furniture were tied in the open box. A table on the rack looked like a roof over the windshield. Whenever she saw his truck parked on Main Street, Emily usually loved to explore Pete's most recent purchases. However, in the shadows of the city lights, she could not discern any particular item to tweak her curiosity. She reminded herself to extract the package of art articles that Rich had given her when they got home.

Pete drove slouched against the door, his hat pulled down over his eyes against the reflection of oncoming traffic. His eyes stared straight ahead without expression. The silhouette of his nose melded with his moustache and large lips, creating an impression of solidity and unwavering confidence. Emily was comforted by his presence, even though she sensed he was annoyed with her. In an effort to lighten the heavy atmosphere created by the silence between them, she attempted conversation on her favourite neutral topic, the weather.

"It feels as if it's been raining for weeks."

Above the hum of the rain and passing traffic, her voice sounded hollow and insubstantial, like unnecessary noise. Usually Emily's penchant for small talk filled awkward silences. Tonight she felt horribly inadequate.

Pete, on the other hand, came straight to the point, "So, Emily, what's this all about?"

"What do you mean?" she evaded him. "So I had a bad experience coming to the city. It could happen to anyone."

"That's not what I mean, and you know it."

"I don't understand," she pretended. "If it's thanks you want ... for coming to get me, then ... thank you very much."

"You don't need to thank me. That's not why I came."

The windshield wipers punctuated the brief statement hanging between them.

"Why did you come?" she asked.

"Don't answer a question with a question."

"What was the question?"

"Don't play games with me, young lady," he said bluntly. "What's up with you, that you need to solve this so-called murder?"

Emily gazed out the window, watching the cars they passed racing backward. Her mind pondered how fast-paced lives could seem to travel so quickly away into the past, like quickly fading memories. The faces of the drivers were fleeting, caught in the headlights for one brief instant, startled with the reality of light, then lost again into a realm of has-been or never-was.

"Emily."

Pete's voice shattered her reveries, bringing her back to the conversation she was trying to avoid.

"I don't know what you're talking about." She tried again to dodge his directness. Purposefully, she tucked that vagrant curl behind her ear and stared at the rivulets of rain flying away from the windshield.

"I'm talking about you ... a subject which you seem to have a lot of difficulty focusing on. What's driving you to be so involved with this Schmidt guy anyway? Did he mean something to you, or is it all just for your own amusement?"

"I guess I do owe you an explanation."

"I guess you do."

"Well I suppose it's a little bit of both."

She paused before proceeding, but then launched herself into the unavoidable explanation.

"First of all, I used to drop in on Schmidt from time to time for a chat. At first I was collecting for the Arthritis Society, the Cancer Society, or the Food Bank, whatever charity I was supporting at the time. He'd always be so friendly. We'd chat, and he'd offer me a cup of tea.

"Did you ever notice how a cup of tea brings people together?" She paused, as if to ponder. Then she continued, "Now it kind of depends on what kind of tea you serve. It must not be too hot or too cold or ..."

"Emily!" Pete snapped her back to the subject.

"Yes? Oh, where were we?"

"Schmidt," reminded Pete. "Why do you care?"

"Well, I always saw him as a lonely old man, kind of broken, you know ... Old and broken. We had some nice chats. He was very well educated. He told me about attending operas in Vienna, Oktoberfest in Munich, about the Black Forest, and the castles built by Crazy Ludwig, Von this, and Von that. He seemed a gentle man in the true sense of the word. It really bothers me to think that I was so naïve."

Her voice sounded childlike, as if she was convincing herself to remain innocent and non-judgmental.

"I find it hard to believe all those awful things they say about him," she continued. "To me he was just an old man looking for someone who would listen to his stories. He knew quite a lot about art and history. We'd talk about his paintings, and he'd explain his fascination for the Medieval Times."

"You didn't tell this to Allard, I take it?" Pete's statement was a leading question.

"Oh, no. It never went any further than casual chatting over tea. I felt sorry for him."

"So why do you care about the so-called murder then?"

"Listen, Pete. There's something you should know about me," said Emily, finally getting to the point. "I'm a pretty simple person really."

"I hardly think so."

"No, really. I never actually accomplished much in my life. I was fond of my husband in a conventional sort of way. We had, shall we say, an agreement. To all expense and purposes we were happily married."

"I believe you mean 'intents and purposes,'" Pete corrected her.

"That's what I said. We got along okay in the end after all."

"Even though he cheated on you?" Pete asked poignantly.

"Well, you know, I'm not the first wife to be cheated on, and I won't be the last. I made up my mind, though, that I wasn't going to let him ruin my life. He wasn't worth it really. No need to cry over milk under the bridge."

"It's water under the bridge, and crying over spilt milk," corrected Pete.

"There, you know what I'm talking about. I made up my mind to be happy in life, so I was."

"It didn't occur to you to divorce him?"

"Oh, goodness no. You didn't do those things in those days. Besides, he looked after me well. Since he had all that hanky panky on the side, I didn't have to bother with putting up with him when I didn't feel like it. He had his way, and I had mine. When he died, I had his pension to live on and my old-age security. I moved to Emerald Hill because I could afford to buy here, and people are friendly. For the first time in my life, I became Somebody. People know me by name. They listen when I speak. I don't want much in life—just to get by."

"Well, as I see it, that's something, 'just getting by.'"

"Because I'm getting older—"

"How old are you then?" Pete asked bluntly.

"Well, let's just say I'm not a chicken anymore," she said, with a flip of her nose.

"A chicken? What do chickens have to do with your age?"

"Well, you could say I'm getting on," she answered.

"On what?"

"Oh, now you're playing with me."

"No, really ..." He puffed on his pipe and spoke through the side of his mouth. "What does a chicken have to do with it?"

She blurted, "You know what I mean. I'm getting old."

"Oh, you mean you're not a *spring* chicken anymore."

"That's what I said." Emily sniffed defiantly with her nose in the air.

"You're only as old as you think you are."

"Well, I'll be damned if I'm going to curl up like a caterpillar, and just fall asleep one day out of sheer boredom."

Pete glanced at her as her voice gained more vehemence. He sensed an urgency, which she had never shown before.

"Now, if I could solve this murder, I'd have accomplished something just a bit out of the ordinary. Besides it gives me something interesting to do. And maybe, just maybe, I can make a small difference in town, a small contribution to a sleepy little place without much going on."

"Well, if nothing else," Pete added to her train of thought, "it'll give those folks at the Country Kitchen something to talk about."

"Yes, that's it precisely. Now you understand."

"Perhaps it goes without saying, though," Emily continued, returning to the subject of Schmidt, "I liked the guy. He didn't deserve to die like that."

"Everybody has to go sometime." Pete's voice was expressionless, but then he added with an edge of bitterness, "At least he didn't suffer like those people he sent to the gas chambers."

Emily was caught off guard. His comment betrayed truth to the inkling, which she had harboured ever since she had known him; from some of his mannerisms, she thought he might be from a Jewish background.

"Do you know people who were sent to their deaths in those camps?" she asked, trying not to assume too much about his origins.

"That was a long time ago," he answered evasively.

"Is Picken your real name then?" she asked.

"It's shortened from something else."

"I didn't think it was local. Not like the Bartons or the Allens on the English side, or the Duvals and the Seguins from the French."

"No, my folks weren't from around here. My father was born on a boat coming from England to the New Country. My mother always said she didn't know where she was born. Depended on which army was going which direction. She spoke five languages, Ukrainian, Russian, Yiddish, Polish, and a little bit of English, but she couldn't read or write."

"What did they do when they came here?"

"Homesteading. In those days you could get a piece of land if you showed up and began farming it."

"Did they have any money?"

"Started from scratch. No money, no experience. Five kids. When I grew up, we could scratch our names in the frost on the walls inside the house in the wintertime. When you've lived without food, you never take eating for granted again. People who never know what it's like to be poor will never really understand what it's like to go without."

Pete leaned his arm on the window and puffed on his pipe contemplating. Emily chose not to delve too deeply into some parts of Pete's background. Although he appeared to like being centred out, she knew that not far below the surface, he was a very private man. He had already revealed more to her, than he did to most people. She appreciated his candor but didn't want to intrude where she didn't belong. Still she couldn't help but ask the next question.

"What about you, Pete? Haven't you ever wanted to have someone to come home to?" she asked gently.

"Having somebody to come home to sounds too much like C 'n R, and I don't mean the railroad."

"CNR?" she asked.

"Yeah, it sounds too much like commitments and relationships."

"Is your life really complete without it?" she prompted him to continue.

"It's like this: You don't have to come home to a truck. The truck's always with you," he said slowly, choosing his words carefully. "There's something pretty special about bein' on the road. It's hard to describe."

He paused, and Emily waited for him to continue. The lights from the oncoming traffic were hypnotic, and the whisper of the pavement murmured in her ears, while she waited for him to resume talking. Silence fell between them, like darkness at night, and she assumed that he had finished speaking.

Presently, he continued softly, as if from a distant time and memory.

"You're up before dawn, when the stars are still out, and night's pitch black. There's no one else on the road. Then you're driving along a long, flat stretch, and you notice that the horizon is beginning to lighten up. Soon you see the sun rising right in front of you. You're driving straight for it. A huge glowing ball of orange is coming up directly in front of you, framed by the sides of the pavement … right in the middle of the road. You're drivin' right into 'er. It's like creation, and you're seeing it. It's like a show put on for you alone 'cause you're the only one on the road. Pretty soon you realize the grass is glowing orange and green, and the shadows on the rock cliffs along the highway are fading. The truck motor's humming, and you can hear the tire treads just singing on the pavement. It's like you're the only person in the whole world, and the universe belongs to you."

He paused to let his poetic images sink in. As if to reaffirm the reality of his description, the tire treads did seem to be singing on the pavement.

There was no response from the passenger seat. He glanced over to see Emily's head slumped onto her chest. She was sound asleep.

He studied the image of the woman sleeping in the seat beside him. For the first time, he noticed the wrinkles around her eyes, and the fragile hands, which were normally alive with gestures and excitement. For the first time, he realized that she looked old and frail. He felt an unfamiliar tingle of affection in the pit of his stomach. He had the ridiculous urge to take her in his arms and to protect her from the evils of the world to which she seemed so vulnerable. Luckily, she stirred and snorted, and he was able to break himself away from the feelings of tenderness that had so unexpectedly crept up on him.

They drove on in silence. He kept his eyes pinned on the road as the wipers beat a rhythm on the windshield. The dotted lines of the passing lane flashed, like a mesmerizing rhythm, punctuating the whir of the truck motor and whoosh of the large treaded tires on wet pavement. Pete felt his attention drifting away from the drive into a hypnotic kind of reverie, but suddenly his focus fixed on his rearview mirror. He realized that the headlights following the truck had remained constant since he had entered the highway. Every time he moved to the passing lane, the vehicle behind changed lanes.

He began to test his suspicions. When he slowed down, the lights remained in his mirror. When he sped up to pass another car, the vehicle following him accelerated. He applied the brakes unexpectedly, and his trackers almost hit his back bumper. For some reason, the pursuers were not trying to hide their intentions. Pete got the impression they wanted him to know he was being tailed.

As they crossed the border between Quebec and Ontario, Pete began to plot a strategy for losing his companions. He didn't want to know what they wanted, and with Emily as his passenger, he really didn't want to encounter them face-to-face. However, they followed too closely for him to outrace their vehicle, especially since his truck was laden down with wind drag, and he was afraid the table overhead might lift in the updraft and break the rope holding it in place.

The stretch of highway between the border and the first exit was barren. Only the visitors' centre, closed to the public at this time of year, served as a rest stop for weary truckers needing a safe place to pull off the highway. Pete hoped, when they approached the cut-off, he would see a few transport trucks parked along the shoulder. Unfortunately there were no vehicles anywhere at the rest stop. He maintained his cruising speed until just before the ramp, and then, at the last minute, he swerved to the right and exited the highway. He was totally disappointed when the headlights in his rearview mirror barely faltered as they followed him into the parking lot. Although no one else was in view, Pete was thankful that the area was well lit. He chose a spot beneath the brightest streetlight within full view of the highway. At least, if his hunters attempted an attack, surely some passersby would witness violence and come to his rescue.

As the truck swerved and slowed, Emily stirred in her sleep.

"Stay down!" yelled Pete. "Don't move!"

But it was too late. Just as he pulled to a stop, and the following car pulled up beside them, Emily lifted her head past the window and peered out to see where she was. The pursuers spotted her and smiled in recognition. Pete's heart sank when he realized that these were the thugs whom Emily had described after her first encounter with them during the broom closet incident.

Slim and Baby extricated themselves from their rusting VW sedan and approached the truck. They each carried a gun.

Without leaving his seat and without turning off the motor, Pete pushed the button to roll down the window on Emily's passenger side. Slim had to lean down to lower his head to Emily's eye level. Baby came around the truck and aimed his gun at Pete. Pete could not tell whether his bald head was wet with rain or sweat from the exhilaration of the hunt. Baby's fingers were poised on the trigger, and his hands shook.

"So," said Slim in his low, slippery baritone, "we meet again, Mrs. Blossom. How convenient."

Emily never missed a beat.

"Pete, this is the nice young man who saved me from being hit by a car when my purse was being snatched. I told you how kind he was to buy me a cup of tea."

She did not mention her encounter with the two in Schwartz's. She preferred to recognize the better side of the two thugs, in the hopes that they would rally to the compliment, rather than fulfill their darker intentions.

Slim nodded a casual greeting in Pete's direction, while he draped his gun on the window ledge, inches from Emily's face. He cocked his other arm on his hip. When he smiled, Emily noticed a space between his front teeth beneath his black, prickly moustache. His breath smelled of smoked meat.

"Call off your pit bull," demanded Pete, tipping his head toward Baby without lifting his hands from the steering wheel. "Didn't anyone ever teach him proper manners?"

Slim indicated to Baby to lower his weapon.

"He's just here to discourage you from getting any silly ideas ... you understand," said Slim. "If Mrs. Blossom cooperates this time, we won't hurt either of you."

"Of course, by all means," said Emily exaggerating her little-old-lady politesse. "I have nothing to hide. Why don't you tell me what you want?"

Slim slowly shifted the muzzle of his gun to point it directly at Emily's jugular.

"You know perfectly well what we're after," he growled. "Hand over those letters you got from Jenny Henderson. We know you have them. We got suspicious after we found the empty purse, and we went back to the apartment. Her son told us he gave them to you to get rid of them."

"Well, why didn't you say so?" said Emily.

"We tried to," Slim pointed out, "but you wouldn't cooperate in the restaurant."

"In the restaurant?" repeated Pete.

"Yes," said Emily. "I forgot to mention our little discussion over smoked meat."

"What are you talking about?" Pete demanded.

"Stop stalling," said Slim.

"Let's get it over with," said Baby. "We can just put a little pressure on the old bag like this."

He raised the gun again to Pete's eye level.

"Now, now," Emily said to Baby, "that's not necessary. Put down your gun and I'll give you what you want."

Emily waited until the gun was lowered and then she unsnapped her seatbelt, to reach into the back seat of the cab.

"I've got them right here."

Pete's eyebrows betrayed his surprise, but he dared not move a muscle.

Emily rummaged through the antiques stuffed into the cub cab anyway they'd fit. Eventually she found what she was looking for and extracted a package of papers wrapped in string.

"Here they are," she said, handing the bundle to Slim.

As Slim reached for the package, Emily dropped it onto the pavement.

"Oh, I'm so sorry," she exclaimed. "How clumsy of me!"

As Slim bent down to retrieve it, Emily continued smoothly, addressing herself to Pete. "Let's go home, Pete. They've got what they want."

Without questioning, Pete put the truck in reverse and backed out of the parking space. He guided the truck onto the highway. In the rearview mirror, he saw Baby lower his gun and approach Slim as he began to untie the package of papers. When they realized that the rain would damage the materials, they decided to return to the shelter of their vehicle where they could safely verify the contents of the package that Emily had given them. By that time, Pete and Emily were speeding west toward the first exit that would lead them on the back roads to the village. Soon they were passing through familiar countryside. The gravel roads were rough and uneven, but they could see the lights of the houses on the hill beckoning in the distance.

"That was quite exciting, wasn't it?" asked Emily, ruffling her feathers proudly.

"So where are the letters then?" asked Pete.

"I have them in my raincoat. The inner lining has a zipped pocket. They're safe and dry."

"What was it you gave them?"

"The articles on art that Rich gave us from Schmidt's things."

"Promise me you'll turn those letters over to Allard in the morning," demanded Pete.

"Do you think they would really have used those guns?" asked Emily, purposefully avoiding Pete's request.

"Those men are dangerous, Emily. They do mean it. They've dedicated their lives to murdering people for less than you've done. They get a thrill out of pulling the trigger; don't kid yourself."

"I have such a hard time believing anyone would really kill me. I haven't done anything."

"You have now," said Pete. "They'd as soon kill you as look at you at this point. The only thing holding them back is that you've got what they want."

"But why? What is it that they're after?"

"Whatever it is, Emily, get rid of it before they get rid of you. I'm warning you—stop playing with fire."

Emily sniffed and watched the lights of the village steadily growing brighter as they neared the base of the hill. The cozy Victorian houses gathered like comforting shadows along Main Street. The peacefulness of the town lured her into comforting denial.

"I don't believe Slim is as bad as he wishes he were," said Emily. "And as for Baby, he's a pushover. Slim really calls the shots. Baby follows orders."

"Emily, promise me you'll contact Allard in the morning."

"Cross my heart and hope to die." She flipped her forefingers across her chest, exaggerating the gesture as if to underline the sincerity of her promise.

"I hope you don't actually," said Pete.

"Don't what?"

"Have to die."

When they arrived at her house, Emily hesitated before opening the truck door.

"The least I could do is to offer you a cup of tea," she said. "Would you like to come in?"

"No, thanks," he answered, puffing on his pipe. "I'm up early tomorrow."

"Pete?" she said, without knowing exactly how to approach a subject that she felt she needed to broach.

"I'm racking up quite a bill with you."

Pete's eyebrows disappeared under his hat in a questioning manner.

"First the truck door getting dented, then breakfast at the Country Kitchen, and now, gas and dinner to the tune of three smoked meat sandwiches and the works. Would you let me give you some money to make up for your extra expenses on my behalf?"

"Thanks for the offer, but no thanks."

"It's beyond the call of generosity," Emily stated.

"I'll getcha later," he said. "Some day I'll need to borrow something."

"Oh yes, I'd help out if I could," she agreed readily. "But I can't imagine that I'll ever be much good to you. You're much too independent."

"I'll getcha later," he repeated, indicating that the conversation was finished. "Write if you find work."

"Pardon?" she said, mystified by the non sequitur.

"Write if you find work, so I can write back and borrow money."

"Write? Right," she said, nodding slowly. "I'll do that. In the meantime, thanks for everything."

She crossed in front of the truck toward her house. Her hair hung straggling over her eyes. Her raincoat drooped from her shoulders like a wet rag on a hanger. Her pocket bulged and bumped against her leg with the awkward weight of a heavy object.

Still Pete recognized the telltale lilt to her step he'd come to recognize. Emily carried herself as if, no matter how beaten and battered by life, she would always recover her optimism.

Suddenly she remembered an important detail she had failed to mention, and she returned across the lane to approach his driver's side. He rolled down the window, but left the truck running.

"Tomorrow is Schmidt's funeral," she said. "Are you planning to go?"

"Funerals are not my thing," he replied sternly. "My mother used to send me and my kid sister to every funeral in the neighbourhood once we moved to the city.

"'One must always pay respect to the dead,' she'd say." He imitated her Yiddish accent as he spoke her words, "'and it's up to you two to go. You never know. Maybe nobody else will show up.'"

Then, returning to his natural way of speaking, he added, "I've paid lots of respects to the dead. Enough for the rest of my life. I've been there, done that. Tomorrow the Purchasing Department is going to encourage Sales to get off his ass and make some money."

"Good plan," Emily said, standing back from the truck. "I'll go for the two of us."

He shrugged and puffed on his pipe.

Realizing there was no more to say, yet reluctant to end the conversation, Emily hesitated once again.

"Sure you don't want a cup of tea?"

"No, thanks. Morning comes early."

He had both hands on the wheel, ready to drive away, but he waited until she was safely inside and had turned on the light in the hall. The stained glass window glowed warmly above the doorway. Then he revved the motor and drove around the corner toward his own home.

Chapter Twenty

"CHARLIE, CHARLIE, where are you?" Emily sang, in the hopes of luring her cat from his favourite hiding place under the couch by the heat vent. "Come on out and say hello. Didn't you miss me all day?"

The cat remained unconvinced, and Emily resigned herself to a cup of tea without company. Although it was approaching her usual bedtime, she was still quite exhilarated from the events of the day. Also, she still had some unfinished business to attend to.

She hung her raincoat in the hallway and went upstairs to change into her nightgown and bathrobe. Then she went back downstairs and unzipped the inner pocket lining of her coat to extract the packet of letters, hidden inside, warm, safe, and dry. She turned on the reading lamp by her comfy winged armchair, plugged in the kettle, and chose a soothing herb tea from the cupboard. A pretty flowered mug with a blue willow pattern was the best mug for evening tea. Mornings were for brightness and strong red patterns; evenings were suited to muted colours and cozy aromas. Moonlight lavender matched her mood perfectly.

Emily wiggled herself in to her comfy chair and pulled an angora afghan around her shoulders. She sipped her tea, cradling the mug in both hands. Then she settled in to investigate the mysterious contents of her package.

About twenty letters were bundled together and stored in one large envelope, bound by a black ribbon. Each letter was addressed to Mr. Ernst Zündel. Each was neatly typed on onionskin paper. The typewriter used was an old one, with the letters t and s slightly off kilter. The first letter on top of the pile seemed a good place to begin.

Dear Mr. Zündel,

I have been reading with interest your efforts to reestablish the facts of history. I support your attempts to set the record straight with respect to the Nazi movement and the history of World War II. I admire your courage and determination to resist the dissemination of propaganda and misinformation, which has become so popular, and especially prevalent in North America since the end of the war. People actually believe that six million Jews were exterminated in the concentration camps in Europe during the war. This so-called genocide, of course, we know, is totally exaggerated.

However, I am greatly disturbed by your contention that the holocaust and extermination of members of inferior races never took place. I feel I must speak out and request that you reconsider your approach.

From personal experience, and as a scientist in medical research, I must clarify the extent to which the world and science benefited from the ethnic cleansing that took place under the Nazi regime. By denying the existence of this selective extermination, I believe that you, Mr. Zündel, undermine our great contributions to science in many fields of research including advances made in the fields of psychotropic drugs, psychological pain thresholds, medical treatments of inflicted and induced hallucinations, brain surgery and lobotomies, and countless other medical achievements which were made possible through the policies of the Nazi government.

Hitler had complete justification for his strategy of protecting the future of the Aryan race at all costs, by whatever means necessary, including the elimination of all races that were historically flawed. However, by benefiting from the situation and using it to full advantage, an additional course of action resulted in a true brilliance, which few historians give him credit for. The Nazis took advantage of the opportunity to use actual humans in previously prohibited experimentation, to advance the cause of research in human medicine. As a scientist in the field of psychology and psychiatry at the time, I was able to make great progress in the pursuit of science, with full knowledge and support from the authorities The Nazi regime provided me, and fellow researchers with opportunities unparalleled in history.

I beg you to reconsider your approach to holocaust denial. Instead, extol its benefits. Then, people will understand the greatness of the Aryan race, and the reason for their eventual dominance over the world.

Should you wish to pursue further discussion, please feel free to contact me.

Sincerely,
Herr Doktor Helmut Schmidt

Emily let the letter slip into her lap as she regained her breath and her composure. She felt nauseated. Her eyes continued to scan the words she had just read, trying to comprehend the horror of the meanings behind them.

Her dear friend, Helmut Schmidt, had been a monster beyond imagination. Not only had he committed unspeakable violence against his fellow man but he was also proud of it. Not only had he acted in the name of scientific research, but he had also inflicted excruciating pain on innocent victims with full understanding of the consequences of his actions.

However, the worst part of the realization for Emily by far was the extent of her own innocence. She had no idea she had been in the company of pure evil, evil embodied in someone she had considered her friend. She shuddered to think that she could have been in the presence of such danger with no inkling of fear.

She could not resist reading the next letter. How could it be worse than the first?

Dear Mr. Zündel,

I am disappointed that I have not heard from you in response to my letter of last month. I thought that I had made my intentions clear enough. I hoped that, upon receipt of my letter, you would be in contact with me to discuss how we could collaborate in future …

Emily was so engrossed in reading Schmidt's letters that she had not heard the approach of footsteps at the door. At first, she did not register that her visitors had not knocked but proceeded to bang at the door immediately. Before she could move out of her cozy nest, the door slammed open, and she was no longer alone.

Slim and Baby burst into the room, this time armed with knives.

"Okay, lady, that's it for you! We've had enough of your games. Where are they?"

Emily tried to get out of her chair, but the blanket, which she had wrapped around her, impeded her movements. The bright light from the reading lamp blinded her to the shadows in the hallway.

Baby sidled toward her. With one arm he pinned her to the back of the chair; with the other hand, he placed the cold edge of his knife blade against her neck. Emily could feel his heartbeat against the back of her head, and she smelled sweat and smoke on his clothes.

"I got her!" he yelled, agitated in the excitement of the moment.

Emily felt the knife trembling on her skin. She felt Baby's spit on her cheek when he spoke.

Slim's smooth baritone voice added to the tangible tension, electric in the atmosphere of the room. Emily sensed an edge to his anger that had not been apparent before.

"Mrs. Blossom, I'm sick of you making me look like a fool," he growled. "You probably think you're pretty clever handing us that bundle of newspaper clippings instead of the letters you knew we were looking for, but you're not as smart as you think. This time we're on to you. Now, cough 'em up! Hand over that package!"

She remembered reading somewhere in her detective research that the smell of fear often encourages predators to be more aggressive. In addition, the dose of reality was still dry on her lips, after realizing the truth behind Schmidt's words, which she had just read.

I think this is the time when I give up and trust Lady Luck, she said to herself.

Then out loud, she surrendered. "It's right here. What you want is right here in my lap."

She tried to keep the tone of her voice steady. Baby's knife blade increased its pressure, and she felt the skin give way to its sharp edge with the speed and surprise of a paper cut.

"Slim, tell Baby to let me go," she commanded. "I'll give you what you want."

Slim chuckled in answer.

"What's the matter, lady? Don't you like a dose of your own medicine?"

"I never hurt you," she said. "I could have turned you in, right at the beginning, when you first broke into Schmidt's house. Did you know I knew you were there? Ever wonder why I didn't squeal on you? You'd be in jail by now, if you didn't have me to thank for covering for you."

She could see Slim calculating her words out of the corner of her eye. He furrowed his brow, and his eyes became slits as he tried to think through the significance of her words. Baby still held her head firmly in his grip. A drop of blood slowly trickled down her neck and underneath her collar.

"Then again, I could have had you arrested in the restaurant. All I had to do was tell the waiter to call the cops. Harassment? Purse snatching? Elder abuse? They would have put you in jail and thrown away the key. Did you ever think of that? Did you ever wonder why I didn't blow the horn on you?"

Slim remained silent, but Baby never wavered. Emily dared not falter.

"Tell Baby to let me go," she said again.

Slim jerked his head, and Baby relaxed his grip. The knife disappeared, and Emily could almost breathe. However she hesitated to move too quickly for fear of sparking another round of aggression.

Her mind raced, trying to stay at least one step ahead of her assailants. Why hadn't she turned them in? Why hadn't she told Pete exactly what they were looking for? The truth was that she didn't know the answer to her own question. Unless she could come up with a reasonable explanation, they'd go after her again; but this time, she wouldn't be able to talk her way out of it.

"Have you read these?" she asked, knowing full well that Slim had never actually seen the objects of his pursuit. She gathered up the letters, and slowly unfolded the blanket from around her waist. "They're very interesting, but I don't actually think they're going to do you any good. In fact, they might make the bishop very angry if he reads them."

Slim grabbed for the papers, but Emily kept them just beyond his reach. She smiled, but not too confidently.

"Let me read you a sentence or two," she said, adjusting her glasses and holding the first letter underneath the light so she could see properly.

"Let's see, where are we?"

The room was hushed. They all waited until she found her place.

"Ah yes, here it is," said Emily, and she read, "'I am greatly disturbed by your contention that the holocaust and extermination of members of inferior races never took place. I feel I must speak out and request that you reconsider your approach.'"

Emily looked up at Slim over the rim of her glasses.

"Is that what the bishop wants to hear?" she asked, fishing for his reaction, before she continued. "I'm not sure that's what he had in mind when he hired you to come searching for evidence to support his position on denying the Holocaust."

"How do you know what the bishop wants to hear?" Slim asked.

"You tell me," said Emily, turning the tables in the hopes of gaining time so she could think.

"I don't know why he wants these letters," admitted Slim, "but he's willing to pay big bucks to get them."

"Let's get outta here," said Baby. "Somebody's walkin' around outside."

Emily read another sentence, "'I beg you to reconsider your approach to holocaust denial.'" She looked at Slim again. "Are those the words of someone who supports the Aryan Guard?"

"How do you know about the Aryan Guard?" asked Slim.

"Isn't that what it says on your T-shirt?" said Emily.

Slim looked down at his chest and read the message upside down: "White Power Why Not? Support Aryan Guard White Pride."

Suddenly, an ear-shattering yowl interrupted the conversation. Baby screamed. He dropped his knife, and his hands flew toward his leg.

Apparently, Charlie had emerged from under his couch, just as Baby had stepped back to push the curtains aside in order to see what was happening outside. As his foot trod on the cat's paw, Charlie protested loudly and dug his claws and teeth into Baby's offending ankle.

At the same time, Slim's attention flew to the doorway, as the police entered with guns drawn.

"Don't move," yelled Allard. "Drop your weapons!"

Emily stood up and raised her hands, as the pile of letters fluttered to the floor. Slim and Baby turned to escape out the back through the kitchen, but they bumped into each other as they fled.

"Stop right there, or I'll shoot," yelled Allard.

The culprits began shoving each other and shouting.

"You f'n idiot!" cried Slim.

"I told you someone was coming," said Baby.

"You shoulda kept the knife at her throat."

"You told me to let her go!"

"Shut up!" commanded Allard, at the top of his voice. "Hands up! This is the last time I warn you."

Slim and Baby stopped their bickering and faced the sergeant with their hands raised in the air. Emily could not help but notice how quickly they changed from dangerous roughnecks to placid, sorry-looking ragamuffins.

Just at that point, Pete sauntered into the room, followed by Cassie and Robert.

Emily grinned sheepishly, feeling foolish in her nightgown. She tried to tame the unruly lock of hair, which insisted on obstructing her view.

Cassie rushed toward her.

"Oh, Emily, are you alright? Did they hurt you?"

Emily tut-tutted, as Cassie fussed over her.

"You're bleeding. That brute did hurt you," cried Cassie, when she saw the trickle of blood on Emily's neck.

"Oh, it's nothing, my dear. I'm just fine," said Emily, who was watching Pete's expression out of the corner of her eye.

Pete leaned against the doorway, legs crossed, with his hands in his pockets. He surveyed the scene as if he were watching the casual greeting of friends in the street; however, Emily sensed his annoyance from across the room. She smiled a crooked smile.

"Hi, Pete," she said, pushing away Cassie's solicitations. "Thanks for coming to the rescue."

"I phoned the police," Cassie was saying behind her. "I heard the door banging, and I got frightened. I phoned 911, but by the time I got through, they said the police were already on their way."

Emily continued to scan Pete's face for some form of conciliation.

"You never did go home, did you?" she said from across the room.

The police were busy applying handcuffs to the intruders. Allard approached her to ask her what had happened. Cassie fussed, and Robert tried to calm her down and encourage her to return to their apartment.

Without a word, Pete turned and left. Emily saw his truck pass under the streetlight outside the window.

For the first time since her adventure had begun, Emily felt lonely and unfulfilled.

Chapter Twenty-One

THE NEXT morning, Emily slept in. Her feather duvet enveloped her in a delicious warm and dry cocoon.

As she woke up, however, she realized her joints ached; her head throbbed; and her heart felt heavy. Between sleeping and waking was the most difficult time of the day for Emily to recoup her energies. Bad dreams and unresolved emotions clouded her perspective. Usually she tried to get up quickly to avoid the doldrums of what she called "the in-betweens." Today she was surprised to see it was already ten o'clock when she rolled over to let the sunshine wake her slowly.

Charlie still wasn't speaking to her. He curled at the end of the bed and avoided her caresses. He was pouting.

"Charlie, my dear, it wasn't my fault. I didn't intend to be gone for so long yesterday," Emily pleaded with him. "Just come up here and give me a little cuddle."

The cat opened one eye without stirring. He flicked his whiskers, as if testing the mood of the day. But he did not deign to displace himself from his cozy nest at the foot of the bed.

Emily did not dare to disturb him. He was not about to be bribed by her undignified pleas for forgiveness. It was a stalemate.

Suddenly the phone rang, breaking the standoff. Since she used the phone so seldom, she had set the ringer to the highest setting. The noise sent everything flying. Charlie leaped to the floor, like a dust mop after a spider web. Emily swung her legs out from under the feathers and reached for the receiver, knocking the phone from its place on the night table. Her duvet slipped onto the floor, taking with it the radio, which turned itself on and began blaring the news of the day. Emily hesitated before she could understand what the voice on the other end of the line was saying.

"This is Jenny Henderson," said the woman in a cigarette-deep tone. "You came to my apartment yesterday asking about Mr. Schmidt."

Emily was trying to listen to the caller, turn off the radio, pull down her nightgown, and crawl back under the covers, all at the same time. But suddenly recognition dawned, and Emily's attention snapped into alert. She sat on the edge of the bed in her nightie, with a blanket pulled over her shoulders, and concentrated on the conversation about to take place.

"Yes, yes, Jenny. So nice of you to call."

"I'm sorry about yesterday," the raspy voice went on. "Sometimes my son Frank goes a bit overboard. I hope you weren't hurt."

"No, no," lied Emily. "I guess I came at a bad time."

"There's never a right time with him," commented Jenny, almost as an aside. Then she added. "I'm on a phone card. I've only got money for a few minutes. Did you say that Helmut was dead?"

"Yes, the funeral's today."

"I won't be there," Jenny said, bluntly. "But you said you wanted to talk to me. What about?"

"Well, he died under very suspicious circumstances," replied Emily, warming to her detective's task. "Is there anything you can tell me about your marriage, or about his past, which might shed light on who might want to do him in?"

With a million questions swimming in her imagination, Emily figured she might as well begin somewhere, even though speaking on the phone was not her forte. She preferred meeting face-to-face because then she could see a person's facial expressions to confirm her intuitions. On the phone, she had to rely on the speaker's inflection to betray hidden emotions. Jenny's voice, however, was like reading an open book. Emily could feel the pain of lifelong suffering. She sensed that Jenny had never really known much pleasure. Her tone was dull, as if she had long since surrendered to a sad fate. Somewhere along the way, she had lost all hope and was resigned to unhappiness.

"Helmut was a tortured man," said Jenny.

"Really?" said Emily, feigning surprise. "He always pretended to be so cheerful."

"Oh, everybody thought so. On the surface he seemed to be a very nice man," agreed Jenny, "except to anyone who ever slept with him."

"Why? What do you mean?"

"His dreams. He always had the same nightmare, over and over again. He'd relive the same thing so often that I got so as how I thought I was there myself. He'd wake up screaming, and I'd know just what was happening in the dream."

"Is this something that actually happened to him?" asked Emily, afraid that the phone card would give out, and she'd never hear the end of the story.

"Oh, he was there alright, and it all happened for real," said Jenny Henderson's hardened voice, edged with bitterness. "It was not about what somebody did to him either. It was what he did to someone else, which was so horrible. I'd never want to live with his conscience."

"Did he tell you the story? Did he talk about what happened?"

"At first we never talked about anything but sex. In the beginning, when we were first married, we were really good in bed together, if I do say so myself. He always fell asleep like a baby after he had his way with me."

Emily was a bit taken aback, but didn't let on. Even over the phone line, she detected a smile in the raspy voice, and a hint of pride. Sex was something Jenny Henderson obviously had taken great pride in doing well.

"But after a while, things weren't quite so exciting, and the dreams started coming back. Sex wasn't so good anymore. He couldn't get it up. Then he'd try hard not to go to sleep at all, so he wouldn't have to have that dream again. Eventually he'd get so overtired, he couldn't help it. The dream would wake him up again and again. He'd get totally exhausted. The more tired he got, the worse he got ... the madder he got ... the more he'd yell, and the more he'd hit me ..."

Emily cringed. Here was a familiar theme, which she recognized from Ruth Schmidt's story. She heard a catch in Jenny's throat, and she could imagine the tears in Jenny's eyes.

"What were the dreams? What happened? When?" Emily was impatient and getting desperate.

"It was back in the old country, during the war, when he was working as a scientist doing research," said Jenny.

So far the story was consistent with what Emily already knew.

"Schmidt had been commanded to experiment on pain, and he was supposed to use real human guinea pigs. Most of them were Jews, from what I could gather. The idea was to cause so much pain that the person would confess to something. Eventually they'd even admit to doing something they didn't do. Then the torture would continue to a point just before death, just to see how much someone could endure. They had to study both men and women to see the difference between the two."

"That's horrible," Emily commented.

Jenny went on in a monotone that she delivered as if she were hypnotized. Finally she had a chance to tell someone what she knew, someone who would listen. She blurted out the words, which flowed like water pouring through a floodgate.

"But then, he recognized one of the victims he was supposed to torture. It was a young woman. It turned out to be his first girlfriend. Mrs. Blossom, he tortured his girlfriend to death! In the end she never confessed the truth to him. Even though they both knew what she was hiding. Of course there were witnesses because he couldn't conduct experiments in private without some upper commander watching to make sure his methods were correct and accurate. Besides, they always had someone there to make sure a torturer didn't back off from the end. They had to see it through."

"What was the secret she was hiding?" asked Emily, suspecting that she knew the truth already. She felt a shiver run through her body when she thought of the photograph that she actually had in her possession at that very moment.

"The woman never admitted to having had a relationship with him. You see, she was a Jew, and he was a Nazi. She knew he'd be punished or killed if she confessed. But on top of that, she would not admit that she had gotten pregnant. Right to the very end, she hid the fact that she had already had a baby as a result of that relationship. She couldn't reveal anything about the child for fear that the SQ would try to find the child and kill her along with all the others. Schmidt never found out what happened to his child. He knew the baby existed because he had seen her just after she was born, but he never let on that he knew anything about the woman or her background."

Jenny's voice lost its energy as if the telling of the story had finally allowed her to empty the flood of emotions that her knowledge had kept welled up inside for so many years.

Emily paused to catch her breath.

"I can hardly believe it's true," she said.

"Oh, it's true, alright. All of it," affirmed Jenny. "I heard it all, over and over. I lived every second with him, night after night.

"He kept a photograph of her on his desk. His girlfriend was pregnant at the time the picture was taken. He was standing next to her, holding her, as if he would protect her forever. Her eyes stared out from the photograph like a ghost haunting him. He used to sit in a chair and stare at that snapshot for hours with tears streaming down his cheeks. He'd never say a word about it when he was awake. Only in his sleep did she come back for revenge.

"That's why our marriage failed in the end. I knew too much. I couldn't stand the sight of the man after a while, and he couldn't stand living with himself ... let alone with me. Especially when he knew that I knew the whole thing. Eventually we couldn't be in the same room together. The truth was like a huge black monster that was always there between us. We could never get away from it, and it was eating us alive."

"Thank you for telling me, Jenny," said Emily gently. "I hope that you will be able to forget it now. You're a good person. It's nothing you did. They were his nightmares, not yours."

"I gotta go now," said the voice at the other end of the line. "My card's almost up. Bye."

"Jenny, just one more question before you go," Emily added in a hurried tone. "Did you and Schmidt ever have any children together?"

"No. We never did. Thank God for that one small mercy," answered Jenny. "I married a better man the second time around. We had a family, and I live with my son Frank now. He cares for me in my old age. We get along alright. I just want to die in peace, whenever the time comes. It won't be long now."

Her voice faded. "I have to go."

"Wait! Wait!" cried Emily. "What about the letters? Where did those letters come from?"

"Schmidt dictated those to me around the end of our time together. He told me what to say, and I typed them, but I knew they were dangerous. In the wrong hands, those things he said would do a lot of damage. He told me to send them, but I couldn't. I never told anyone about them. I just wanted it all to go away. Now they're your problem."

The line went dead before Emily could say any more. She held the phone to her ear in the hopes that Jenny would somehow get reconnected, but the dial tone hummed unremittingly, dashing her hopes for more information. She sat on the edge of the bed and shivered with cold and dread.

Presently Charlie seemed to pity her, and he jumped up onto the bed beside her, purring. He pushed his head under her hands, which lay inert in her lap, holding the empty receiver. His purring and prodding revived Emily from her stupor, and eventually she came to herself enough to pet the insistent cat.

"Like I told her," she said to Charlie, "it's his nightmare ... not mine."

After a moment of recovery, Emily began to chatter again in her normal fashion.

"Okay, mister, let's get on with our day. You need something to eat, and I need to get dressed. Time's a-marching on."

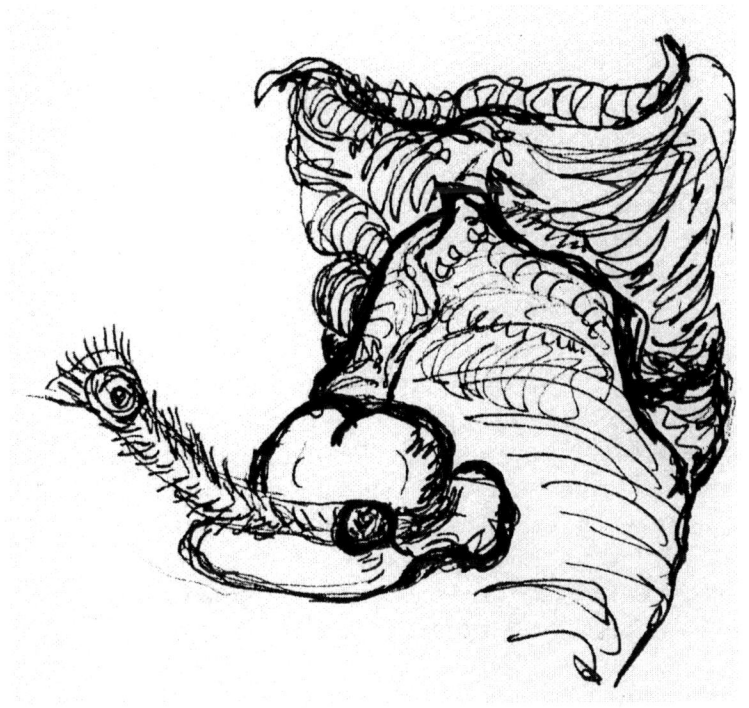

Hat with Peacock Feather on Pillows

Chapter Twenty-Two

IN SPITE of her resolution to get up and begin her day, Emily sat on the edge of the bed and stroked Charlie absent-mindedly.

She surveyed the mess at her feet. Her duvet lay rumpled on the floor. The reading lamp had fallen on top of the radio. Emily kept a stack of books by her bed.

The variety of titles reflected a potpourri of subjects to satisfy whatever she happened to be in the mood for. There was one book on the history of disease and war, another on the philosophy of religion. She kept a collection of Robert Frost poetry in case she wanted to practice memorization, and of course, there were three detective novels by three different authors for research.

The cat had his way with her, demanding to be petted in exactly his preferred spots. First he brushed under her hand with his back, insisting on being scratched behind the ears. Then he rolled onto his back on her lap and held her fingers gently in his large, furry paws so that she would massage his belly where the fur was warm and soft. Eventually, he used his claws to remind her in no uncertain terms not to move too quickly, or to press too hard. He took her forefinger between his teeth, and rather than biting, he pressed just hard enough to hold her hand in place. All the while he purred so loud that Emily's ears were vibrating.

"I can see why they say that a cat's purring has a healing effect," she mused. "The vibrations are supposed to create soothing waves of healing energy. Charlie, you produce enough energy to sink a ship."

She petted him, concentrating on each stroke, trying to discern which method he preferred, how hard the pressure, how fast the movement, how gentle the touch.

"If I believed in reincarnation, Charlie, I wonder what person you were in previous lives. You probably were a haughty and naughty prince at one time, living in Europe in the sixteenth century. With those steely eyes and determined character, no doubt you gave your nannies quite the run for their money."

Charlie purred and snuffled contentedly, while lying upside down and kneading her palm with his claws.

"Then again, you must have done some good things in your past lives. I always figure that cats must be returning souls. They're so otherworldly, don't you think, Charlie? Surely you're being rewarded for having lived virtuously in another life since you have such privileges here and now. Imagine, you don't have to worry about working for a living. You don't have to worry about earning money or doing the dishes. All you have to do is to tell me when it's time to eat and what kind of food you want. You've got it all figured out, you and most house cats.

"Mind you, not every cat on earth is as lucky as you! Not by a long shot. If you were an alley cat, life would be much harder. Then you'd have to fight for your dinner, and learn to avoid getting hit by a car, and find out where to stay warm and where the mean dogs live. You'd have mange and scars from fighting with other tomcats. Your ears might even get frost bitten and fall off. Imagine if you had to live as an alley cat, Charlie! You'd be in real trouble."

Emily mused quietly while she stroked the cat, who now desired to be massaged under his chin.

"I think Schmidt would come back as an alley cat. It would serve him right."

She reconsidered her premise.

"On second thought, he probably lived on the Great Wall of China as a Siamese watch cat thousands of years ago. Maybe that's where he learned to attack and torture people."

Rousing herself from her mental gymnastics, Emily gathered the cat up like a pile of dirty laundry and deposited him on the mattress. Then she replaced the radio and lamp next to the books and collected the duvet from the floor. While Charlie lounged, she covered his hunk of fur beneath a heap of the feather duvet. The purring grew even louder as his lump gradually made its way toward the edge of the bed. His paws thudded on the floor when he landed out from under his hiding place.

In the meantime, Emily threw her bathrobe over her nightie and slid her feet into terrycloth slippers. She headed downstairs to put the kettle on and fill Charlie's cat dish.

She did not dare to glance toward her cozy armchair. She did not want to be reminded of the night before, when her safe haven had been invaded by danger and hatred. She had turned the letters over to Allard, and after everyone had left, she straightened the living room, returning everything to its proper place. Emily was quite adept at shutting out unpleasant memories. She disciplined herself to focus on immediate matters and to ignore nagging regrets and self-recriminations.

"I have to choose something appropriate for a funeral," she explained to the cat, who studied her every move as if she were a mouse. "I don't think black is in anymore, but I know not to wear light and cheery. It looks like a cold and blustery day. Wool would probably suit the occasion. I don't imagine there will be a large crowd in the church. I haven't any idea how many people knew him, but I guess we'll find out."

Eventually she chose her grey flannel dress with a lace collar and long sleeves. In front of the mirror, she noticed two parallel red marks on her neck.

"Another quarter of an inch, and you'd be dead," Allard remarked when he saw the cuts left by Baby's knife. "You're a lucky woman."

Emily fingered the scars gently, and then selected a scarf, which would match her dress, lend colour to her cheeks, and highlight her hazel eyes. She carefully arranged the scarf around her neck to hide the scars left from the previous evening's encounter.

Then, she placed her hat carefully so that her hair would appear neat and tidy underneath. She tipped the brim just low enough to highlight the peacock feather pinned with rhinestones to the hatband.

"I don't want to look too severe," she said to Charlie.

Her unruly wisp of bangs insisted on escaping from underneath the hat brim. After several attempts, Emily gave up trying to tuck it into place. She paused to stare hard into her reflection to see if she could determine what kind of person lived behind her familiar façade. A solemn face patterned with wrinkles returned her gaze. Although her eyes were officially listed as brown, they were actually pale green with ruby and gold flecks around the pupils. No matter how long she studied the face in the mirror, she still could not recognize the person she imagined herself to be.

"It's hopeless," she said out loud, turning away from the mirror. "If I can't see who I am by now, after all these years of living with myself, then I'm not going to figure it out this morning. Funny how a person can live with a stranger in the mirror all one's life without ever really seeing oneself underneath."

Then she paused to stroke the cat. "You haven't got that problem, have you, my man? You don't need to wonder who you are. You've got it all figured out without complicating things any more than they need to be."

When she returned downstairs, she realized she had left the kettle on the stove too long. The water had boiled away; steam filled the kitchen, which smelled of scorched aluminum.

"Oh dear! Oh dear!" she exclaimed. "When will I ever learn not to put the kettle on the stove when I'm not in the room? That's the third one ruined this year. I keep forgetting to use the timer I bought at the dollar store. Next time I'll buy one of those electric gadgets with a thermostat. Just for that, I'll have to go without my tea this morning. Maybe that'll teach me to be more careful."

With that resolve, Emily donned her coat and left the apartment, heading for the Anglican church on the other side of town.

In the parking lot, there were only three cars, one of which belonged to that nice Mr. Underhill, the funeral director. Emily's awkwardness faded when she saw Mr. Underhill standing at the door as a greeter. His cultivated smile was designed to make her feel welcome and as much at ease as possible under the circumstances. His cologne smelled like funeral lilies and lavender. His skin was the colour of sand.

"Hello, Mrs. Blossom. So nice of you to come," he said in a soft, clinging voice.

Mr. Underhill and his wife bought the undertaking business around the same time that Emily bought her house. They moved to town, and soon after they arrived, they joined the Curling Club and volunteered at the school. Before long, they became an integral part of the community, and everyone forgot they were newcomers.

He guided her into the church and bowed as she made her way down the aisle toward the front. Only one pew was occupied. A lady dressed in blue sat beside a dark-suited younger man. Neither head turned to see her choose her seat five rows back. Emily sat beside a post, which held the rack of hymn numbers. She had a good vantage point but did not want to sit conspicuously in the open. Old Mrs. Noteworthy, the minister's mother, played the organ. Occasionally she missed a key and produced a high-pitched dissonance.

Somehow that sounds just right, thought Emily. *Otherwise I might think we'd all died and gone to heaven by the sound of that peaceful droning.*

To get herself in the mood for grieving, Emily studied the figures in the stained glass windows. Sad, solemn faces clad in purple and red robes gazed down at the churchgoers.

Whenever there are any churchgoers, Emily footnoted her own observations.

The crucifixion was such a tragic affair, she thought. *Imagine the pain that poor young man had to suffer with all those nails stuck in him and that crown of thorns, with blood dripping down his face. He couldn't even reach up and wipe it from his eyes. The weight of his body on that cross must have caused excruciating pain. And what about the flies? There must have been flies buzzing around him in all that heat. You never see the flies in any of the pictures. You can just imagine the smell of those rotting and infected sores*

His poor mother! To see her son suffer so! All because he wanted to help the world and show people how to love one another. Just goes to show how inhumane humanity really is.

Just as Emily was about to begin to study the artistic merit of the statues around the altar, Mrs. Seguin slid into the seat beside her.

"Hello, Mrs. Blossom. You don't mind if I join you, eh?"

She settled her ample body into place beside Emily and scanned the church for information.

"There's nobody else here then?" she whispered loudly, and then answered her own question. "He must not have had many friends. But then again, he didn't really go out all that much, did he?"

The statue of Mother Mary gazed mournfully at her son's corpse lying at her feet. Emily admired the texture of the flowing robes.

It's amazing how solid marble can look so fluid when sculpted by a sensitive artist, she thought, trying to ignore Mrs. Seguin's distracting comments.

"I recognize the Blue Lady from the Country Kitchen," whispered Mrs. Seguin. "But I don't know the man sitting with her."

Mrs. Blossom, the detective, snapped to attention.

"The Blue Lady? Who is that? I saw her on the Montreal-bound bus the other day? Does she live in town?"

"I don't think so," answered Mrs. Seguin. "She's not from around here. I'm sure of that."

Mr. Underhill glided down the aisle and whispered to the couple in the front. The woman smiled somberly and nodded. The funeral director disappeared to summon the minister to begin the service. The organ droned louder, but Emily could still hear the rustle of the minister's robes as Reverend Halloway approached the altar and turned to face the meager congregation.

"Dearly beloved, we are gathered here to celebrate the life of a loved one who has passed on to the Kingdom of God."

Emily prepared herself for a torrent of mixed emotions.

"Every time I go to a funeral, I have such a hard time keeping a straight face," she whispered.

"I know what you mean," said Mrs. Seguin who obviously misunderstood her meaning when she added. "I always bring extra Kleenex just in case."

"Our Father who art in Heaven, hallowed be thy name." Halloway's voice filled the nooks and crannies of the highest church pinnacle.

Emily imagined that he would even wake the cluster flies in the ceiling cracks by shouting so loud.

However, the minister's words reverberated as a hollow sound. Automatic words flowed as if he had repeated the prayers so often they had lost all semblance of meaning.

"Thy Kingdom come, Thy will be done, on Earth as it is in Heaven."

I wonder if He's all that happy with the way things have turned out, mused Emily as she carried on a running commentary in her head to the prayer, which she had learned so earnestly as a child. *Back then I believed in God so hard it almost hurt.*

"Give us this day our daily bread ..."

According to Pete, we better not take that one for granted, thought Emily. *And now we come to the hard part.*

The minister's voice slithered smoothly over the phrase she was waiting for, "And forgive us our trespasses, as we forgive those who trespass against us ..."

That's the biggie, she thought.

"For Thine is the kingdom, and the power, and the glory ..."

"Forever and ever," Emily and Mrs. Seguin joined voices. "Amen."

Mrs. Seguin crossed herself, forgetting that she was not in a Catholic service. The minister's tone changed to simulate casual confidence.

"We are here today to celebrate the life of our dear friend, Helmut Schmidt. He was a good man, a kind husband, and a loving father."

Halloway's voice rose to the very heavens, as he warmed to his task of celebrating life, now that it was over. Emily marveled at his talent for exaggeration.

That man missed his calling when he decided to go in for the ministry, she thought. *He should have opted for acting.*

"Dr. Helmut Schmidt's contributions to science were many. He was a scientist in the true sense of the word, highly respected by his colleagues in the field of medical research."

Little does he know, thought Emily.

"Helmut lived his life here on Emerald Hill in peaceful harmony with his friends and fellow citizens."

"That's true enough," whispered Mrs. Seguin. "We all liked the poor man."

"He was proud of his adopted country. He was a proud Canadian. We shall miss his cheerful enthusiasm and his stories about the old country where he came from."

"He really seems to believe what he's saying," commented Emily.

"He's a very good minister, you know," stated Mrs. Seguin simply.

"Now Helmut Schmidt has gone to join his Maker in Heaven above. May he rest in peace. Amen."

"Amen," repeated the voices from the pews.

"What's Allard doing here?" whispered the Would-be Mayor.

Emily glanced over her shoulder. Sergeant Alain Allard sat in the back of the church, almost hidden by the shadows cast behind the light streaming through the stained glass arches. He was dressed in street clothes, but still looked imposing and intense. He caught her eye and nodded politely. She acknowledged his greeting and turned back to the service, striking what she hoped was a casual pose of rapt attention to the words of the minister.

"Detectives always attend funerals of the victims," she whispered to Mrs. Seguin. "They're looking for suspects."

"Really?" gasped Mrs. Seguin. "Do you really think that's what he's doing here?"

"Murderers often show up to view the results of their handiwork."

"You don't say!"

Mrs. Seguin's astonishment was very satisfying, so Emily continued to reveal her professional expertise.

"It's true. Every good detective knows that," Emily asserted.

The minister glared at the two ladies, whose whispering competed with the sound of his own pious voice.

"Now let us turn to the twenty-third psalm for comfort in this time of our grief."

Emily repeated the words as Reverend Halloway read them. She was surprised and pleased that she could still remember them. Sometimes she doubted whether her memory was as good as it used to be.

"The Lord is my shepherd; I shall not be in want. He makes me lie down in green pastures. He leads me beside the still waters. He restores my soul. He guides me in paths of righteousness, through the valley of the shadow of death. I will fear no evil, for you are with me. Your rod and your staff, they comfort me. You prepare a table before me in the presence of my enemies. You anoint my head with oil. My cup overflows."

Emily heard herself repeating the last phrase out loud, joining the minister in his litany, "Surely goodness and love will follow me all the days of my life, and I will dwell in the house of the Lord forever."

"Amen."

"Amen," the churchgoers echoed in unison, filling the church with holy inspiration.

"Thank you all for coming," said the reverend. "There will be cookies and tea served by the ladies of the church in the basement."

Old Mrs. Noteworthy took up the familiar strains of the funeral march. The organ droned obediently. She only made five mistakes in the refrain.

Church on the Hill

Chapter Twenty-Three

NEITHER EMILY nor Mrs. Seguin was in a hurry to leave. The Blue Lady turned to slip out of the pew a few rows in front of them. Her face was streaked with tears, and she clutched a laced handkerchief in a blue-gloved hand. Her long-haired companion was solicitous and took her gently by the arm to support her in her grief as she made her way up the aisle past Emily and the Would-be Mayor.

"I wonder if Schmidt went to church," Emily whispered.

"I saw him at the turkey dinner at the Presbyterian church last fall," answered Mrs. Seguin. "He complimented me on my date squares. He said he ate five of them."

"I think he liked sweets," Emily said.

"Oh, yes, yes. A good church supper makes most bachelors into churchgoers."

"It was nice of Reverend Halloway to agree to do the service even if Schmidt wasn't a regular member of the congregation," said Emily, returning to her ordinary tone of voice. They were alone in the church. There was no longer any need to whisper. Besides, one could always voice a compliment loudly, in case anyone, who would appreciate a kind word, did happen to be listening.

Mrs. Seguin's reply was still whispered, "A small church like this one can always use the extra income."

Emily's eyes widened. She whispered again, "You mean they charge for funeral services?"

"Of course they do," asserted her busybody friend. "Weddings and funerals are a very good source of income. How else can they keep a little church like this one going? They're all so strapped for cash these days. It costs a lot to heat these old buildings, and the minister needs to earn a salary, too. That's why Halloway serves two congregations. He gives two services every Sunday. The nine o'clock service is here, and the eleven o'clock service is in Apple Wood."

"That must be a lot of work," said Emily, suitably impressed.

"I've heard he sometimes gives the same sermon in both churches," confided Mrs. Seguin. "The Apple Wood congregation feels a bit put out that they don't get their own personal sermon, especially on Easter and Christmas. They feel they deserve better than a recycled sermon for the important holidays."

"I see," said Emily. "I'm sure they do."

"Old Mrs. Noteworthy," Mrs. Seguin continued, "only plays for funerals though. That's her specialty. They have one of the local music teachers for the regular Sunday services."

Emily winced.

"Does Old Mrs. Noteworthy always play the funeral music this well?"

"Oh, yes. She's been playing all her life. Arthritis, though. She has arthritis in her fingers," explained Mrs. Seguin. "It happens to all of us old folks eventually, doesn't it?"

Emily rubbed her own fingers lightly, checking to make sure that she had not yet been afflicted with a disease of old age.

The two ladies realized that there was nothing more to learn by remaining in the church. They found the stairs to the basement and followed the smell of coffee to the dining hall. Sergeant Allard was chatting with the Blue Lady and her companion near the coffee urn. As they neared the group of three, the detective signaled to Emily to join them.

"Emily Blossom, have you met Helmut Schmidt's daughter, Ms. Smith?"

Emily suppressed a gasp of surprise. The Blue Lady regarded her with a pleasant smile and offered a blue-gloved hand in response to the introduction.

"Ms. Lily Smith, Mrs. Emily Blossom." Allard let the names run smoothly off his tongue. His manner was slick and polished.

"And this is Mr. Henry Greenacre," Allard continued his introduction. Jokingly, he turned to the dapper younger man. "How does one introduce a lawyer, by the way?" he laughed. "The honourable Mr. G?"

"How do you do?" said the younger man, shaking Emily's hand heartily.

Emily felt her knuckles being crushed in his strong grip. She tried not to wince. His face was vaguely familiar, but Emily could not place where she had seen him before.

"May I introduce you to my friend, Mrs. Seguin," said Emily politely, not wanting to leave her friend standing forgotten in the background. She knew Mrs. Seguin was itching to be introduced. "She's known about town as the Would-be Mayor."

Everyone chuckled at the term, and Mrs. Seguin beamed proudly.

"We didn't know Mr. Schmidt had a daughter," admitted Mrs. Know-It-All. "Have you been to Emerald Hill before?"

The Blue Lady paled just slightly, her skin taking on the pallor of her suit. "Actually," she stuttered, "I only recently saw my father for the first time in my life."

"You don't say!" said Mrs. Seguin delighted by the new tidbit of information.

Emily could hear all the details repeated in full colour for the benefit of the diners at the Country Kitchen.

Allard covered his mouth and coughed to dislodge a cookie crumb and to divert the conversation away from Ms. Smith's obvious discomfort.

"Her father's death came quite suddenly, you understand," he explained. "Mr. Greenacre knew him quite well though, didn't you?"

"Oh yes, a fine man," asserted Mr. G. "Helmut Schmidt was a fine, fine man."

There's something very familiar about that man's face, Emily said to herself. *I know I've seen him before under unusual circumstances.*

Then aloud, she asked politely, "Have we met before?"

Greenacre squinted his eyes askew, as he studied her countenance.

"No, I rarely forget a face," said the lawyer. "I don't believe I've seen you before."

While she listened to the conversation about the kind words Reverend Halloway had offered at the service, Emily racked her brain to try to figure out where she had encountered Greenacre so recently. Suddenly a spark of recognition struck her. She could not help but blush. The lawyer was the man in the coffee shop who, with his wife, had mistakenly gotten into Suzanne's car. She did not want to cause him any embarrassment by reminding him of the awkward incident.

To hide her self-conscious discomfort, Emily turned to the table to help herself to a cup of coffee. The homemade cookies looked delicious, but she shied specifically away from the date squares.

If date squares contributed to Helmut's weight problem, then I'd best avoid them.

"With all these lovely desserts," she said out loud to no one in particular, "a person has to watch her girlish figure."

While helping herself to another Nanaimo bar, she carefully avoided the recollection of having downed three smoked meat sandwiches in a row, the day before.

While the Would-be Mayor engaged the Blue Lady and her lawyer in not-so-private conversation, Allard motioned Emily aside, out of hearing distance.

"Allo, Allard," she said loudly. "Fancy meeting you here. Isn't this a pleasant coincidence?"

Allard held his finger to his lips and motioned to her to keep her voice down. His intensity surprised and intrigued her. Finally he was paying her some well-earned respect.

"Detectives should stick together, right?" said Emily gently teasing him. "Perhaps you finally realize how helpful I've been at getting to the bottom of this murderous affair."

"Emily Blossom, I want you to keep your mouth firmly shut from now on," he demanded angrily, glancing over his shoulder to make sure that no one was listening. "There has been no murder."

Emily could not help but gasp out loud. They looked at the others to make sure no one had noticed her reaction. Mrs. Seguin had both visitors firmly in her grip.

"The guy died of natural causes," Allard whispered. "He was killed by a massive heart attack. There was no murder and no perpetrator of crime."

Emily could feel distress well into her eyes. She fought back disappointment and frustration by gripping her fist to her teeth. She felt suddenly faint, and Allard gently guided her to a nearby chair and sat down beside her.

"There's more to it, but I can't explain it all at this point," he whispered. "I just didn't want you to blurt out anything which would make the situation even more awkward than it already is."

Emily reddened. "You think I'd be so crass as to say anything to *her* about this?" she muttered with a surreptitious nod of her head in the direction of the Blue Lady. "I've got more class than that."

Allard backtracked in an attempt to mollify her. He preferred that their conversation appear like idle banter.

"I didn't mean it like that. I know your intentions have always been above board."

She looked at him askance, and he backpedaled again. "Well, most of the time. I admit that you're a bit of a nosey parker, and that you stick your nose in where it doesn't belong, but your heart is in the right place."

"Well, thanks for that much," she replied indignantly.

"It's just that the situation is rather delicate," he said, nodding toward the grief-stricken daughter. "She's quite fragile at the moment, and it's a very difficult time. I'll explain more later."

Emily pulled herself together, smoothed down her grey flannel skirt, and readjusted her lace collar. She reassured herself that her hat was properly cocked to display the peacock feather to its best advantage, and she tucked the stray lock of hair behind her ear. Then she stood up and accompanied Allard back to the little circle of mourners.

By that time, Reverend Halloway, Old Mrs. Noteworthy, and Mr. Underhill had joined the group. They all politely sipped their coffee and munched cookies, taking small, polite bites so as not to devour them all at once.

As soon as it was polite to do so, Emily excused herself to pay a visit to the ladies' room. She needed a bit of a breather to recover from the shock of Allard's revelation.

She gazed into the mirror to assure herself that the peacock feather was properly displayed. She plucked her scarf higher to hide the scars on her neck. Then she attempted a pleasant smile and practiced relaxing her eyebrows to disguise her disappointment in the recent turn of events. In the mirror's reflection she saw the door open behind her. Lily Smith entered timidly.

"There you are. I was hoping you hadn't left already. I wanted to have a little chat," said Ms. Smith in a soft, lilting voice.

Her diction was almost too perfect. Emily surmised that English was not actually her mother tongue, although only a well-trained ear would detect the slight guttural edge to her consonants.

"Inspector Allard tells me that you were good friends with my father."

"Yes," said Emily gently. "We often had tea together. He liked to chat, but he rarely had visitors."

"What was he like? Can you tell me a bit about him?"

Emily was taken aback by the question, since she assumed a daughter would have known her father intimately. However, she didn't question the implications of Lily's inquiry.

"He was a friendly man. He liked to talk about history. He told me a lot about the development of ideas and science. He was fascinated with the medieval period in Europe especially in the realms of art and music."

Lily hung on her words, as if trying to absorb them into her inner core. She had dark eyes, and a nose that seemed too large to match delicate features of high cheekbones and fine lips. Her mouth moved in sync with Emily's expressions, and she nodded encouragingly, as if to say, "Go on. Go on. Tell me more. Speak to me forever, as long as you tell me good things about my father."

When Emily realized that the woman listened like a sponge, she tried to share more details. There was something about Lily's gentle manner that made Emily want to please her.

"He was a connoisseur of paintings, and he owned quite a few original pieces. We had our love of art in common, since I'm an art collector myself. He was very knowledgeable."

Emily grasped at straws of her memories.

"The afternoons passed so quickly I can't seem to remember the details of our conversations. I never intended to stay as long as I did, but Helmut enjoyed having someone to share his ideas with. He was always reading and studying. Did you know he practiced calligraphy?"

"I did find some of his practice notebooks among his belongings," asserted Lily. "I want to know so much more about him."

"You didn't know him then?" asked Emily, intrigued.

Lily's face clouded over with grief. Her black eyes became darker behind tears that welled up with no warning.

"I searched the immigration records for years before I found him," she explained in a tired and distant tone. "Finally I found out where he lived, and I wrote him a letter. I explained how my mother had smuggled me out of the country at the beginning of the war. I was only a little baby. It must have been so hard for her to let strangers take me away, but she knew it was the only way for me to escape. I think she knew she'd never see me again. It's the ultimate sacrifice a mother could give to her only child.

"The only possession my mother left me was a copy of my birth certificate. She was identified as my mother, and beside the name for my father was typed 'Unbekannt.'

" 'Helmut Schmidt, Heidelberg Deutschland' was written in my mother's handwriting beside the entry. When I located Helmut Schmidt in Canada, I asked him if he would submit to a DNA identification to confirm that he was indeed my father. You can imagine how ecstatic I was when I received an answer to my letter.

"Schmidt complied with my request. I arranged for the tests to be done. Then it seemed to take forever for the results to confirm what I already suspected in my heart. I think he was even more surprised than I was when the results actually proved without a doubt he was my father. I'm not sure he was as glad to find me, as I was to find him. Perhaps the truth was more complicated in his life."

Lily reached into her blue purse and pulled out a tattered piece of paper with exquisite calligraphy scribbled on both sides. She handed the letter to Emily, but the sentences made no sense.

"It's in German," explained Lily, but I know the words by heart. "He begs for my forgiveness and tells me he loves me and that he never meant to do me any harm. He writes that my mother was the only person he ever loved."

By this time, tears flowed freely down Lily's cheeks. Her words caught in her throat and then tumbled into the open like splashing water.

"But then he asked me not to try to find him. He said he couldn't bear to see me after so many years."

Lily's eyes pleaded with Emily for understanding and compassion.

"Mrs. Blossom, can you imagine how impossible it was for me to accept that he didn't want to meet me finally, just to see what kind of a person I've grown into, just to see that his seed produced a good and kind human being? Can you understand why I couldn't stay away?"

Emily did not quite comprehend why Lily was so adamant that she corroborate Lily's conclusions, but she agreed anyway.

Anything to soothe such a tortured heart, she thought.

"I wanted to tell him that I forgave him." Lily confessed. "I just wanted to be able to say the words out loud. To tell him that it was okay. It was okay that he deserted us, that he couldn't look after us during the war, that war ruined so many millions of lives, and ours was just one example of the tragedies wrought by the Nazis on the world. He was as much a victim as I was, as my mother was."

Emily knew instinctively that Lily was repeating to her what she would have told her father had she had the chance. Emily was Lily's only real link to the living father for whom she had been searching. She needed to say the words of forgiveness out loud.

Emily dared not say a word for fear she would betray the terrible secrets about Helmut Schmidt that she had discovered over the past few days. Allard's words echoed in her head: *Keep your mouth shut!*

However strongly she felt about protecting Lily from the truth, she could never have prepared herself for the whole truth behind Lily's confession.

"I disregarded his wishes," Lily was saying. "I tracked down the address and I went to his house here on Emerald Hill. He was sitting in his armchair when I walked into the living room."

Emily felt shivers running up her spine, and her face flushed with realization of the words she was about to hear. Of course she knew exactly when Lily's visit had taken place.

"He took one look at me standing in his living room, and he choked for breath. He reached for his throat as if it someone had sliced his jugular vein."

Lily's tone was flat as she succumbed to the memory of the shock, which had overwhelmed her at the time.

"His only words were, 'You look just like your mother!'"

Lily's eyes scanned Emily's eyes, trying to trap them into understanding the full meaning of what she was saying. Their gazes met, and Emily's hand strayed to cover her gasp of astonishment.

"And then he died," Lily whispered. Her voice petered into the silence of finality.

Emily could not resist enveloping Lily into her arms. The grief-stricken woman- child finally succumbed to the sobs that had been threatening to burst her heart. Emily rocked her in a soothing embrace, and then Lily continued her story.

"His breath gurgled in his throat, and his head slumped to the side. I didn't know what to do. I ran out of the house, leaving my umbrella on the floor beside the chair. I jumped in my rented car and drove away. I couldn't think straight. Finally, when I came to my senses, I phoned the police. I told them what had happened, what I had done, and then I hung up without identifying myself. Inspector Allard took the call when I phoned back the next day. We met, and he questioned me in more detail. He was very understanding. He told me that once the autopsy report came back, he was sure there would be no charges. It wasn't even manslaughter. How could I have known that my father's heart could never stand the shock of meeting me?"

Before Emily could find suitable words of condolence, the bathroom door opened, and Mrs. Seguin rushed in.

"Oh my dears, I'm so sorry to interrupt. My kidneys are just bursting. I drank too much coffee. I knew you two were in here having a chat. I just couldn't hold it in any longer!"

The Would-be Mayor rushed indecorously for the first stall, slamming the door urgently and shoving the lock into place. Emily knew that this was just an excuse for her to eavesdrop on the conversation between her and Lily Smith. She held Lily's trembling body for a little while longer without speaking. Presently Lily recovered her composure and let go of their embrace. She ran some cold water into the sink and splashed her face several times to wash away the tears.

Mrs. Know-It-All was just drying her hands, when Lily finally whispered, "Thank you, Mrs. Blossom. I needed to speak to someone. Thank you for listening."

Lily Smith made her way back to her lawyer, who still stood beside the coffee and cookies chatting to the good reverend and his aging mother. Emily said her goodbyes to Allard and headed toward Main Street.

The Would-be Mayor ran after her to catch up, saying, "My, my, that looked like quite an intense conversation you were having with Ms. Smith. What on earth was that all about?"

"Actually, my dear," said Emily, who was finally completely fed up with meddling, "it's none of your business."

Mrs. Seguin gasped and fussed, "Well, there's no need to get all huffy about it. I was only asking a simple question."

"Go poke your nose into someone else's business for a change," said Emily curtly. "Leave that poor woman alone. She's gone through enough."

Chapter Twenty-Four

THE SIGHT of Pete's truck parked on Main Street was such a relief to her that Emily thought she would cry. When she saw his boots on the dashboard, she was even more elated. She opened the passenger door and climbed into her seat beside him. Pete looked out from under the newspaper, which covered his face to shade him from the sun as he napped.

"Can't a fellow get any rest around here?" he muttered, replacing the newspaper over his eyes without lowering his boots from the dash.

"Sorry," said Emily. "I didn't mean to disturb your beauty sleep."

"It's okay. I'm just glad it's you!" he said with relief. "I was hiding."

Emily looked around. There was no one on the street.

"Hiding? Hiding from who?"

"I saw Marie Cartier heading for the truck," he explained. "I was so glad she ducked into the post office before she saw me here."

"What's the matter, Pete? She's got a crush on you," teased Emily. "She told me so herself."

"Tell her to go you know where. I'm not interested."

"She seems like a nice person, Pete."

"That's what you think," said Pete. "She's crazy. I've known her a long time, and I know she's totally off her rocker."

"Are you sure that's not just your opinion? What do you know about women?"

Pete lowered his boots from the dashboard and put his hands on the steering wheel.

"I know a lot more than you think I do, and that woman's nutty as a fruitcake. Is that clear enough? I don't want anything to do with her."

"Okay, okay. I was just teasing. Besides, there's something important I want to say. I'm just not sure how to begin."

"How about at the beginning?" he suggested, leaning back again and placing his boots back up on the dashboard.

Emily stared ahead, soaking in the warmth of the sun and of Pete's presence. He waited, eyes closed, arms crossed, with his pipe perched between his lips.

"Pete," she began.

"Hm?" he responded, to let her know he was listening and not really sleeping.

"How can I ever make it up to you?" Emily tried unsuccessfully to keep her voice from quavering.

"What? What are you talking about?" he said from under his hat.

Her fingers strayed to the scarf at her neck and ruffed up the folds around her chin.

"Look, Pete. I'm sorry. I really am. I didn't mean to cause you so much trouble."

No answer.

"I want to thank you for everything you've done for me," she continued.

No answer.

She tucked the stray bangs behind her ear and patted the bun into place.

"Pete?"

"Hm?"

"Are you being difficult?"

Pete cocked his hat, cupped his pipe in his fist, and peered at her with one eye.

"I'm listening."

Then he disappeared underneath his hat again and puffed a cloud of smoke into the air.

She folded her hands in her lap and sat quietly.

"You are being difficult," Emily said, answering her own question.

"Difficult? Me, being difficult?" He snorted. "You're one to talk."

"Well, I can't think what to say."

"Then don't say anything," he said.

From the truck, Emily surveyed Main Street. The red brick houses baked in the warm, soft sun. Pedestrians jaywalked from parked cars to the post office, without worrying about passing vehicles, which always slowed to let them cross. She studied the townspeople going about their daily errands without looking over their shoulders or feeling threatened by strangers.

"Can I ask you a complicated question?" she inquired, changing the subject.

"Hmm," he acquiesced.

"When does a person know how much truth is a good thing?"

Pete lifted his hat and gazed at her face. Although he must have realized that she was distressed, he didn't let on. His face disappeared under the hat again.

"The whole truth is never a good thing," he said simply. "Too much of anything is hard to take. Why do you ask?"

Emily went on, without coming directly to the point.

"Even if a person says they're searching for the truth, isn't it okay to lie a little, to protect that person, if the whole truth would hurt too much?"

"That depends on whether they really want to *know* the truth, or whether they only want to know what they *think* is the truth."

Emily was quiet for a moment while she translated his answer to suit her.

"Pete?"

"Hm?"

"Do you believe in justice?"

"Depends on what you mean by justice? An eye for an eye? That kind of justice?"

"No, I guess I really mean, do you believe that a person gets what's coming to them in the end? Just retribution, and all that?"

Finally Pete sighed, tipped his hat back, and sat up, leaning against the door facing his interrogator.

"Okay, Emily, what's all this about? Does it have something to do with your murder investigation?"

Emily glanced at Pete contritely.

"How can you look so dumb, and be so smart?" she asked.

"It takes talent," he retorted. "Now, what's this all about?"

Emily sighed and glanced out the window again. Now that she had his attention, she was reluctant to answer too quickly. Evidently she paused too long, and Pete thought she was stalling.

"Emily!" Pete's voice hardened with scolding. "Get to the point!"

She took a deep breath and looked at Pete's face. His eyes were steel blue and shallow. He stared her down. She lowered her glance and spoke softly, so he would have to listen to hear the truth of what she was about to tell him.

"Schmidt was so evil, he didn't deserve to be murdered. He brought it all down on himself. No one else could have been more evil than he was. Eventually the truth caught up with him, and he couldn't stand to stare it in the face."

"Is that so?" said Pete, without taking his eyes off her.

"Yes ... and you know what else?" Emily continued confidently. "I thought I wanted to solve a murder mystery, but that's not what I really wanted."

"No?"

She looked at him again and confessed, "I just needed a good dose of reality to wake me up. This town is a bit too quiet. What I needed was something I could get my teeth into. Something significant."

"Did you get what you wanted then?"

Emily nodded, "I'm glad there wasn't a real murder, and I'm really glad there wasn't anyone around town mean enough to commit a murder."

He looked away and slouched against the steering wheel.

"Those men last night were perfectly capable of doing you in, Emily," he chided.

She grinned self-consciously and shrugged her shoulders.

"They didn't though, did they?" she answered, and added, "Thanks to you."

"Good timing that's all."

"They weren't from around here anyway," Emily said. "I still say there's no one around town mean enough to commit murder."

"Are we supposed to argue this point, too? Get real," said Pete, opening the door. "Let's go for a cup of tea. Then you can tell me all the details."

Chapter Twenty-Five

THE BUZZ of conversation paused when Emily and Pete entered the Country Kitchen. The Would-be Mayor had cornered Inspector Allard at the table by the pastry counter. Suzanne and her mother were just finishing up the last crumbs of their afternoon croissants.

Pete chose a seat in the corner, from which he could survey all the other patrons in the restaurant, and, when he spoke, he could address everyone present. He slumped into a pose with his elbow on the table and his forefinger teasing his moustache. He propped his boots on an empty chair beside him. Emily sat facing him, so she could command his wandering attention, when necessary.

"So, let me get this straight," said Pete. "There was a murder, but there was no murder?"

"Right," said Emily.

"Those guys were thieves, but they didn't know what they were supposed to steal?"

"Right."

"This lady was Schmidt's daughter, but she didn't know her father?"

"Right."

"Does any of this make sense to you, Allard?" Pete yelled across the room.

Allard was glad to escape the curious clutches of Mrs. Seguin and excused himself to sit with Emily and Pete. The Would-be-Mayor stayed put but eagerly eavesdropped on the ensuing conversation.

"If I may point out the obvious, we've been trying to tell you there was no murder right from the beginning," said Allard, "but Mrs. Blossom really didn't want to give up the chase."

"I knew there was more to it than a person dying, just like that," Emily defended herself.

"Now, just how did you know that?" asked Allard, with raised eyebrows.

"Careful, Allard," warned Pete. "You might not want to know the answer."

"I do, I do," piped up Mrs. Seguin, from across the room.

Suzanne and her mother were gathering up their coats to beat a hasty retreat. Suzanne believed that she should protect her mother from the rumours, which flew around the town quite regularly. Her mother was oblivious to most conversations, but was also happy to comply with her daughter's whims.

Ilsa approached the table, and the three ordered coffee.

"Why don't you start from the beginning," suggested Pete. "What do we know about Schmidt?"

"I think I've got it figured out," said Emily, like a schoolchild with the answer to a teacher's question in class. "There are a lot of pieces to the puzzle, though."

"We're listening," said Allard.

"All ears," added Pete.

"Me too, me too! I want to know everything," said the Would-be Mayor.

"Well, there are the photos," said Emily. "Those were a dead giveaway."

"Photos?" asked Allard.

Emily looked at Pete, as if she had been caught in the act. The photo was evidence, which Emily had taken from Schmidt's desk, unbeknownst to Allard. Pete shrugged.

"It's your dime," he said.

Emily took a deep breath and resigned herself to continuing what she had begun.

"Okay, this is what I have figured out.

"Helmut Schmidt had a photo of himself and a young woman on his desk. The woman was pregnant. Ruth Schmidt had a photo of her and Schmidt with the same background, but several years later. The photos gave me the first clues. Then I spoke with Ruth Schmidt, and then Jenny Henderson, and their stories were similar. Schmidt was a tortured man with a lot on his conscience, to say the least. The letters helped me put it all together."

"Put what together?" said Pete. "So far, you're talking gibberish."

"Begin with what you know," suggested Allard.

Emily cupped her hands around her coffee, and began the story of Helmut Schmidt, the details of which she had pieced together over the past few days.

"Helmut Schmidt was about twenty-five years old before the Second World War broke out in Germany. He was well educated, and as a promising young scientist, he began his career in medical research. About that time, he had an affair with a young lady. My guess is that she was only about fifteen or sixteen, but the relationship was serious enough that she got pregnant. So far, so good?"

Pete and Allard listened patiently, as she gathered momentum in the storytelling.

"However, when the war broke out, everything changed drastically. Schmidt was enlisted by the Nazis to continue his research, but they had a pretty sinister agenda. Primarily, they wanted him to study the effects of torture on innocent victims, in order to determine pain thresholds. His subjects were Jews who had been rounded up, destined for concentration camps. As fate would have it, one of his victims was the young woman with whom he had had an affair. She died as a result of his torture techniques, never having confessed.

"Shortly after the war, Schmidt met a young Canadian nurse, Ruth, who was in Germany as a volunteer. He spotted an opportunity to come to Canada. So he married her, and together, they moved to Montreal. With his extensive knowledge in the field of medical research, he didn't have any difficulty finding a job with a pharmaceutical company. He was even hired to work at the Allan Memorial Hospital on a highly secret research project sponsored by the CIA. Ruth and Helmut might have lived a happy life together, if he hadn't been plagued by nightmares related to his horrible past with the Nazis. His guilt became anger, and he took out his frustrations and pangs of conscience on Ruth. To say it was an abusive relationship would be putting it nicely."

"That's what Ruth Schmidt was going on about then?" interrupted Pete. "When we saw her at the Seniory Lodge."

"Yes," agreed Emily, "she couldn't let go of him, even in hate."

"That lady was cuckoo," said Pete to Allard, making circles by his head with his finger.

"After you guys got through with her, we didn't have a chance to get any information. She was a mess by the time we got there," said Allard. "Go on, Emily. This is all very interesting."

"Actually there's a local connection, in a weird sort of way. It has to do with a good friend of Pete's," continued Emily, sending a wink in Pete's direction.

"Marie Cartier and her mother, Clarisse."

Pete groaned.

"When Schmidt worked at the Allan Memorial Hospital, it just so happens that Marie's mother was one of his patients. Instead of treating her for postnatal depression, Schmidt included Mrs. Cartier in his LSD experiments."

"That explains a lot," exclaimed Pete.

"You see, Pete," Emily had to rub it in, "Marie has good reason to be a bit ... shall we say ... complicated."

"That's putting it mildly," said Pete.

"So where did the letters come from?" asked Allard. "Is that why you went to Montreal?"

"Yeah, what was that all about?" echoed Pete.

"Actually, I didn't know anything about those letters," admitted Emily. "I kind of fell into that angle by mistake."

"You can say that again," said Pete. "You are all about mistakes."

Emily ignored his taunt and continued her story, directing her explanation directly at Sergeant Allard.

"Jenny Henderson worked as a secretary for the pharmaceutical company where Schmidt was employed. So when his marriage was on the rocks, whom should he turn to but his private secretary? He left Ruth and took up with Jenny, in the hopes that he could escape the ghosts that haunted him. But there was no rest for the weary."

"Rest for the wicked," Pete corrected her.

"Yes, that's what I said," Emily said. "There was no rest for the wicked."

"Was that any better?" asked Allard. "Usually second abusive marriages are as bad, if not worse, than the first."

"Out of the proverbial frying pan," said Pete.

"Yes, well, Jenny lasted a bit longer than Ruth, but the situation was just as tormented. Jenny's the one who told me about the torture chamber. He relived his evil deeds every night, would wake up screaming, and rarely slept through the night. Jenny's also the one who told me about the letters."

"The ones those thugs were after?" asked Pete. "You never did tell me what those were all about."

"Apparently, Schmidt read about Ernst Zündel in the newspapers, around the time when he was being investigated in Edmonton for hate crimes. Schmidt wanted someone to know about his accomplishments as a Nazi scientist. He couldn't resist the temptation to justify his actions to a fellow Aryan. He dictated the letters to Jenny and told her to send them to Zündel. He hoped that his articles would be published in Zündel's newsletter."

"So how did Jenny end up with them after all?" asked Allard.

"I'm not sure exactly how it all worked out," admitted Emily, "but this is my guess: When Zündel never answered Schmidt's letters, Helmut contacted a bishop in Europe who was famous for his speeches on denying the Holocaust. The bishop expressed an interest, but Schmidt died before he could locate Jenny to find out what happened to the copies he thought she had."

"Jenny still had the letters?" asked Pete. "That's how you got them? When you went to Montreal?"

"Jenny never sent the letters after all," explained Emily. "She knew they were dangerous in the wrong hands, and she typed them out, but kept the originals all those years ... even after she and Schmidt broke up and he moved to Emerald Hill."

"So that's the bishop who hired Slim and Baby?" asked Allard.

"Slim and Baby?" piped in Mrs. Seguin. "Who are they? There's nobody by that name in town."

Allard ignored the Would-be Mayor's question. He would prefer that she never heard about the break-in at Emily's the night before.

"They broke down in questioning, but I couldn't make out what they were blabbering about. Slim said the bishop located them through the Aryan Guard in Alberta. He figured they'd be amenable to trying to get those letters back."

"Little did he know how brilliant they weren't!" said Emily.

"Thank goodness," said Pete.

"So, what happened to Schmidt in the end?" asked Pete. "I gather that Slim and Baby were not the murderers either."

"I can fill in that part of the story," said Allard. "Lily Smith turns up in town looking for her father, Helmut Schmidt, whom she had tracked down by studying immigration records."

"Lily is the unborn baby in the first photo," Emily piped in. "She's also the Lady in Blue we've been seeing around town lately."

"Lily was an orphan, shipped out of Germany, before her mother was arrested. She contacted Schmidt. Their DNA matched, and then she came to see him. He died of a heart attack at the sight of her."

"She looked just like her mother," said Emily. "It must have been like seeing a ghost in real life. Schmidt's worst nightmare come true."

"Funny how it all fits together, now ain't it?" said Pete.

"Allard, how did you feel when you found out it wasn't murder?" asked Emily.

"Not as bad as you," he answered. "Personally, I'm quite happy not to have to investigate murders in this town. It's a quiet, peaceful village, and I'd be happy if it stayed like that."

At that moment, Cassie and Robert came in to the café and chose the table for two by the door. They were holding hands. Robert held the chair for Cassie, and she graciously accepted his invitation to sit opposite him.

Pete and Allard were glad for an interruption. As far as they were concerned, the story was sufficiently explained. They looked at each other in unspoken agreement; neither one of them wanted to encourage Emily's inclination toward any more adventures.

"So I see you found him again," Emily said to Cassie, who was beaming with excitement.

"You were right, Emily," Cassie admitted. "I told Robert you knew all along that he'd be back."

Robert looked sheepish. He had round cheeks and a boyish grin. His blond crew cut and blue eyes contributed to his cherubic charm.

"Do you know where he went?" Cassie announced, manipulating her left hand out from under Robert's firm grip.

"He had to visit the jewelry store three times before he got it right."

She proudly displayed a sparkling diamond ring to everyone in the restaurant. Ilsa emerged from the kitchen with Maria right behind her just in time to ooh and ah about how beautiful the ring setting was.

Pete and Allard remained seated, watching the others happily circling the young couple in the middle. Emily and Mrs. Seguin, Ilsa and Maria, all gathered round to admire the ring.

Mrs. Seguin squealed with glee.

Pete unsuccessfully suppressed an audible groan.

"Aren't they just about as cute a couple as you've ever seen?" Emily gloated.

"Let me take a picture of the beautiful couple. Don't move. I've got a digital camera in the kitchen."

Ilsa disappeared into the kitchen and reemerged with a camera. Robert put his arm around Cassie's shoulder, and Cassie held up her ring finger proudly for the snapshot. They posed self-consciously.

The Would-be Mayor declared, "Say cheese," and the couple obliged with toothy smiles. There was a cheer, and a round of applause when the photo shoot was over.

"I'll send it to you by email," said Ilsa. "Give me your email address, and you'll be able to put the photo on Facebook with your engagement announcement."

Pete thumped his fingers on the place setting. Emily could not help but notice the sudden onset of his bad mood.

"What's got your tongue all of a sudden?" she asked.

Pete glanced at the young couple in the corner.

"Tell him to take two aspirins and lie down 'til the feeling passes."

"Pete, that's not nice. You don't really mean it," Emily protested, immediately regretting her impulsive response.

"Don't I?" he asked. Then he called across the room, "Why don't you take a couple of aspirins and lie down until the feeling passes, son?"

Robert grinned foolishly. Cassie beamed. They were obviously in an invincible bubble of intoxication.

"It's too late now," he quipped. "Where were you when I needed you?"

"Now you stop that," scolded Cassie.

"It's a beautiful ring," said Mrs. Seguin, adding her two cents to the discussion. "Don't you think so, Inspector?"

"I'd have to consult the opinion of my fine assistant here," Allard said, nodding at Emily. "What do you think, Mrs. Blossom? Are they well suited to each other?"

Emily was flattered by Allard's reference to her as his "fine assistant." She glowed. Anything was fine with her at this point.

"There's nothing like true love to cure a tortured heart," she said.

"Who said that?" asked Pete. "I don't recognize the quote."

"I said it," pronounced Emily. "It's an original."

"Suit yourself," answered Pete. "Ilsa, give me some gooey-in-the-middle …"

And then he added as an afterthought, "Please."

The End